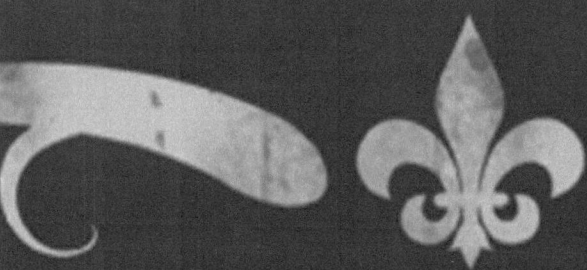

The GHOST of VIMY RIDGE

SEAN STOKES

IN LOVING MEMORY

PATRICK McKEEMAN
ROSALIND 'ROZ' WATTERS
JIM WHITE

All you need is love.

THE WAR TO END ALL WARS

SPECIAL THANKS TO:

Rob Woolsey, Colin Wiley, Joshua Buckton, & The Billy Bishop Museum
Your incredible research salvaged this story.

Sandra & Quinn Kirton
Thank you for keeping My head above water during the writing process

Tara Sutherland
Thank you for not firing me when I prioritised my phone over working.

Sabaton
Thank you for using heavy metal to preserve history.

My Aunt Mary
You have been the saving grace
of my future.

Mom
Ditto.

Caleb, Cody, and Kenzie.
I love you all and miss you so much.

To old and new friends
You are all my second family

Pony Boy
"For good times and bad times, I'll be on your side forever more.
That's what friends are for."

And to my adoring wife
I love you... always.

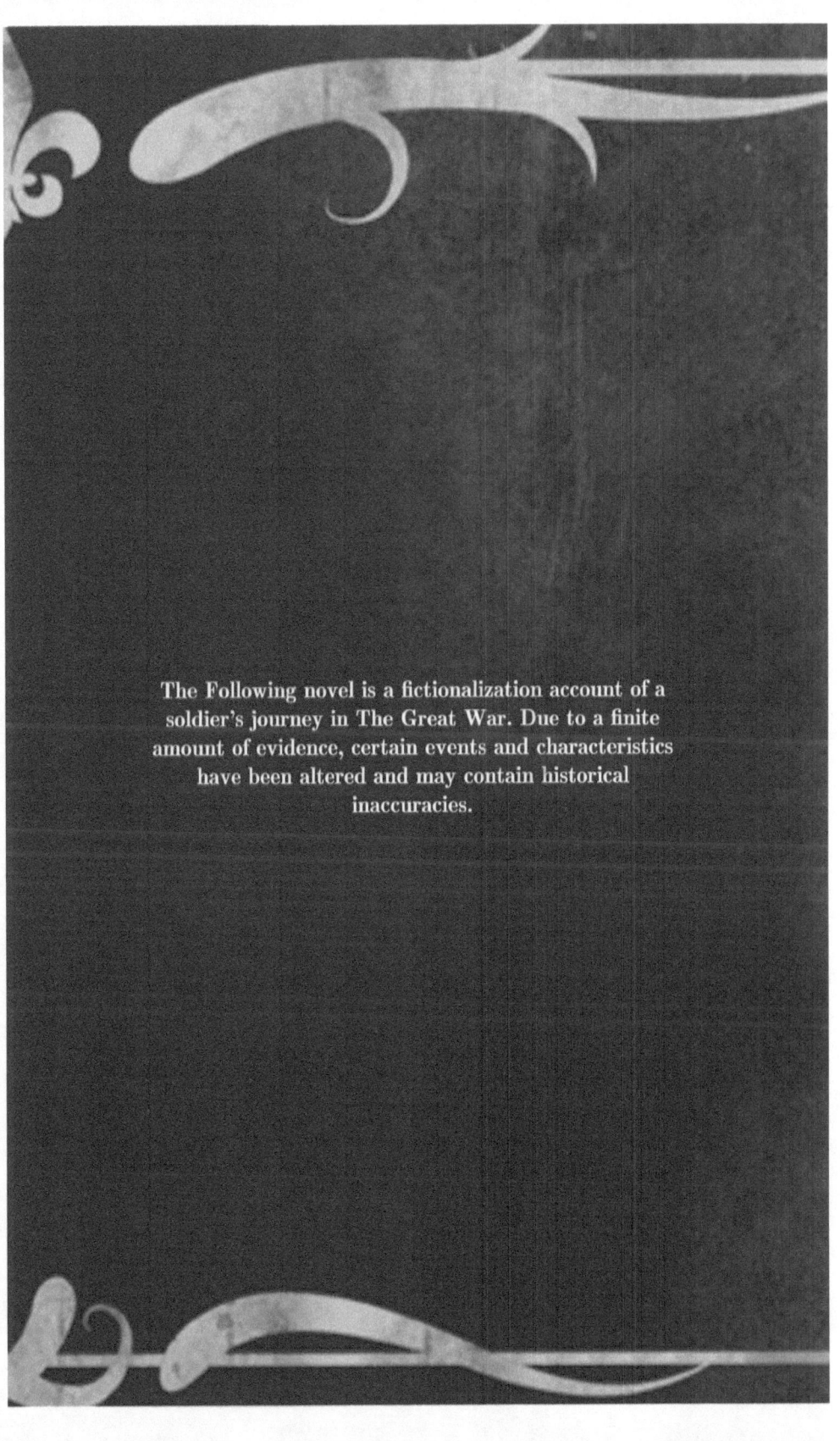

The Following novel is a fictionalization account of a soldier's journey in The Great War. Due to a finite amount of evidence, certain events and characteristics have been altered and may contain historical inaccuracies.

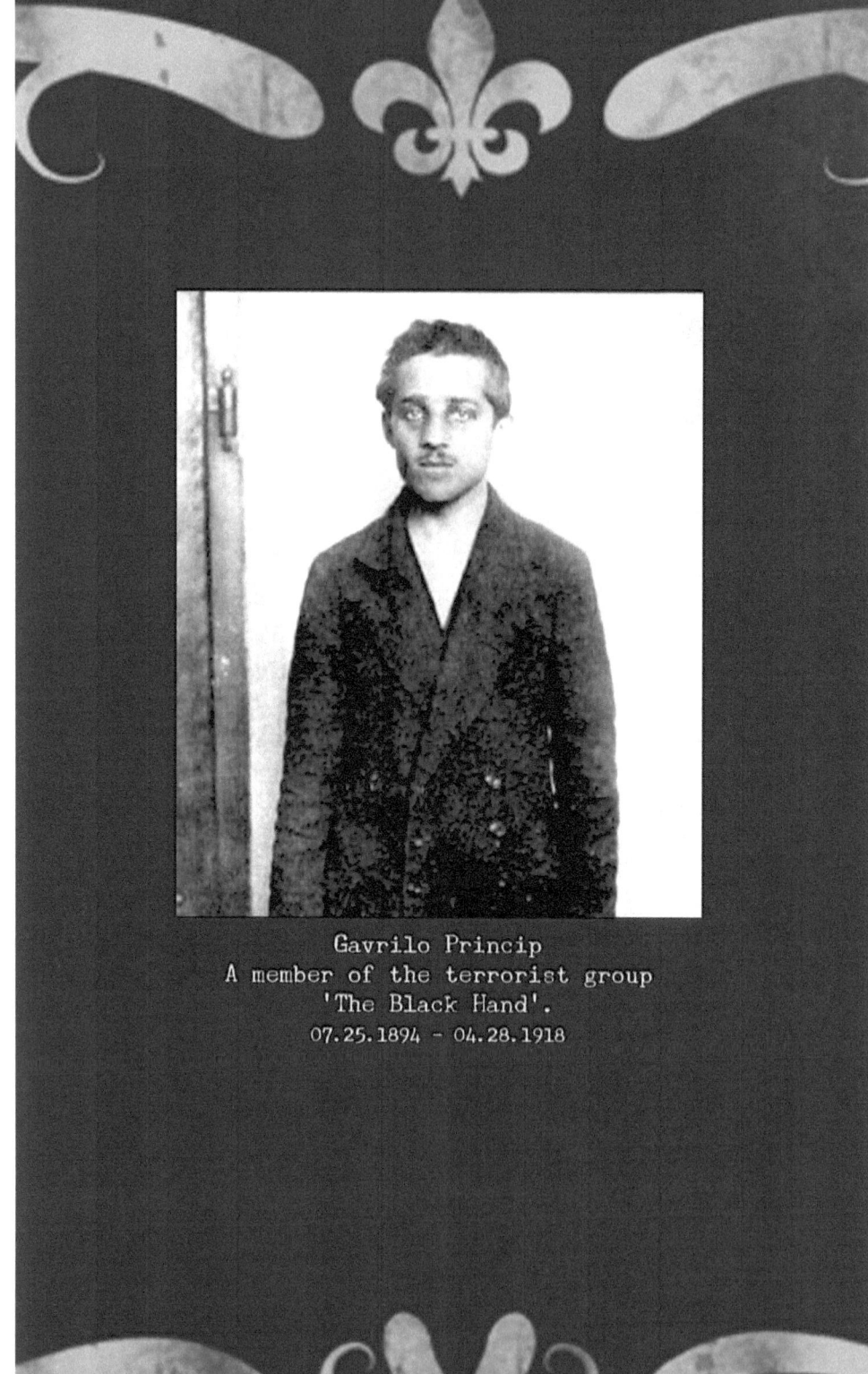

Gavrilo Princip
A member of the terrorist group
'The Black Hand'.
07.25.1894 - 04.28.1918

OVERTURE TO WAR

JUNE 28TH, 1914

SARAJEVO
AUTHOR

It was early in the morning and the train from Tulza was docking into Sarajevo Station. The distance between the two cities is minimal but carries many patrons as they tend to their daily routine. They all share a silence in the air as the world is asleep and unaware of the events that will transpire in their beautiful city.

There were six men in total. Muhamed Mehmedbašić, Vaso Čubrilović, Nedeljko Čabrinović, Cvjetko Popović, Trifko Grabež, and Gavrilo Princip. They were associated with a group named the Black Hand, a criminal organisation in Serbia whose leader "Apis" had deep ties to the Serbian government and used his powers for evil instead of good. The man took the dreams of a liberated Serbia and used it to poison the minds of disenfranchised youth and trained them to be soldiers. This wasn't Apis's first attempt at removing someone from power. In 1903 he murdered both the King and Queen of Serbia to prove Serbia had evolved from a monarchy government. This ultimately backfired as the emperor Franz Josef, the antiquated ruler from Austria with one foot in the grave seized control of the Balkians and instilled the locals with so much hatred that June 28th became a predetermined date in history.

The six men arrived in the city carrying the following items: a pistol, a grenade, a single cyanide pill, currency, and security uniforms. They were given only one order, to kill the archduke. Each man took this command to heart and swore a blood oath to ensure completion. Gavrilo more so than the others. The boy was only nineteen and hadn't experienced life outside of pain and misery. In his formative years he and his family lost six out of nine children who passed away in infancy while being riddled with Tuberculosis. This way of life on any level is bleak and when you add the racial inequity into the mix, you get someone who's willing to become a martyr at any cost

At the time the media had published Ferdinand's trip days in advance so the people could make time to attend the Archduke's visit. It also gave time for the Black Hand to be meticulous with their target. They found Appel Quay was the best place to set the ambush and positioned the men accordingly. Mehmedbašić was the first man on point, Čabrinović was second, and so forth until Princip was placed at the end of the street. Princip stayed close to the road so he could keep an eye out on his comrades and hoped the plan would work. From his perspective he saw the crowd grow when it came time for Ferdinand to arrive. His blood flowed with adrenaline.

They expected to go smoothly until Muhamed Mehmedbašić stood down and didn't make a move. He had a grenade in his hand ready to strike but he yielded. Could have been nerves, could've had a change of heart, nobody truly knows for sure. What we do know is this prompted the second man Čabrinović to take his turn. What he failed to remember though was the grenade he used had a ten second fuse. When he threw the bomb, it bounced off the motorcade and detonated underneath the car behind them.

The explosion injured 16-20 people and left the streets in a panic. Ferdinand's car sped away while Čabrinović ingested his cyanide pill and jumped into the river to claim martyrdom. This all backfired as the pills' effects were minimal due to expiration. To add insult to injury the river was shallow and was too shallow for Čabrinović to drown. He was arrested by authorities and Ferdinand made a clean escape.

Gavrilo was crushed. He missed an opportunity of a lifetime because someone got cold feet. From speculation one can see him being filled with rage and unable to cope. Nobody knows how he was feeling. Nobody can understand his mentality as history didn't take the time to understand his hatred for the empire. We only know that he found himself in a café down the street while Ferdinand made his way to the governor's residence. Ferdinand was irate over the ordeal but chose to continue with the visit with an extended stop at the hospital to visit the wounded. To get to the hospital from the governor's residence the driver Leopold Lojka went back onto Appel Quay assuming it was the safest route. History may have 20/20 vision, but in that current moment, little to no other options were available.

Gavrilo was unaware of Ferdinand's next move. He remained at the Cafe for a lengthy period before he felt the need to get up and leave. As fate would have it, right when Gavrilo Princip left the café, the Archduke's motorcade had pulled in. The street was a dead end and back then, automotive vehicles were primitive and hardly drove in reverse. If you shift the gears abruptly you risk stalling the engine. That is what happened in Appel Quay, and it gave Princip the opportunity of a lifetime. He seized the moment and approached the car, firing two shots simultaneously. The first bullet hit the Archduke in the neck while the second hit The Heiress Sophie in the abdomen. A crowd quickly gathered around while Princip was tackled and arrested. After a brief trial Princip was found guilty on October 23, 1914, and eventually died in prison on April 28th, 1918, from the same illness that killed his siblings; tuberculosis.

After the assassination the world changed. The Austro-Hungarian empire sent an ultimatum with demands that Serbia deemed to be unfair and propelled the empire to invade the small country. Unfortunately, this pressured Russia to attack Austria to which Germany's ruler, Kaiser Willhelm II, came to Austria's aid. This in turn made Russia call upon their allies in the Triple Entente thus beginning an unforeseeable slaughter no previous generation had seen. One out of every ten men who served in the great war had perished, millions more wounded, and the survivors permanently scarred both physically and mentally.

This story is not going to be casting anyone in a positive light. It is not meant to vilify any race, creed, gender, or even species. This story is to honour the men and women who survived The Great War, and to those who paid the ultimate price. My hope one day is that we evolve beyond the need for war, but as the world currently stands, I feel we need to go back to 1915 and give ourselves a history lesson. Maybe if we learn from our past, we can find a better future. I'll be honest. For myself I find the future to be bleak. For as the British philosopher Bertrand Russell once said:

War is not determined who is right - only who is left.

Appel Quay
06.28.1914

1915

I

JUNE

Tradition does not mean to look after the ash, but to keep the flame alive.

JEAN JUARES

OWEN SOUND, CANADA

TOMMY

Stand firm, hold your position, and see the salvation of the Lord on your behalf, O Judah and Jerusalem. Do not be afraid and do not be dismayed. Today go out against them, and the Lord will be with you. In our Lord's name I pray; amen.

Every morning, I would speak the Chronicles' prayer before I walked into the chicken coop. I would stroll amongst the animals carrying a burlap sack hoping to get one by the neck without losing a finger. When I caught one, I used the wrist technique Father showed me to give the animal a painless death. At least that's what he claimed to be true. Truth be told, the technique made my job easier because If I were to use a pistol or tomahawk it would either scare them all off or worse, attack. The sound of their neck's snapping just made my stomach queasy.

After several birds were collected, I would drop them off at the carriage, then go back into the barn and start the process all over again beginning with the prayer. If the quota demanded it, I would've spent the whole day chicken picking. Mr. Boyd liked to run things down at his shop so what he would do is give me the list in the morning and then have me deliver the meat in the afternoon. I kept track of my numbers with a notepad and a dull pencil as the numbers were based on what we sold the day before. Some days it would be chicken, others would be beef, and the rest were pork. The days I disliked the most were pork. You see, beef was easier than pork because the cows were shipped to us already dismembered from the abattoir. With pork, we had to do it all by hand and seeing the carcasses weighed as much as me I'd have to be more resourceful than just lugging and gutting.

The hike to the shop stretched over five miles by horse & carriage. Minutes felt like hours travelling down that dirt road. On horseback it would've taken a fraction of the time as Luna and I did with the carriage. To her it didn't matter, she was so smart and so well-trained all I had to do was bring out her blanket and salle and she was galloping for joy. For me the benefit to the carriage was the view on the horizon. If you were to pass the tallest hill at the precise time you would see the sun gaze down on Owen Sound as if God himself looked down upon us. I could've taken the scenic route across the ridge to enjoy the view, but Mr. Boyd's living was determined by the schedule, so I cut off an hour by taking the main road to get to town. I would take this same route to go back to my home several hours later.

I arrived at the shop and parked Luna at the back entrance. Mr. Boyd was waiting outside while he smoked from his pipe. He wouldn't lay a finger on the sacks or else his back would tweak. At least that's what he claimed to be true. For a man who with a muscular figure and fit he spent little time doing any form of physical labor and used every excuse in the book to get out of it. I took it on the chin and thought it was for my benefit. His wife on the other hand was rather distraught by his laziness. I lost count after both hands and feet the number of times Mrs. Boyd walked into the back and tore Mr. Boyd a new hole in his behind. On the day of their anniversary, I was howling like a husky. The Boyds were yelling at each other in the back room. Mrs. Boyd yelling at the top of her lungs, "you just got blood on my new dress you dingus!" and all the patrons laughed until their bellies were sore. The shades of embarrassment on Mr. Boyd's face were all sorts of red.

After I unloaded all the sacks of poultry my brother Roy showed up to help. E is one of four other siblings I adore. Charles is the oldest, followed by Elizabeth, then Roy, then me and lastly, there's Essie. Charles was an honorable, upstanding Canadian that enlisted when England declared war on Germany. We don't know what happened to him, just got a letter in the mail from his captain stating he was missing in action. My mother hopes he will return but after a few months of no letters, my heart was weary. It affected Elizabeth deeply. She hid herself in her room and shut out the world for days on end. Father on the other hand would never shed a tear, and he expected Roy and I to follow in his example, "tears are a form of weakness in men. The day a man cries is the day he becomes a coward." My mother detested this logic, but you would expect nothing less from a man who served in the Boers and came into Canada with less than two dollars in his pocket. When he met my mother, they were living in Montreal up until Essie came along, so we headed west and found our paradise. He told us stories of glory on the battlefield at night, filling our dreams of one day having our own glory to share when we have children of our own. Roy took it to heart more than I did; however, I couldn't help but feel smitten with the idea of exploring the world beyond the day-to-day struggle of being a laborer. Roy wanted to follow in Father's footsteps so badly he spent his eighteenth birthday at the recruitment office. That was where he was coming from before work.

"How did it go?" I asked.

"I'm fit as a horse. We ship out to Niagara on Friday," he answered.

"What's your regiment?"

"The 58th. I looked at all the other recruits and it'll only be a matter of time before they make me a captain." Mr. Boyd overheard us talking and wasn't impressed.

"Ya keep flapping your jaws you'll be shipped to the hospital to yank my boot out yer arse!" he barked. Roy and I stood straight like we were already soldiers.

"Yes sir," we said together.

"Good. I'll be out front with the customers." Mr. Boyd left us to do the work in silence.

We finished unloading the poultry and began cleaning them up. We got a large pot full of water and put it over the fire. This was to help make the plucking easier. Roy took one half while I took the other and got it done in under an hour, a new personal record for me. Roy was the one who deserved the credit. His charisma and intelligence made him a natural-born leader. He could look at any problem faced and find the solution within seconds. The only downside was his temperament. Roy used to lose his temper over anything minuscule and Charles took full advantage. There were days Charles would steam up Roy something fierce and it would result in my brothers fighting inside the house. Whenever that happened Mother threatened them with her broomstick, and they stopped instantly. She never beat us with it, just used it to trip the son who started the row. When we didn't listen to Mother. Father brought out his belt, that's when you know you're in trouble. I still bear a scar on my back from the belt after I broke one of Elizabeth's dolls. It was an accident of course but according to Father I needed to be taught a lesson. The house went through a change after that happened. Father still blames us for the event getting out of hand. I guess you can say it was the beginning of my resentment.

After we finished the plucking Roy went up to the front while I stayed in the back and worked on some of the orders. Some customers now and then would want custom cuts and that's where my specialty shined. Out of the three sons inside the Holmes house, I am the most meticulous. My sight is far more refined than my two brothers to where I could cut a flank into strips with the most precision. Roy and Mr. Boyd struggled to make the cuts even but when I used the knife it was like duck soup. There were a few customers like Mrs. McClung that only visited Mr. Boyd's shop for my cuts. She was a strong-willed woman whose opinion was vastly different than most, more specifically the idea of women having the same capabilities as men. I lost count on the number of times the Boyds got into an argument because of Mrs. McClung's influence. In Mr. Boyd's eyes, a woman must be at home with the children and doesn't deserve the same freedom as men. In my eyes, it didn't make sense for him to blame the women for being a bad influence when he was the one being a terrible husband.

We finished the day with a little over one-hundred dollars. It was a good day by Mr. Boyd's expectations, but Roy and I only got a couple of bucks each for the labor. On our way home Roy and I gave each other earfuls about it while poor Luna was stuck in the middle. "That old cheap bastard," Roy uttered. "When I'm in the army I'll be making twice as much."

"You won't be able to spend it here though, Roy. You'll be too busy killing Huns in France," I retorted.

"That's okay. I'll have enough money after the war to bring home a French girl and get her a big house in the countryside." I gave Roy a shove and uttered an insult.

"That's if you find a girl just as ugly as you." Roy laughed at my remark and punched me in the shoulder.

"You laugh now but you've never seen a French girl. You can't compare."

"You've never seen one either, Roy." A row was brewing.

"I have!" His snap had some bite behind it.

"Oh yeah?! How many French people do you know?!" I asked, calling his bluff. Roy got defensive and stuck his chest out.

"A lot more than you chicken picker!" Roy gave me a shove out of spite which compelled me to push back. He fell to the ground, and we began to wrestle on the dirt road while Luna laughed at our expense. It was over before it began as Elizabeth found us and broke up the scrap.

"Thomas quit beating up your brother! He can't get injured before he leaves." She grabbed us both by the scruff of our necks and dragged us home. Elizabeth was a tough woman like Mother, but her heart was always in the right place as she didn't tell our parents when we got home.

* * *

The night before Roy had shipped off the whole family gathered at the dinner table for one last feast. Mother went all out when she heard the news of Roy's enlistment. She cooked her famous roast with boiled potatoes, different sorts of vegetables from her garden, freshly baked bread and apple pie for dessert, Roy's favorite. Annie and Elizabeth set the table while the rest of us gathered over the fireplace. Father of course poured himself a drink from his secret bottle. Father loved whiskey more than the government. When the town went dry in 1906, he resorted to making day trips down to Toronto to get his favorite bottle. Lately he's been reduced to buying brandy instead of whiskey and offered some to Roy at the last supper.

"I want you to take a few sips and tell me what you think." Roy did as he was told. He took a few sips and coughed it back up. Father patted him on the back as if to comfort his favorite son. "You'll get used to the taste." Father snickered and took a sip from his glass. "You're fighting a different war than I was, son. Those Huns sure are a crude type."

"Yes sir," Roy responded. "You don't have to worry about me, though. I'll be back home before you know it."

"I know you will. England has some amazing officers that will teach you how to be a great soldier. Perhaps one day you'll be better than I was."

"When I come back home, I'll be sure to wear the sharpest uniform for you." My Mother called out to me and interrupted the conversation.

"Tommy, it looks like rain's coming. Do me a favor and lock the stable for me?"

"Yes, Mother," I answered. I rushed out back to the stable where I saw the dark clouds coming in. The latch we had for the stable doors was a long piece of wood carved to fit into the metal slot on the other side. As sure as rotten luck would have it, the rain started just as I finished locking up the stable. I hoped the weather only called for rain because Luna was afraid of thunder and lightning. I kept my mind distracted with gossip.

"Did anyone hear about Billy Bishop joining the Flying Corp?" I asked the family.

"Yes, I heard! That kid's a daredevil I tell yuh!" Roy answered. "You watch. It'll be a matter of months before he's a certified ace."

"What's an ace?" Essie asked.

"It's when a man shoots down seven Germans," I said, imitating the sounds of a machine gun. Mother gave me a dirty look, subconsciously telling me to stop. Father recognized Mother's look and took control.

"Back in the Boers we never dared to use those deathtraps. If the Huns were bold enough, they would stick to the open field instead of using mechanisms built for the circus." Roy spoke up in my defense.

"But Father, the airplanes do a lot more than just shoot each other. They also do reconnaissance and take pictures of battlefields so the officers can guide the soldier through the trenches. I even read in the paper that the Americans are in talks of using planes to transport people across the planet and would get there faster than a ship." Father controlled his disdain towards Roy's retort.

"A real man doesn't need help with technology when his mind is the most powerful weapon of them all. Remember that when you're on the battlefield, Roy. Not when you're at the dinner table speaking against your father. Do you understand?"

"Yes Father," Roy said in a defeated tone. The table conversation soon died off, leaving only the sound of metal scraping the ceramic plates.

* * *

The next morning Roy was up and ready to go before any of us were awake, double-checking his luggage to ensure he got everything. I was the first one up because his suitcase made a loud thud when it hit the ground.

"Sorry, Tommy," he uttered. "Just a little nervous this morning." Mother woke up after hearing me take the lord's name in vain. She came marching into our room to see what happened only to walk away, sighing in an annoyed tone. I gave him peace of mind by going through his luggage to verify everything. He sighed in relief. "Thank you," he said.

"Don't mention it. Just write to me and tell me all about it. I want to hear everything," I said back. He was leaving this town behind to look for adventure on another continent. I can't deny that I wanted the same for myself. Sadly, I wasn't old enough to enlist.

"I will, Tommy. Soon enough you'll be over in France and I'll be your commanding officer." Roy laughed and gave me a nudge, then walked into the living room with his suitcase by his left side. Father was awake at that point and had his morning cup of coffee, Mother was in the kitchen making breakfast, and the girls were in the yard tending to their garden. The only one still in bed was Essie, she was the heaviest sleeper of us all. She only woke up when she smelled the bacon cooking in the cast-iron pan. Little Essie ran into the room and got herself ready at the table before everyone else in her typical fashion to make sure she got the first piece. On this occasion she gave the first piece of bacon to Roy instead. It was a heartwarming gesture that made everyone smile, even Father.

We loaded up the carriage with Roy's things before he gave each member of the family a personal goodbye, starting with Mother. "I'll be back soon, Mother. Father, I'll make you proud." He hugged our older sisters together. "Goodbye, sisters. Please help Mother around the house." He picked up Essie and gave her a bear hug "I'll be back real soon!"

"You promise?" Essie asked him.

"I Promise," he said then gave her a kiss on the cheek. He saved his last goodbye for me, the little brother.

"Don't kill all the Huns without me," I said, jokingly.

"Not a chance," Roy said back. We shook hands and then gave each other a firm hug. "I'm gonna miss you, little brother."

"I'll see you soon," I said back. We let go of each other, then Roy walked to the front of the carriage with Father. We waved each other a final goodbye as we watched another son of England go off to war to serve King and country. My mind flooded with the image of Roy coming back home, decorated with medals. Some days after I pictured myself standing next to him, decorated with the same number of accolades.

Pier 21
Halifax, Nova Scotia

II

AUGUST

Perfectly ordered disorder designed with a helter-skelter magnificence.

EMILY CARR

HALIFAX, CANADA

ANNIE

I watched from the pier and waved goodbye to my brother and father with the sun blocking my vision. My heart was heavy with worry, but I focused on the journey home. I waited until the ship was the size of a pebble before I rode my bike through the crowd full of high-strung men.

Since the war broke out last year, hundreds of thousands of soldiers have used our ports to sail across the Atlantic. They come to Halifax from all parts of the country, looking for adventure while bargaining to have fun along the way. With the war as grim as it's been, I fear we will see more wooden coats than men if they don't get their act together. The one man I never have to worry about is Dad. He is impervious to bullets and stupidity. Dad was one of the first to ship across the ocean to fight but when the army heard of his leadership skills, they sent him back home to train the new recruits. When Conor turned eighteen Dad appointed himself as commanding officer. He felt he was the only one qualified to do the job properly as he never trusted a British officer, not even with a pack of smokes as he would say. He wouldn't dare utter these opinions in public where the crown could hear him. He only spoke freely about the king amongst his closest friends over a bottle of Newfie Screech.

My father moved us here from Cape Breton after he did his tour in South Africa. Dad wanted us to socialise with other children so he found this house over on the south side of Lucknow street and called it home. It's not quite the same as the farm as the scenery is just a winding river of people wandering around the city. One similarity is the amount of sheep roaming around while the wolves barked orders. I find myself a bit of an oddball whenever I see a soldier. With Dad and Conor, it's one thing. I am obligated to support them as they are my family. If I didn't know the man I would greet him with disdain. Especially if they're British or French. Our local boys I try to be hospitable but it depends if they're drunk or sober when I meet them. Before my work at the recruitment office, I served them over at The Billa Tent; a ghastly place filled with buffoons who can't hold their liquor and scrap over any reason under the sun. Whenever I had to deal with them my caper accent came out angry enough to scare their ancestors. "B'y I'ma goin' rip yer bushwacker off and shove it down ya trap if ya keep shootin' off. G'way withcha!" I loved it when I told off the French, they looked at me like I had a head injury for not sounding like the ideal *Canadian.* It's whatcha dealt with, ya know?

I was coming up to the final intersection before my home when I saw a crowd gathered around a house filled with smoke. Policemen and the fire brigade were rummaging through the decimated O'Brien's house. I was not sure what caused the damage, but the small crowd exacerbated itself with ludicrous theories while the real witnesses were secluded behind an ambulance. "What was that you said?" One man asked a young mother.

"I said 'The Germans must've attacked us. It's the only explanation," the mother answered. Another man added his two cents to the debate.

"No, you are wrong. It was a spy. The Huns smuggled secret soldiers onto our ships to kill us when we least expect it. There's no way our navy wouldn't see a U-boat coming through the canal." Another woman looked at that man like the buffoon he is.

"Oh, don't be so dim-witted. It is clearly a failure in the weapon system itself. If women were in charge there would be no bloody war to begin with!" The crowd roared with opinions while I snuck past and hustled my way home to hide behind my front door. I sighed in relief when my cat Mindy greeted me with her adorable pink nose and purrs while her long, fluffy fur rubbed up against my legs. As I fed her chicken I petted her soft coat, giving my large kitty the affection she deserves. We suspect she came off a merchant ship from Norway given she's the same size as a beagle. She was timid of me in the beginning but over time she adjusted nicely and became a respectable, cuddly pillow. If I were to leave Nova Scotia behind, her royal majesty would be the only one coming with me.

I did a small cleanup of the house to drown out the image of the destroyed home. I started folding the laundry, then washed some plates, ironed my dress for the next day, and once that was all done, I made myself dinner, leftover chicken soup from the day before. Mindy's favourite protein was chicken so as the soup was boiling, I put an extra thigh for her dinner. Conor teased me all the time for letting her sit at the dinner table with us, mocking me for treating her like a family member instead of a mouse hunter. Dad always came to my aid as he loved her more than I. "You go before the cat goes," he would say.

Later in the evening I sat down with a book and a cold ale. Mindy later joined me on the couch to make biscuits in the blanket Angeni knitted for me. Angeni is an old native woman that used to look after Conor and me while Dad served in the Boers. Because our mother passed away when she gave birth to me, Angeni took it upon herself to fill the shoes of the mother figure. She taught me how to brush my hair, sew my clothes, clean the house, and everything else until I turned sixteen and began to fend for myself. The fifty-four-year-old is still alive and lives by the harbour in a little house she and her late husband Paul had purchased to raise their family. Paul was not native like Angeni. He was a Scottish fisherman that saved her from drowning in the harbour some years back and were inseparable until Tuberculosis took him in 1908. Paul left the house to her along with three wonderful children; Kimi, Dakota, and Sakari, who are many years ahead of me in age. Dakota works in Ottawa as a translator, Kimi is a nurse for the Red Cross in Montreal, and Sakari still lives in the home. She helps Angeni get around to places that are difficult for the adorable little old lady. About once or twice a week I'll swing by to visit. Sometimes those visits require a few bottles of wine and good humour. One day Sakari and I drank two bottles to ourselves while we assembled Angeni's bed. Sakari and I used pieces of wood to compare Sakari's former lovers while Angeni kept one bottle to herself and laughed at our expense. The thought of them distracted me so much that I lost my point on the page and gave the book up for the rest of the evening.

* * *

The next morning was steady at the recruitment office. Captain Cockburn was preoccupied reading the news articles from the front lines while I sorted through the applicants. The ones that were scheduled for the day were at the top while the walk-ins remain at the bottom. On average we would receive thirty candidates a day during the week and over fifty on Saturdays. The ones who didn't make the cut failed for any reason under the sun. Some had high arches, some had rotted teeth, a few were over the age of forty-five and many were under the age of eighteen. So many younglings are filled with patriotism and wonder without realising their shoelaces are untied until they trip down the stairs. One after the other their eyes filled with tears, begging to be treated like a man and exempted from the army's prerequisites. "I'm sorry, lad. Come back in a couple of years when you turn eighteen." I know I'm calling the kettle black on this as dad lied on my paperwork saying I was eighteen, but after hearing some tales from the battlefield, the boys would be in luck if the war ended before they became of age to serve.

Some time had passed and I was ready to go for my lunch before a Canadian major walked into the office looking for the Captain. "Good morning," he said.

"Good morning, sir. May I please have your name?"

"Major McFarland here to see Captain Cockburn." He was well-mannered and dressed himself with distinction as a Canadian soldier. I told him to wait as I interrupted the captain's lunch by knocking on his door.

"What is it?" Cockburn asked shrewdly.

"I have Major McFarland to see you," I answered. The Captain's lip's quivered and told me to give him five minutes so he could gather his senses. When I returned, the major was playing with his hat, spinning it around his fingertips with one hand while caressing his lapel with the other. I kept my focus on my work and ignored the major. He looked faintly familiar but I couldn't put a finger on it. Two minutes of silence had passed before he said something.

"May I ask you a personal question?" He asked, cautiously.

"Yes, sir. What is it?"

"Is your father Otto Middaugh?" He asked, making me blush from embarrassment.

"Oh god, am I fired?" I asked, frozen in fear. The major chuckled.

"Ha ha, not a chance. He's a good man." By the sounds of it, Dad only showed the Major his good side. Just before I was about to respond, Captain Cockburn approached us.

"Good morning, sir," he uttered.

"Good morning, Captain. Thank you for the last-minute audience." I was impressed with the Major's demeanour. I couldn't imagine why he struck fear into the captain's heart.

"Yes, sir. Right this way," Cockburn said. The major put on his hat and walked into Cockburn's office confident and relaxed. The relaxation was momentarily as the Major started yelling at the captain. His voice was so thunderous he left Cockburn speechless, a valiant achievement to other soldiers who felt the petty wrath of the British Captain. I've even been subject to demeaning threats because the old man was having a rough day. In the beginning, I just took his character at face value, over time the fuse had been whittled down by a couple of inches. In the limey's eyes, sure, one could argue my opinion oversteps some boundaries or ruffles some feathers. On the other hand, the man's stuck in the recruitment office for a reason. He's the kind of coward that would send a boy to take his place on the front line and then lie to his superiors to save his image. The only reason why I stuck around the stunned officer was purely for monetary purposes. Everywhere else around town paid significantly less compared to the BEF. Especially for a woman.

The major walked out of the office with his head held in distinction. He bid me a fond farewell while Cockburn came out of hiding moments later with a note. "Ensure this telegram gets to Major Griffith." I took the note and translated the message into morse code.

`Major Griffith. Send 200 Ross to Ottawa HQ.`

Minutes went by on the clock before I received a bleak response.

`Splendid.`

I got up from my chair to relay the message, only to speak to an office door. Whatever the major said, it ruined the captain's day.

As the day wore on Cockburn became more irritable. He greeted every recruit with scathing insults over the littlest flaws. "Your big toe is two milli-metres too big; you'd be killed before you get to the front line." The old man was making my blood boil. How dare a limey bastard insult my countrymen. Just because his empire colonised our land it doesn't give him the right to treat them like cannon fodder. I wanted to say this so badly, but Dad has repeatedly warned me to mind my mannerisms around men, saying a young woman can piss off the wrong man if she isn't careful. I'm sure though if he heard what the captain said, he would've done the same thing as I. "You're better off killing yourself with your height, boy. You're so tall the Huns can spot you a thousand metres away." I heard that disgraceful remark and broke my pen out of anger. I stormed into that office and humiliated the petty excuse for an officer. He was in the middle of measuring his waist size when I pushed him hard against the wall while shoving the rope down his throat.

"The boys can live without your sarcasm, Captain!" His skin was white, and he clutched his heart with his right hand as if it was going to implode. He fell to the ground like a corpse, uttering gawd-awful gurgling noises before he was rendered unconscious. My rage turned into desperation. I dropped to my knees and took the rope out of his mouth. His breathing didn't return so I shook him violently, begging the man to wake up. "Come on you old man, wake up!" The recruit stood on the other side of the table unsure of whether to laugh or cry. After a minute of endless shaking, I resorted to punching his chest as hard as I could. By the fifth punch, the captain gasped for air and coughed so violently foam was coming out of his mouth. I rolled him onto his side and praised God the man didn't die on me. Captain Cockburn sat up slowly, breathing heavily. He looked around the room in confusion, muttering to himself before seeing me, and then came back to his senses. "Get out of my sight and never come back!" He yelled with a thunderous tone. I took the long, scenic route around town so nobody could see me cry on my bicycle.

* * *

The next morning, I woke to a knock at my door. I grabbed my housecoat and hustled down the stairs, expecting the military police. I was about to open the door before second-guessing my outfit. If I was going to be lured away in handcuffs, I wanted to look respectable. I ran upstairs, quickly threw on my green floral summer dress and put on some makeup. Minutes went by and I heard another knock. This time it was more forceful. The force of the knock made my lipstick tube slip out of my hands and fall to the ground. I grabbed it in a panic and finished without looking at the mirror, applying the lipstick to my bottom lip as I walked down the stairs. When I got to the front door, I took a deep breath before I opened it. I kept my eyes closed as I heard the creak of the door echo in the hallway. On the other side I heard a familiar voice. "Uh, miss Middaugh?" The man asked me. I opened my eyes to see Major McFarland dressed in full uniform.

"Yes?" I answered.

"Do you mind if I come in?" He asked, calmly. My fears got the best of me and I panicked.

"He was an arsehole! I couldn't deal with that crude man anymore. If I am being arrested for it then so be it! I will take culpability for my actions." I held my hands out in front of me, waiting for soldiers to drag me to prison. The major just looked at me confused.

"I don't follow. Who is the arsehole?"

"That belligerent Captain Cockburn. He must've told you what I did so you're here to arrest me." The major was even more confused.

"I haven't seen the captain since yesterday morning when I yelled at him for misplacing two-hundred rifles." My face went through various shades of red from embarrassment.

"Oh," I uttered. The major looked at the street and asked to come in.

"I hope you don't mind but I'm on a tight schedule and need to make this quick. Can I come in?" I composed myself together and invited the major into my home. I guided him to our dinner table and sat him down.

"Do you have time for coffee or tea?" I asked.

"I'll take a glass of water please," he answered. I fetched him a tall glass and filled it up with cold water, then poured myself my own glass to swallow my pride. We sat down at the dining room table on opposite ends.

"So, if you're not here to press charges. May I ask what you are doing here?" I asked the major.

"Well, I was going to ask you if you would consider transferring over to my office in Toronto, but, by the sounds of it, Captain Cockburn would not be a reliable reference." I was confused. What was it about me that made him interested? He wasn't the pervy type, I've seen plenty of those. He kept his distance and kept the conversation professional. It was a rare commodity for a Canadian soldier.

"I'm not sure how well I'll fare outside Nova Scotia, sir. Halifax is my home, and I would prefer to keep it that way," I said, causing him to snicker.

"You know something? I can't help but say I was expecting that. You're like your mother in that aspect." His words penetrated a deep wound, pushing me to speak up for my late mother.

"With all due respect Major this isn't the appropriate time to talk about my dead mother. I wish I can help you but I'm afraid it is not possible. I cannot pack up my things and leave for another province halfway across the country." I was scared that what I said had angered him, however he remained calm like Mindy.

"My apologies, Miss Annie. It was not my intention to cause you grief. I appreciate you taking the time to meet with me. I have gathered the wrong impression of you." His last words had me confused.

"I'm sorry, come again?" I asked.

"Well, when I spoke to your father last, he said you were an impeccable secretary and that is what I need. My commanding officers request the best Canada has to offer. And since I cannot recruit your father or brother, I figured you would be the next best thing."

"I appreciate the offer, but I'll be okay. I will find work elsewhere where I don't have to deal with soldiers."

"Well, I can respect your decision, Miss Middaugh. The one thing I would have to question is, and don't take this as an insult, but is there anyone here in town that will hire someone who tried to kill their boss?" The major got up from his seat and walked towards the door. "It's okay though, I have worn out my welcome and would rather see my own exit before I cause any more distress. It was wonderful to see you again." The major was one step out the door before I pulled him back in.

"I have some terms and conditions before I say 'yes'," I said. The major closed the door and listened carefully.

"I'm listening," he retorted.

"I want the same pay as before. Actually, no, I want a ten-cent raise."

"Done." I was in shock that he agreed so blindly. I felt I had to test him more to see if he was legitimate.

"I want my own accommodations."

"Naturally."

"I don't tolerate belittling or flirting. Especially from older men."

"I'm a happily married man, Miss Middaugh, but if I were to see another soldier behaving in such a way, I will take care of it." He passed every test with flying colours. "Is there anything else you request?" I was lost in the moment, perplexed by the level of independence The major is giving me. It made me forget all about Mindy who jumped onto the table and gave the cutest meow, as if to ensure her opinion was included in the conversation.

"She's the most important. Without her you have no deal," I said. Mindy meowed again to concur with my statement. The major was outnumbered two to one, and he knew it.

"It's not a normal request I encounter... but I can't foresee a reason why it couldn't be arranged." Mindy looked over to me and licked her lips, as if to give me permission to accept the major's offer. We left the province that following week. I got Sakari to look after the house while Mindy and I took the ferry to the mainland, then boarded the first train to Ottawa.

Sir Sam Hughes

Former Minister of Militia
and Defence of Canada

01.08.1853 - 08.23.1921

III

OCTOBER

It has too often been too easy for rulers and governments to incite man to war.

LESTER B. PEARSON

OTTAWA, CANADA

GEORGE

There are two kinds of leaders. One is made to build civilisation, and the other is to destroy it. How you utilise your time and resources will determine what kind of leader you will be.

I learned this invaluable lesson from my mentor, General Arthur Currie. It was unusual for a man of his character to be given command of an army. He is large in stature, clean-cut without the need to shave, awkward amongst others, and unusually quiet for a general. With all that taken into perspective the man is an expert tactician who holds integrity above the politics of war, unlike other generals who scrutinise his tactics. It's a travesty that those men let their egos get in the way of his leadership. If they had the humility to see beyond the tip of their swords and let the artillery reach its potential, thousands of soldiers would still be standing at the front instead of rotting in No Man's Land. Arthur does his best to ensure we are given the right resources we need. He gave us fresh uniforms when needed until Prime Minister Borden sent him to the front to train our boys overseas, leaving me to command the militia alone. We held a long handshake the morning he left and wished each other the best of luck, knowing he may never return. I'm not a cynic by nature, it's just what war does to men. I'm grateful I haven't become a complete pessimist after seeing the carnage at the front. There were soldiers like Otto who made those devious times bearable. During our tenure in Neuve-Chapelle, his imitations of the British officers kept the men's spirits high and gave them the courage to charge across No Man's Land repeatedly and survive the grotesque ordeal. I expected the same characteristics from his daughter Annie, and she exceeded tenfold. She is so meticulous with her work it made the best of captains hide in shame. One flaw they have in common is their grievances towards England and our monarch. On the train ride to the capital, she called a Limey soldier every vile name in the book because he was being rude to her.

We arrived in Ottawa on a cold, rainy October. 4th to finalise the formation of the 147th Battalion. The purpose of this trip was to give the war minister the signed documents to establish a battalion in Owen Sound. I wasn't the first pick to be the commanding officer. Major Begy bought his way into becoming C.O. courtesy of his political friends. The decision was overturned a week later when Arthur used his influence to reverse the vote. With me came Major Thomas Corrie, my second-in-command. He was waiting for us at the station with a bottle of whiskey and a fresh pack of smokes under the light post. Thomas is one of the few men I would trust with my life. He has a certain level of calmness that's only disrupted when he's faced with incompetence. As we walked to the hotel Thomas was giving me updates on the front.

"Huns took Loos," Thomas answered.

"What's Loos?" Annie asked.

"Loos is a village in France. Brits coordinated an assault last week and failed." We were within 50 metres of the Hotel and it started to rain. Neither Thomas or I were bothered and continued with the conversation. "Casualties?" I asked. Thomas gave me a grim look.

"You don't want to know."

"Tell me," I ordered. Thomas lit up another smoke, then pulled out a slip of paper. He covered it with his hands while I read the telegram. My face was whiter than a ghost. "fifty-thousand," I uttered.

"No one knows for certain, but rumour has it French is being replaced."

"That's only a rumour, Tom. The Brits would've told us if they replaced their CO."

"That is true," Tom retorted. "Unless a certain major happens to be good friends with a Lord's daughter."

"Well, regardless of how you or your private acquired this information we should tend to Canadian needs before foreign politics."

"Unless someone like Douglas Haig were to be the replacement?" Tom asked sarcastically. I sighed in anger upon hearing that name. 'Butcher' Haig we used to call him. My first encounter with him was in South Africa during the second Boer mission. Hundreds of men were killed in that campaign because of the man's incompetence.

"That's a problem," I said.

"It is. I expect you'll be hearing from General Currie once the decision has been made." Poor Annie was freezing to death and interrupted our conversation.

"Gentlemen, would it be possible for us to talk about this in a dryer setting? Perhaps inside the hotel?" She asked us, shivering from the rain. We failed to see we were steps away from the hotel. Thomas snickered and let her run in.

"She's a smart one," he said.

"She's Otto's daughter," I retorted. Thomas was stopped dead in his tracks.

"That's good to know." Thomas knew Otto well and all his mannerisms. They had great respect for each whenever alcohol was not involved. Any time it was conversations turned into tests of strength and manhood.

We walked through the doors and checked in at the front reception. The army put us on the top floor of the hotel, looking over the Rideau Canal. I felt insulted that they put us in such a luxury suite. The kind of money spent on us for one administrative trip could've been spent on a new pair of boots or a day's ration for a soldier. The same results would've been achieved through telegrams. We spent the rest of the evening sitting in silence, overlooking our Nation's capital and all its scenic architecture.

* * *

At 8.40 Thomas, Miss Middaugh and I arrived at Parliament Hill with nothing more than optimism and a briefcase full of signatures. The signatures came from fellow officers in the 31st regiment who didn't hesitate to answer the call to arms. They had waited many months for this day to come, for the ever-almighty Samuel Hughes to put his name down on a piece of paper to mobilise the battalion. We just hoped the immoral leader would make this process as painless as possible.

We arrived at city hall twenty minutes ahead of schedule. It gave Thomas the opportunity to enjoy smoking while I described the minister to Annie. I told Annie Hughes is the type of man who expects his pockets to be filled before he can give you what you want. If you didn't have anything lucrative to offer him, you best hope you have a general or political ready with a signature. She asked why the media portrayed him in a different light and all I said was, "If the man can look at himself in the mirror and honour his word as a patriot then he would at least give us a better rifle to use."

Thomas and I left Annie in the hallway when Hughes' secretary escorted us into his empty office. Hughes was running behind schedule, so we waited in the two chairs along with a British Major sitting alone with a cup of coffee. His lack of medals told me he's spent much of his military career behind a desk. He only had his Mons and silver coin drooped down his jacket in poor fashion. If I were his commanding officer, I would have scowled at him for disgracing his uniform with such tardiness. Alas, more important tasks took priority over my ego. I cannot deny I felt more frustrated when Mr. Hughes disregarded the officer's appearance. "Good morning Major McFarland. How was your trip to Halifax?"

"Couldn't get away from the fresh air, Sir," I retorted.

"Lovely," he said, sarcastically. "Would either of you gentlemen like a cup of coffee or tea?" Hughes offered. We collectively declined while he asked for coffee from his secretary. When she left, he turned his attention to the business at hand. "Well, I guess you would rather get on with it then. Do you have all the signatures required?" I opened my briefcase and handed the war minister a folder filled with the names and ranks of every officer I personally recruited. Hughes took only a few minutes to look over the names and close the folder. "Good job. There is just one thing."

"What is that, sir?" I asked him. The Major took the liberty to answer the question.

"You're a man short," he uttered. I gave him a look of disbelief, *such rudeness*, I thought. Hughes jumped in to dilute the tension.

"This is Major Harold Griffith. He is going to be your liaison officer." I was thrown off by his remark.

"I beg your pardon, Sir, but you did not give us this information in previous correspondence." Hughes stirs his coffee cup like he was thinking of an answer.

"I am aware, Major. This is a new concept we are implementing due to circumstances involving the men." Corrie spoke up firmly.

"What circumstances, Sir?" He asked them. The tardy Major took the liberty to answer with a fragile ego.

"Some of your men have been behaving like barbarians." He pulled out a stack of files and threw them on top of Hughes' desk. "Go ahead and see for yourself." I grabbed the first file from the stack and looked it over thoroughly. I recognize the incident from a story I heard a few months before. There was a company on leave in Paris that got into the whiskey and picked a fight with several members of the French army. The report gives a grisly detail of a young private pistol-whipping a captain over a girl. The drunken private was sent back to the front as a form of punishment instead of being court-martialed. My guess is the Brits felt he'd make a good human shield.

I set the file down and grabbed a few more. The second report involved a lance corporal looting a store in Brussels, and the third deserted his post at Mount Sorrel, was found then executed by his commanding officer. At the bottom of the pile was a report consisting of a Canadian Lieutenant organizing a game of hockey as a training exercise. I found this finding ridiculous.

"With all due respect Major Griffith, but how does a sport qualify as an act of hedonism?"

"I have seen this depravity you Canadians call Hockey up close in person, Major. How would you expect those men to be able to fight if they're beating each other's brains out with sticks?!"

"Major Griffith, soldiers get injured in training all the time. Perhaps this officer felt it would be good for morale."

"Able-bodied men are good enough for morale, Major." Hughes stepped in again.

"George, I understand your trepidation over this but you will concede and you will accommodate. Major Griffith is your liaison officer and that will be the end of it. Do we have an understanding?" I took a second to collect my thoughts and drown my emotions. A true soldier follows the orders given by his commanding rank, regardless how the soldier feels about the objective. A heavy price to pay for freedom and liberation from colonialism.

"Yes Sir, I understand," I said, swallowing with pride. Hughes knew that he won and he gave a cocky smile for victory.

"Good. Major Griffith will accompany you and Major Corrie to Owen Sound, and you will report to me once the battalion is established. Any questions?"

"No Sir, no questions," I answered.

"Good. Meeting adjourned." I stood tall and shook Hughes' hand. It was out of respect for my country, not for this pompous fool. Once we parted ways with Griffith, Thomas and I united with Annie and left.

"How did it go?" She asked.

"To hell with the Brits," Corrie answered. No other words were needed.

* * *

The next morning, we reconnected at Union Station to board our train. The four of us shared three cabins. Annie and her feline companion had their own separate suite. We felt this was best to make Annie comfortable. As a civilian, she should take higher priority of seating compared to two soldiers accustomed to sleeping on piles of dirt. Major Griffith took the liberty of having his own room because in his mind he felt officers should be entitled to luxury as their years of service to the motherland were paid forward. I was expecting him to show up at the station alone, however, another gentleman stood next to him. The man's face was disfigured. His nose and left eye were missing with horrendous scar tissue taking its place. He was silent in every sense of the word. We didn't ask what happened to the fellow and he doesn't care to share. We wouldn't even know his name if it wasn't for Griffith. Sergeant Osgoode would greet you with silence or a hand-written note asking for something. And of course he was sitting with us in the last cabin. For the next four hours we sat in an uncomfortable silence.

* * *

From the train station to our hotel across the river, men, women, and children were in awe of our presence. It felt damn good to be home. Both Tom and I were from this area, Tom more so than I. What makes Owen Sound so unique compared to other cities as it retains its core values. If you were to look at other cities like London or Hamilton, they were quaint in their formations but grew to adapt ideology from the major cities. Owen Sound went in the opposite direction and became recluse and self-sufficient. It's the perfect breeding ground to form a battalion.

We spent the night in the local hotel and then went to headquarters at sunrise. We had a lot of work to do. From posting campaign posters to rallies to meetings with the local politicians, our schedule was tight as hell. The first man I was introduced to was the Mayor, John McQuaker. John and I had a history with each other when he was a captain of the 31st. He was another man like Arthur who put the needs of his people before political gain and ensured his office was available to us along with any external resources, we require for the 147th, "Our boys deserve only the best and nothing else," he told us. After we left the meeting Tom, and I wanted to host a fundraiser at city hall for the elites to contribute their share to the war. In order for them to buy war bonds we needed to manipulate them into believing their contribution will give their social status more influence on policy. It was all nonsense of course but in times of war, it's sometimes best to tell the people what they want to hear rather than give them the truth.

Mercer was put in charge of hosting the event as he was the one most connected to the elites. We took the offer from the Mayor and gave Mercer his own office next to the mayor. I tell you the mayor regretted offering us his office after the first week. The man spent his time running errands and scheduling meetings with all the officers I had personally requested to lead the battalion. Including Corrie, Mercer and Finley, there was Major Jucksh, Captain Smith, Captain Howes as our medical officer, Captain Morrison, Captain Richardson, and Captain Ritchie. Each man served in the 31st regiment under my leadership and is impeccable with their skill sets. They are the reason why the 147th will be the best battalion in the Canadian Corp.

The fundraiser took a mere two weeks to plan and execute. We had several challenges stuck in our path. First, our motorcade broke down in the first snowstorm. It was Griffith's idea to use the motorcade to travel around the city and ignored the local's suggestion of using a horse carriage. It was infuriating trying to debate with that imbecile, but he was the one holding our finances. He soon learned to adapt but his irritable attitude towards anything that disrupted his comfort stayed the same. Captain Smith pulled me aside multiple times asking my permission to hit the British buffoon.

Griffith put us in a bad predicament near the end of our planning for the fundraiser. The man's only responsibility was to collect the meat for the caterers which he failed to do so then waited to mention it until the cooks arrived. I was furious and felt obligated to resolve it by myself.

I had less than an hour to grab all the meat from the butcher shop across town. I took the horse carriage along with four buckets filled with snow. I wasn't sure if I needed any burlap sacks, so I grabbed several from Mercer just as I was leaving. I arrived at the butcher shop within ten minutes in the middle of a snowstorm. When I got inside, I was greeted with a lineup of angry patrons. They had been waiting in line for several minutes and the man behind the counter was an irresponsible manager. I spotted him being aggressive towards an old woman who was looking for some fish for supper. He argued with her for a few minutes until he called out to one of his employees for help. "TOMMY!" The young man barged through the saloon doors and rushed to his employer's aid. The young man handled himself exceptionally, serving each individual with grace and fortitude. "Two rib eyes and four tunas coming right up." It took seconds for the kid to get her order together and she left smiling instead of screaming. When she saw me she made it a point to speak with me.

"Excuse me. Are you one of those recruiting officers I keep seeing around town?" She asked me.

"Yes ma'am. I am," I answered.

"Well good because you need to get that boy away from this place. He's too damn good to be working for a swine like Boyd." I asked her if he was of age to serve, and she couldn't give me a definitive answer. It was something I was going to investigate when it came time for my turn to be served... at least that's what I hoped. The manager sent him home a few minutes after. It infuriated me more than Major Griffith forgetting the meat. The meat problem was resolved in minutes, missing the opportunity for a strong, potential soldier can be devastating.

december

2nd Avenue east (fka Poulett Street)
Owen Sound, Ontario

IV

DECEMBER

Nothing in life is to be feared, it is only to be understood.

MARIE CURIE

OWEN SOUND, CANADA

TOMMY

On Fridays I left early from work to get a good spot in line for the casualty list.

Whenever a man gets killed in combat their identity tag gets collected and brought to the war department where hundreds of clerks sift through the names and make them available to the public. I had never seen the facility myself, but this is what I was told by one of the officers. If you found a loved one on the list, they were either dead, or wounded. Knowing this fact gave everyone a lump of coal in the back of their throat whenever it was their turn to look at the list. The ones who made it through the end without spotting a name were filled with joy and optimism. The ones who didn't, like the elderly couple standing in front of me, suffered such a cruel fate. Before they stepped up to read the list The old woman was so tense she was shaking. The man was silent and held his wife's hands. When it was their turn, the old man left the wife to the side while he looked so closely at the list he could've smelled the ink. He got through the first two pages before stopping his finger on the top part of page three. He wiped his hand on the page as if to clean off accumulated dust. He looked at the name one more time then sighed. He turned towards his wife and nodded his head. The old woman collapsed onto the floor from grief. Her screams could be heard across the store. The death cry of a mother losing her child. I rushed to assist the elderly couple in their time of need. To the old man's credit, his pride refused him to receive any help. "She's okay, Son. I'll take it from here," he said. He picked up his sorrowed wife and they walked out the door together while the people inside stood out of their way. It was a bittersweet sight to see as a patriot. When it was my turn, I only focused on the last names starting with the letter H. The top of the page began with Harris and the bottom ended with Hurley. The name Almer Roy Holmes was nowhere in sight. *Thank God,* I thought. It would've broken my mother's heart.

From across the hall somebody called out my father's name. "Holmes!" I turned around to see Coleman Adams waving a letter at me. He was a good friend of the family and when he didn't spend his time running the post office he was in church. He always encouraged our family to go but Father's relationship with God only comes when Father needs something. At first, I thought he'd mistaken me for Father because we look identical. It wasn't until I felt a nudge in my shoulder that probed me to turn my head around to see Father standing behind me.

"Did you check the list?" He asked me.

"I did. He wasn't on it," I answered.

"You're certain?"

"Yes, I'm certain." The look on his face confused me. I was expecting him to sigh with relief like Mother would. Instead, he had a look of dismay on his face. I found it odd but remembered the man has a short temper and isn't a fan of crowds. So much so that I was tasked with retrieving the letter from Mr. Adams on his behalf. He pushed the mail into my hands before my fellow townsfolk bombarded him. I tell you, walking through that crowd was like squeezing oil out of an olive. Father was waiting for me outside the building with his cigarette half-smoked. He grabbed the letter from my hands and read to himself while we walked. I tried to see what Roy said but father wouldn't allow it.

"When I'm finished you can have your turn." He was so preoccupied with the letter a horse carriage almost ran him over. Luckily for him, I was paying attention and pulled him back at the right time.

"Watch where yer going!" The rider yelled. Father didn't acknowledge the aggravated driver. His eyes were fixated on the letter while we walked on Main Street without care for anything else.

"Roy is in Paris," he said. He folds the letter and puts it in his inner coat pocket.

"Why can't I read it?" I asked him.

"Because we have more important things to address than a letter. I'll give it to you when we get home," he retorted. We turned the corner onto 2nd Avenue and walked up to the tailor shop Father goes to for his suits. He opened the door and instructed me to go inside.

The owner of the shop Stan was another one of Father's connected friends. Stan was the man all the elites went to for their suits and paid top dollar for his craftsmanship. He's someone who loved and respected the Crown as much as Father but was more liberal in his beliefs. Whenever he would visit our home all he'd speak of is Germany's war crimes. "That fat bastard Will-Helm should be quartered in Buckingham Palace. Only a monster would dare use gas against his enemies. What a disgrace!" I'm unsure if he realises, we use gas as well but who am I to disagree.

Stan and Father made me try on several different types of suits. It was the first one I had ever owned, and they wanted it to be perfect. From all different types until the last one that was made from wool. They said it added years to my age and gave me a respectable charm. The wool kept itching my skin and making mobility almost impossible without the risk of tearing the seams. I raised my discomfort to Father while he felt the need to supervise Stan's work. Every so often Father would pick at little details over my suit. "Change the cufflinks. He needs to wear the Lionshead. Change the Jacket. The three buttons make him more prestigious." Stan was growing tired of these alterations while I stood in the center like a statue in a museum. Everything was confusing to me and my patience grew thin.

"Father, why are we doing this? I don't need a suit." Stan gave Father a concerned look.

"You didn't tell him?" Stan asked him. My heart began to race while my mind filled with questions.

"Tell me what?" I asked in a panic. Father groaned and gave in.

"We're going to the Christmas ball," he answered. I was in awe. The Christmas ball was held every year at Morland Place, the most elegant mansion in town. Only the richest of the rich were allowed to go.

"Why?" I asked. His smile extended from ear to ear.

'Well, that was part of the surprise. There are going to be many officers at this ball and as your father, I took the liberty of putting in a good word for you." I looked at him as if he was mad.

"Father, I'm not old enough to serve. Why would you do that?"

"Well, that is why we are here, boy. We need to make you look older and more sophisticated or else the army will see through you." Stan stopped hemming my pants to chime in his two cents.

"He's right. It's just a political card to help the cause." He changed my jacket to the three-button overcoat that draped down to my kneecaps.

"What do you think?" Stan asked me.

"Something's off with it," I answered. Father gave me a dirty look.

"What do you mean 'something's off with it'?" He asked.

"It feels heavy," I answered. Both Father and Stan laugh at my grievances.

"It's supposed to feel heavy, my boy. That is one-hundred-per-cent wool you're wearing. You can't get any better than that," Father said.

"How does wool stand above the rest?" I asked, annoyed.

"It's what the army uses," Stan answered. Father had enough of my attitude.

"Listen Thomas. I don't want to hear any more of your grievances. Our objective is to serve our King and country, and you WILL act in accordance with it. Do I make myself clear?" I thought of the conversation at the dinner table on the day of Roy's deployment. Roy may have been a push over, but he also knew when to concede to Father's demands.

"Yes, Sir. Crystal clear," I said. Father was about to say something before I cut him off. "There's just no glory in lying is what I'm trying to say." Stan distanced himself from us to avoid being involved in our dispute. The look on Father's face was murderous.

"Look in the Mirror, Thomas. Tell me what you see." I looked into the full-body mirror on my left. I looked twenty-seven instead of seventeen. A patriot old enough to serve his country. I hate to admit it, but it convinced me to go along with his plan. Father stood behind me, hovering over me like he was re-establishing his authority. "Age is irrelevant when it comes to glory, son. Don't ever forget that." He chuckled and grabbed my shoulder with pride. "I'm proud of you, son." I smiled with pride.

"Thank you, Father," I said back.

* * *

We rode into town on horseback in the blistering cold. Father's horse George wasn't trained as well as Luna and rebelled against every command Father gave. The front greeters were timid of the horse and asked us to move George to the back. Father's response to their request was "Sure, shoot him if you need to! Lousy good-for-nothing-" Mrs. McClung and her husband approached us in their formal wear and bright attitudes.

"Why good evening, Master Holmes. How are we doing?"

"Good evening, Mrs. McClung. How was the tuna?" I asked her.

"It was fantastic! You let me know when you get in some more, eh?" Father was dragging me away from Mrs. McClung.

"Come along, Thomas." He commanded. I was on my way inside the house when I was waving goodbye.

"What was that for?" I asked him, annoyed.

"That woman is vile, Thomas. You best keep away from her if you don't wish to be castrated." We approached the front door where Father stopped me to examine my suit. He dusted the snow off my shoulders and then banged the doorbell. A colored man I'd recognized as Albert Hall greeted us in full uniform. Normally this would come as a shock to Father, but he was on his best behavior, so he gave Albert the respect he deserved. Albert saw me and shook my hand.

"Good evening, Tommy. Welcome to Morland Place. Do you have your invitation?" I looked at Albert confused.

"Uh, an invitation?" I asked. Father reached into his pocket and pulled out a piece of paper.

"Yes, right here," he said to Albert. Albert looked it over and guided us into the mansion. Inside was filled with guests and live music. The ambience was deafening as the doorman closed the front door behind us. I felt like a lost puppy in the middle of a crowd, with all senses on overload. A butler approached us with food from his silver tray. Father took the hor d'oeuvres with glee while I was coerced. I savored the food too much. As I was finished eating, I found myself alone while Father walked amongst the crowd like the King he thought he was.

LATER THAT NIGHT
GEORGE

I despise parties, absolutely hate them with a passion. The powers that be felt it would raise morale if we hosted a Christmas dinner over at Morland Palace, and I was dreading every second. Griffith went mad with the expenses, spending invaluable resources on frivolous decor that went to waste and illegal alcohol only the soldiers could consume. My boys did their jobs up to my standards as always and painted a beautiful picture of war to encourage new recruits. Mercer and Smith were especially gifted in seducing the rich with their tales of "grandeur" from the front. A gentleman whom I forget his name was fixated on living his glory through his son.

"How many Huns did you kill, son?" The man would ask them.

"Oh, I'm not sure, Sir," Mercer would answer. "We weren't trained to count that high."

"Outstanding! Hey, listen, would there be any chance you can help my son enlist? He's not the brightest but his head's as strong as a bull." Smith would chime in.

"As long as he's eighteen the army's got a home for him." The man smiled and carried on his merry way. Mercer looked at me and I gave him a nod of approval. He disappeared amongst the crowd while I walked around the room, shaking hands with the locals and smiling while the live music drowned out the sound of senseless conversations. While I roamed around the palace, I found an old colleague from the 31st regiment, John Holmes. He was a fellow soldier from the Boers but not one worth remembering. He was exceptional in his marksmanship but lacked the ability to see past his ego. He recognized me instantly and approached me with an ear-to-ear grin.

"George McFarland, is that you sir?" He asked me.

"Mr. Holmes, good to see you. I heard about your son Charles at Ypres. My condolences."

"Thank you, George. It has been difficult but my younger sons will give justice to his memory."

"Are they both serving?"

"One is while my youngest is days away from enlisting."

"Good for them both. What are their names?" I asked.

"Roy is the one at the front and my youngest Thomas is with me." John looks out into the crowd, unable to find him. "Well, he was at least."

"Well, if you by chance happen to find him, send him my way. It was good seeing you, John. Give my best to Edith." I shook his hand and bid him farewell. John disappeared amongst the crowd while I took my time and observed the room. There were two young girls performing a Celtic dance in the center of the room with the crowd surrounding them, impossible to find someone I don't even know. I guided my eyes to find the people I knew and did a process of elimination. The first person I spotted was Corrie, talking to a young harlot, Mercer and Smith were talking to a small crowd at the end of the bar. On the opposite end sat Sergeant Osgoode drinking his sorrows away while a young boy approached him from the side. I recognized him as the boy from the butcher's shop. He was dressed as a young entrepreneur looking to impress the crowd. I waited to see how long the boy would last. My plans were diverted as Osgoode's anger got the best of him as he consumed more from his flask. He grabbed the boy by the collar and yelled in his face, projecting a thick Scottish accent that had the room silent.

"I'll tear ya limb from limb ya keep yapping yer mouth!" I didn't step in Bruce would've killed him. I approached the conflict from the left flank to catch Bruce off guard.

"That's enough, Sergeant!" I ordered. I grabbed him by the shoulders and gave him a small shake, bringing the man back to earth from his troubled mind. Bruce snapped out of his daydream and walked away ashamed of his actions. The boy's breathing quickly subsided when Bruce left, giving him the space he needed to breathe. I sat on the same stool and ordered myself a beer, noticing the boy had a glass of water in his hands.

"You want a drink?" I asked him.

"No thank you, Sir. It is illegal for me to drink," the boy answered.

"Fair enough." The bartender set a tall glass of ale on the counter. "Don't mind the Sergeant. He's been at the front for too long." The boy looked at me and gave a small smile.

"It's okay, Sir. It wasn't a lively conversation anyway." He took a sip of water and introduced himself.

"I'm Thomas Holmes." Another piece of the puzzle came together.

"George McFarland. Pleasure to meet you, Son. Your father is John Holmes if I'm not mistaken."

"No, sir. You are correct. I haven't seen him around but I'm sure he's somewhere."

"I was just talking to him as a matter of fact. He spoke highly of you and said you were days away from enlisting." Thomas put his head down, as if he was ashamed.

"I'm sure he did. I'm not sure what else he told you Sir, but it was exaggerated." I looked at him with confusion.

"What makes you think that?" I asked him.

"He's never spoken highly of me." His face went pale when he realized what he said. Me knowing who his father was, I would take his word as truth.

"He still likes to boast about himself, doesn't he?" Thomas uttered a small chuckle.

"Yes, Sir."

"That's unfortunate, but such is life, right?"

"I guess."

"That being said, anyone who can hold a conversation with our fellow Sergeant has to have iron for skin. Can we agree on that?" The boy nodded and chuckled.

"Yes, Sir."

"So, what were you and my friend talking about?" The boy sighed in frustration.

"I'll be honest Sir, it only got to an introduction before he lost his mind. I'm not sure if it's worth repeating."

"Try me." The boy looked at me with fear in his eyes, like he feared what I was going to say in response.

"I can't lie to you, Sir. I'm not old enough to serve. I turned seventeen back in October and by the time I'm eligible the Germans will be on England's doorstep." I looked at the boy perturbed.

"What makes you say that?" I asked him.

"I read the news every day before work, and the casualty list whenever it's posted. Father wants me to enlist because it is what he deems as tradition but the way I see it, tradition isn't enough to stop the slaughter." I chose my next words carefully.

"What do you think it is?" I asked him.

"Evolution," the boy answered. I looked at him oddly, so he elaborated. "Canada is struggling because our leaders are stuck in the last century. Forgive me if I project any ill will towards England, but if they keep telling us where to go and where to die based off out-of-date warfare, Canada won't have any men left. At least that's how I feel, Sir." This boy may have been too young to serve in the army, but he had as much insight into the war as General Currie. I was captivated by the way this boy's mind worked. He hit every note in my concerto of what it takes to be a soldier, except for him not being old enough to serve. The punishment for lying about your age would result in an immediate court martial. Not only for the soldier who enlisted but for everyone else who enabled him. On one hand If I was to recruit this young man and he would be caught, I would lose all credibility in the army and have my battalion taken away from me. On the other, he would make a terrific soldier one day and if he could keep his nose under the guns long enough until he turned eighteen, the army would be less forgiving. I rolled the dice and took a chance. I took out my notepad and pencil and wrote down the address for the recruitment office along with a time, 9.00. I slid the note back to him and he looked at it carefully. "It was good to meet you, Thomas Holmes. I will see you in the morning." I got up from the stool, shook his hand and walked away, hoping the lad would be waiting for me the next morning.

THE NEXT MORNING

ANNIE

I was the first one into the office after the party.

Perfectly fine by my stature, this gave me the chance to catch up on work orders from George, including ordering the new NCO uniforms I was supposed to do two weeks ago. George arrived ten minutes shortly after I and informed me a recruit was scheduled for 9.00. The Major said things would've gotten easier once the battalion was formed. I pray for him he is right. I've grown tired of dreaming of names on paper.

Once I moved on from the uniforms I went to process the order for guns. The request is set at seven-hundred rifles for the battalion at a cost of twenty-five dollars per Ross. George nearly keeled over seeing the bill. "Eighteen-thousand-dollars for seven-hundred clubs? Spare me!" The Major was never shy over his grudges against the politicians. He was a soldier's soldier, someone who respected his country enough to look at it honestly, and not to line his pockets with greed like Major Griffith who waltzed into the building like an overdressed pig. He informed me he had a recruit coming in at the same time as George's recruit and delegated the task to me to start his file. Griffith being as thorough as a wet sock only gave me his last name and nothing else, Grieve. I got a file started on the man and waited for him to arrive.

Minutes had passed and the clock came close to 9.00. A young man walked into the building dressed for the cold. He looked my age, someone too young to enlist. He approached the desk and took off his hat. "Good morning," he said.

"Can I help you?" I asked him.

"My name is Thomas Holmes, and I am here to see Major McFarland." This was a surprise. I would expect Griffith to bend the rules for enlisting, not the good Major.

"Alright. Take a seat on the bench and I'll grab him for yuh." I got up from my chair and walked to George's office and knocked on the door.

"Send him in," was his response. I walked back to my desk and instructed the young man to walk in. I was in my chair for not even ten seconds when another man walked into the building. His wardrobe was like his ego, too big for his britches. He walked into the room with an arrogant smile, a trait I despised instantly.

"G'mornin' darlin'," he said with a coy tone.

"Can I help you?" I asked.

"Yes Ma'am. Would you be a doll and tell Major Griffith that Mr. Grieve is here to see him?" I kissed my teeth and did what the little man wanted. Naturally Major Griffith was ill-prepared, so I had to entertain this imbecile for twenty minutes. By the time the Major was ready George was walking out with his recruit. George gave me the file and told me to process Master Holmes and get his measurements. I took the file with zeal and instructed the recruit into the empty office across the hall. I instructed Master Holmes to take off his shoes and shirt. Thomas did as I asked and stood in the center of the room, looking uncomfortable standing in front of me.

"Something the matter?" I asked.

"No, Miss. Just anxious is all." I grabbed measuring tape and a clipboard.

"Tell you what, you help me keep track of the numbers and I'll make this as painless as possible. Sounds good?" I handed the clipboard to Thomas and gave him the pencil I had placed in my bun. I took out my measuring tape and went shoulder to shoulder, then hip to hip, shoulder to hand, and lastly toe to head. For the last one I had Thomas step on the metal tip for assistance. "Thirty-four-inch chest, thirty-inch waist, Overall height five-foot-five inches. One scar in between the shoulder-blades. Have you been vaccinated?"

"When I was a child."

"Thank you. No spots from Smallpox. Have you ever had Polio or Tuberculosis?"

"No, Miss, lungs are clean."

"Good. have you ever been committed of a crime?"

"No, Miss, never even cussed either." *The Huns are going to eat this boy for breakfast.*

"Right on. I just need to collect the Major for the oath. Just stay here for a second and I will be right back." I went down to George's office where I overheard Griffith bragging about his "accomplishments".

"This medal I got from South Africa. Hundreds of those Zulu characters swarmed us until a few of us were able to flank them. Their blades were sharp, but my mind was sharper." I had to resist the urge to vomit as I knocked on George's door. When he walked out to come into the recruitment room, he shook his head in annoyance upon hearing Griffith STILL bragging about the same medal. "I rassled with one of them to save the colonel from being slaughtered by those savages." George said in response.

"I'd love to see him try that against a German bayonet." Thomas was waiting in the same spot, with his shirt and shoes back on. I pull out the King James Bible as the Major locked eyes with Thomas and made him repeat everything the Major said.

"I, state your full name."

"I, Thomas William Holmes."

"Do solemnly affirm."

"Do solemnly affirm."

"That I will be faithful and bear true allegiance to His Majesty King George the Fifth, King of Canada, his heirs and successors according to law. So, help me God."

"That I will be faithful and bear true allegiance to His Majesty King George the Fifth, King of Canada, his heirs and successors according to law. So, help me God." George shook Thomas' hand and asked him one more question.

"Are you a man of prayer, Mr. Holmes?"

"No Sir, why do you ask?"

"Because you just joined the Canadian Corp." George walked out of the office as I escorted Mr. Holmes out of the building.

The 147th battalion
Meaford, Ontario

1916

V

JULY

We had grown up in material age, and in each of us was the yearning for great experience, such as we had ever known

ERNST JUNGER
IN STAHLGEWITTERN

CAMP BORDEN, CANADA
GEORGE

Every day is a good day to train.

Before I'm dressed in PT gear, I do my thirty-thirty-ten workout; thirty push-ups, thirty sit ups, and ten squats. Depending on the day I would hold a plank for thirty seconds over the push-ups to save time. At 5.00 I'm on the three-mile gravel track around the tents. I enjoy starting my run when the troops wake up to the sentry's trumpet. I would circle around the tents and observe the battalion from afar, studying their characters and seek out the best amongst the crowd. After my laps I change into my uniform and walk to the range for 0700. I detest using the Ross Rifle but as commanding officer of the 147th it is my duty to set the standard for the men, so I use it for a few minutes before I pull out my Colt .45. It's unusual for others to see me switch from rifle to sidearm. When I use my rifle, I shoot from the right. When I use my pistol, I shoot from the left. The reason being is because I am left-handed by nature. Sometimes I think that could be why I despise the Ross rifle s but then I remember Ypres and my heart changes tune. Unfortunately, Minister Hughes sent out a telegraph stating any soldier who criticized the Ross would face severe punishment. Little did he know many officers in the Canadian Corp shared my beliefs and used the memo for toilet paper.

The 147th is divided into four companies, first to fourth. Each company is headed by a Captain as per my request, not a lieutenant. The Lieutenant's I made platoon leaders with two Sergeants for support. This forced the Lieutenant's to focus on mission tactics and development for the troops. Griffith contested the idea every way from Monday to Sunday. "How are the men supposed to win the war if their leaders aren't leading them into battle?" If he were to ever clean the cobwebs out of his skull, he'd realize it's an officer's job to ensure the mission is a success. How are they supposed to do that if they're picked off by snipers before the battle even begins? Sadly, the man made a few calls to his connected friends in Ottawa, and I was ordered to follow the training designed by men who will never step foot into a trench. To add further insult to injury when we arrived at Camp Borden half the men didn't have their uniforms while the rest weren't assigned a rifle because Griffith was late filing the request order. Newly appointed Captain Finley had the idea to cut down some trees and carve out some make-shift replicas so we could at least get some knowledge into the men while we wait for the big shipment. If the training stays at this pace the men will be too old to fight at the front lines.

The men started their training at 9.00, the time I had my breakfast and read the daily reports. We were waiting to hear the results of our attack in the Somme to alleviate the French in Verdun. For days on end the Brits hit the Germans with every type of shell Army intelligence has created yet over fifty thousand killed or wounded on the first day of combat. The report was three days old, only God knows how many more had been killed since then. Corrie saw the look on my face and walked over with a flask in his hands. "Care for an extra kick in your coffee?" He asked me.

"A little early to be drinking, Tom?" I retorted.

"Normally yes, but I figured you'd need the extra kick." Griffith overhears our conversation and intervenes.

"What's the news from abroad?" He asked. I handed Griffith the report and his face went white.

"This is supposed to be a gentleman's war, not an act of slaughter," he uttered. He looked further down the report and read out loud "only six percent of the Newfoundland Regiment remain. The rest are missing, wounded, or killed." Corrie gave me a grim look.

"Otto's part of that outfit, right?" He asked.

"He is," I uttered. This would've explained the pale look on Annie's face.

"When should we tell her?" Corrie asked, reading my mind.

"Tell who?" Griffith asked.

"My orderly," I answered bluntly. "I think she already knows." Griffith diverted the attention back to himself.

"Doesn't matter. Soon enough the world will know who's responsible for this catastrophe." Corrie's tongue escaped him and poked back to Griffith.

"And just who might that be, Major?"

"Germany, Major Corrie! Germany! Germany! Germany! Every ounce of evil that is in our free world comes solely out of Germany! They conquer foreign land to enslave its inhabitants and use the innocent as fodder for our machine guns. They need to be eradicated!" Corrie was in a mood to fight back, but he looked at me first.

"Permission to speak freely?" He asked.

"Granted."

"Let me ask you a question, Major. Based on what you just said, how do you feel about letting Canadian's run their own Corp instead of Great Britain? We seem to be a bigger problem for the Germans. Why not let us be independent instead of colonial forces?" Griffith's face went red.

"Major Corrie these may be Canadian men, but this is the King's army, and you will be sure to remember that when you speak ill of Great Britain again." Corrie chuckled and chose to enjoy his coffee over debating with the hot-headed Limey. Griffith didn't get the answer he was looking for, so he stormed off back to HQ. Corrie drew his attention back to the reports.

"Does this mean training gets rushed?" He asked.

"No. General Byng is adamant we take the boys to the limit. We don't sail over until he says we're ready," I answered.

"Good, means I get to stock up on rum before we go." Griffith comes back to our tent at a feverish pace.

"What is it now, Major?" I asked, annoyed.

"Our weapons have arrived," he said with a smile. Corrie and I jumped to our feet and walked to the front of the building where soldiers were unloading the crates into the main lobby. Inside stood a British Captain taking inventory and counting the rifles being taken out of their cases.

"Good morning, Colonel. I expect you are ecstatic to see these." I looked down at the freshly crafted rifles with their matching bayonets.

"Ecstatic wouldn't be a word I would use but relieved, yes."

"Relief is good," the Captain said. I looked at Corrie and gave him the command to send an update to General Byng. Corrie left the building while I oversaw the delivery. "Colonel, these guns aren't going anywhere. You can trust me," the Captain said with a coy attitude.

"What's your name, Captain?"

"Alfred Winston Talbot, Sir. I just transferred from the 58th."

"Well, Captain Talbot. As much as I appreciate the support you will go fetch me Captain Finley as it is his men that need the weapons." Judging by the look the Captain made, he wasn't impressed by my order.

"Consider it done, sir. Where can I find Captain Finley?"

"Second Billa tent from the edge of the track." Talbot repeated my order word for word as he walked out of the tent. I kept a close eye on him as he grew smaller in the distance. I didn't receive any paperwork on a transfer from the 48th. I felt a stern conversation with Major Griffith was needed to get some answers.

LATER THAT MORNING
TOMMY

I thought training was going to be a lot more rigorous than routine chores.

We started our day with preparing our bunks and presenting ourselves in full uniform. The Sergeants would walk around the camp and seek out any infractions they could muster onto the men, something even as small as an unwanted crease in the shirt they would use to punish us. Grieve was the first victim, he woke up late and didn't tie his shoes. Sergeant Bradley took no mercy and screamed at the American two inches away from his face. "Private Yank, why are your shoes untied?!"

"I wasn't aware they needed to be tied this early, Sir," Grieve said with droopy eyes. The Sergeant gave Grieve a strong headbutt to wake him up.

"The Huns will turn you into schnitzel, Private Yank. For your punishment you will run the three-mile track."

"Yes, sir!" Grieve kneeled to tie his shoes to prepare himself for the run. Sergeant Bradley looked confused.

"Private Yank! Did I give you the order to tie your boots?!" Grieve looked at the Sergeant more confused.

"No, Sir."

"Then why are you tying your shoelaces when you are fifteen seconds late?" Unable to give the Sergeant an answer, Grieve followed his order and took to the track. He wasn't even a quarter of the way through before he tripped over himself and ate the dirt. Sergeant Bradley relished in every second of it.

"You see, boys. That is why we come prepared for war. A good soldier is prepared to fight no matter the time of day." His yelling could be heard from across the camp. "You are now a minute late, Private Yank! If you do not complete the track in twenty-eight minutes the whole company will be joining you!" Sergeant Bradley turned his attention back to the rest of us, walking up and down the lines observing our posture and attire. When it came time for him to spot me, I stood firm and proud, praying he doesn't find something to punish me with.

"Private Holmes!" He screamed.

"Yes, Sir!" I screamed back.

"Why is your shirt inside out?! Are you trying to make a mockery out of my company?!" I looked down to see my shirt and the Sergeant gave me a slap on the chin to lock eyes with me. "Do you not believe me, Private Holmes?!"

"No, Sir! I was just looking to –"

"Never take your eyes off the enemy, Holmes! Three miles!" I sighed then joined Grieve on the track. As I was running, I looked down at my shirt and saw I was wearing it correctly. I grew annoyed and took my aggression out on the track; bypassing Grieve who was struggling to keep up. When I looked back, I saw the rest of my company, wheezing and panting the rest of the way.

* * *

After our run we lined up single file at the weapons depot to get our guns. Lieutenant Dobie was standing at the front with a clipboard in his hands. He would ask each soldier their last name followed by the first.

"Name?"

"Bowman, James, eight-tree-eight-eight-oh-one." Once the said name was found, he would cross it off and hand the soldier his weapon. Most of the names I've come to know personally as most of the men in the company were from Owen Sound as well.

"Name?"

"Redfern, Frederick, eight-three-eight-three-eight-seven." Freddy was friends with Roy and knew me only as the little brother. He was tall and built thin like a stock of corn but had a rabbit's foot in his pocket. Only luck would bring him to the front of the line and me behind 200 men. I had some comfort in standing behind my old coworker David Reekie. He was the same age as me and joined up a week after but signed up with the British major instead of

Colonel McFarland. When we saw each other getting on the train to Camp Borden we shared a laugh over committing the same crime and have been close ever since. He was a lot calmer than I, when we worked together on the farm, he could be standing next to you and be so quiet you wouldn't even know he was there, which is a lot more than what I can say about Grieve who stood behind me and complained over peanuts.

"Why can't they just leave the trunks open and let us grab them?" He asked, out loud.

"It helps them keep track of who gets one," David answered.

"Tell me how that makes sense. Every officer knows that we are here and accounted for." The man from Montreal named Holloway was standing across from Grieve and muttered something in French under his breath. Grieve took offence and started to poke the bear.

"Ya got somethin' ya wanna say Frenchy?" Holloway chuckled.

"I just said I will give you ten seconds before your incompetence gets somebody shot." Grieve was confused.

"What do you mean incompetence? Are you calling me stupid or something?"

"If the shoe fits, Yank." Grieve took a second to breath before he went on the attack.

"You think you're funny, don't you? Well, I'll tell you what. How about we settle this on the range. Best shooter gets bragging rights and three packs of smokes. How 'bout it?" Holloway was bold and confident, like he's ready to play his ace.

"Five packs of smokes, a bottle of wine, and twenty-dollars," he counter-offered. Sergeant Bradley caught wind of their bet and marched over to Grieve with the fury of a woman scorned.

"Is there something useful you want to add to the list, Private Yank?!" Grieve stood straight in fear of Bradley's wrath.

"No, Sir!" He answered.

"Good. Because If I see any sound exit that trap of yours PT will be etched into your tombstone! Do you understand me?!"

"Sir, yes Sir!"

"Good! Eyes on the prize, Private Yank." Bradley walked back to Lieutenant Dobie and the lineup resumed. It took only seconds for Grieve to accept Holloway's offer.

"You're on," he whispered. Holloway nodded and gave a tap to Charlie, our corporal who organizes all the gambling for the soldiers. Holloway whispered into his ear which prompted Charlie to get his notebook out and write down the stipulations. He then passed the notebook amongst the company and gave them the opportunity to cash in. By the time the notebook was given back to Charlie it was his turn to collect his rifle.

"Name?"

"Elvidge, Vernon, eight-three-eight-five-oh-five." Reekie got his gun at the same time. My heart pumped with adrenaline. The only gun I ever used before this was Father's old Winchester. It was good when I was a child until he had no use for it and allowed it to get rusted up. This was a new weapon, and it was mine.

"Name?"

"Holmes, Thomas William, eight-three-eight-three-oh-one." I held the gun in my hands, and I was in awe. It was top-heavy thanks to the 30-inch barrel, the stock rested comfortably in my shoulder, the grip was smoother than butter and the bolt was foolproof. I didn't understand why some of the officers complained about it. It's the perfect hunting rifle.

There was a crowd of soldiers waiting for Holloway and Grieve to be the first to test out the new toys. The one thing us Canadians love during a competition is the psychological warfare between the two rivals. We would hurl insults to each other that made all the British troops blush from discomfort.

"Go back to your country, Yank!"

"The Huns will make a fine feast out of you, froggy!"

"Hey Yank, this ain't cowboys and Indians, you gotta shoot your gun like a real man!"

"Hey Yank! Ya better do the cavalry charge first in case you shoot yourself in the foot!" Even our Irish and Scottish comrades joined in on the action.

"Yer a waste of skin, Yankee Doodle! Froggy's going to leave you in the dust." The men carried on with the belittling until the instructor Sergeant Broadhead fired his sidearm into the air, forcing everyone to go silent.

"That's better," he said. He threw his cigarette on the ground and grabbed Grieve's rifle from his hands. "Gentleman. This is your standard issue Ross-Mark-Two rifle. The first rule of this gun is that it DOES NOT leave your sight. You will take it with you everywhere you go. If you are on sentry duty, it stays by your side. If you are taking a morning glory, your gun stays by your side. If you're thinking of sweet rosemary in between your bedsheets, your gun is there with you tugging away at the seams. If I catch ANYBODY without their rifle by their side, you will be subject to field punishment. Are there any questions?" Nobody said a word. "Good. Since there's some competition between Private Grieve and Private Holloway, you guys are up first." Grieve and Holloway walked up to the Sergeant and were used as demonstrators. "Gentlemen you will each be given a clip that contains five cartridges. As you can see down range there are ten targets that you must hit in a precise and timely manner. Grieve you will demonstrate how the gun fires in the prone position, Holloway you will be in the upright position. The current record is held by Sergeant Bradley with five headshots in ten seconds. I do not expect you to reach at his level today but by the end of your training you will become marksman worthy enough to serve in the Canadian Corp. Any questions?!" The company was silent. "Let's get started." Sergeant Broadhead handed out clips to each of us and demonstrated how to load the gun. "Once your weapon is loaded you will apply the safety. That way nobody gets stupid and gets somebody killed." He turned his attention and ordered Grieve and Holloway to get positioned. Broadhead called down the line as loud as he could; "Shooter's on the line!" Both men were naturals and took aim at the same time. The two exchanged competitive banter before the guns fired.

"It's too late to back out Yank, I'll enjoy the wine in your honor."

"With the twenty bucks I'll buy you a bottle and serenade in its glory, Frenchy." Broadhead intervened.

"Get ready!" He put his trusty whistle in his mouth and blew the signal. The two fired their weapons at a rapid pace, hitting each target simultaneously within seconds of each other. The smoke from the barrels carried a distinct odor of burning gunpowder spreading across the field. Once the men emptied their clips, Sergeant Broadhead yelled: "Cease Fire! Fingers off the trigger!" Grieve and Holloway set their weapons down and waited for the Sergeants to check the score. Bradley inspected Holloway while Broadhead inspected Grieve's. Both men scored almost identical headshots across the board. The Sergeants were stunned when they came to this conclusion. The other American in our outfit Alex Donaldson called out from the back of the crowd.

"Who won?" The two sergeants had a private conversation with each other before making a ruling.

"It's a tie. Change positions!" Sergeant Bradley yelled. Grieve got up to his feet while Holloway hit the deck. They were given another clip to break the tie while The Sergeants cleared the line of fire and gave the order to fire at will. Both Grieve and Holloway empty their clips into the wooden statues across the field. The men were practically drooling while the Sergeants examined the bullet holes. While the Sergeants talked amongst themselves, Grieve and Holloway were in shock to see they were an equal match.

"Where'd you learn how to shoot?" Holloway asked.

"West Point," Grieve answered. "Yourself?"

"Africa." Grieve nodded with respect then turned his attention back to the two sergeants. They walked back up to the men and shook their heads.

"Seems we got ourselves a couple of sharpshooters," Broadhead said with glee. "To decide the official winner, you guys are going to run the obstacle course while carrying your weapons. Whoever finishes first with the last kill wins." He pointed to the obstacle course 50 yards away. Grieve and Holloway walked to the start of the course while the rest of us waited impatiently for them to start. Some went as far as upping the ante in the betting pool. Even the NCOs were getting in on the action. Broadhead put up three packs of smokes for Grieve to win. I think he did it for morale support because only a few placed their bet with Grieve. I made it a personal rule not to spend my earnings on frivolous gambling or liquor, so I enjoyed the show with the minus without the risk of losing. Most of the men poked fun at me for it but today it was Grieve's and Holloway's turn to be under the magnifying glass.

"Get ready!" Sergeant Bradley called out. The men got into position and were ready to charge. Bradley blew his whistle and the final test began. The two men shot the first target then charged in with their bayonets, stabbing and ripping the burlap sack apart. Before the sand could fall to the ground the men threw their guns on their backs and charged up the ramp grabbing the rope and swinging to the other side. Another target was at the bottom of the ramp and was cut to pieces by the men's impeccable aim. They shouldered their weapons and continued with the course. Holloway was ahead of Grieve by only a few inches when they got to the monkey bars. Grieve was grabbing each one as fast as he could to keep up while Holloway skipped a few bars to widen the gap between them. In the end it backfired as he missed one of the bars and fell into the mud, rifle first. Cheers and boos came from the men, more specifically all the privates. The Sergeants and Lieutenants stood with an eerie calm, waiting to see what was going to happen. Holloway got to his feet quickly, finishing up the course far behind Grieve who was already at the final obstacle, shooting multiple targets at a rabbit's pace. When Holloway got to the final checkpoint, his gun didn't fire. In a fit of rage, he threw his gun onto the ground and lit up a smoke to calm himself down. Grieve was over the moon with excitement.

"That's how it's done, boys!" Grieve danced around like he was riding a horse while Charlie collected all the cash and cigarettes from the pool. Grieve got over half the pot while everyone took a percentage of the winnings. Out of the corner of my eye I could see Major Corrie walking towards us with Colonel McFarland and that receptionist woman from the recruitment office. Her face was as white as if she saw a ghost, with tears flooding down her eyes. More privates looked in my direction to greet the calm major.

"Attent-ION!" Sergeant Bradley commanded. We stood proud in front of Major Corrie while he took long drags from his cigarette.

"At ease," he said softly. He looked at Holloway and walked in his direction. When they stood shoulder to shoulder the major shook Holloway's hand and said, "Good try." He walked back over to the men and finished his cigarette. He looked at Grieve and shook his hand. "Good job, private. What's your name?"

"Private Grieve, Sir!"

"You got a first name to go along with that?"

"Yes Sir. It's Gordon, Sir."

"Right on. Why don't you do me a favor and hand me your rifle, Gordon?" Grieve handed his rifle over and Corrie looked at it thoroughly. He cocked the bolt back to look inside. "Looks clean, private. Well done." He walks with the rifle over to the monkey bars where Holloway fell. He took out a clip from his pocket and loaded the weapon. Instead of firing it though, he threw the gun down in the same spot, letting all the mud seep into the components. He rolled the gun around before picking it back up and handing it back to Grieve. "Private Grieve, shoot the targets." Grieve looked at Corrie with a cock-eyed grin.

"Yes Sir!" Grieve grabbed the rifle and wiped the dirt off the trigger and guard. He walked back over to the target range and took aim. When he fired, nothing happened. Grieve looked puzzled then tried again.

"Is there a problem, Private Grieve?" Sergeant Bradley asked him.

"Uh, the gun seems to be jammed, Sergeant. It won't fire," Grieve answered.

"It was working fine a minute ago, Private. Why the change?" Corrie asked him. Grieve looked scared to give him an answer.

"I don't know, Sir."

"Does anyone wanna take a crack at why the gun doesn't fire?" Holloway shouted from the back of the crowd.

"It's because of the mud in the chamber." Corrie smiled and looked at Frenchy.

"That's correct. There's mud in the chamber. I want everyone to remember this because all it takes on the battlefield is a single stroke of luck to determine whether you live or die. You best make sure you're the one still standing, eh?" Corrie left the company and joined up with the Colonel and the girl, driving away from the camp while the rest of us stayed and absorbed the harrowing wisdom the Major gave us.

Beaumont Hamel
07.01.1916

VI

AUGUST

It was a magnificent display of trained disciplined valour, and only failed because dead men can advance no further.

GENERAL ALYMER HUNTER-WESTON, COMMANDER BRITISH 4TH ARMY
VIII CORPS

HALIFAX, CANADA
ANNIE

The train was arriving at the station and my hands wouldn't stop shaking.

It was an indescribable feeling that I wasn't prepared to handle so I locked my hands in between my thighs in hopes of retaining my composure. Back in Ontario, I had control of myself. I was able to focus on the task at hand in welcoming Dad back to Canada... that was until we passed the Quebec border then the shakes began. Heavy thoughts flooded my mind, daydreams of Billy and I playing together as children, with Father standing on the porch of our home smoking his pipe and enjoying an ale. I know nothing of how Billy died, the letter Dad sent was short and bleak. He just asked for me to meet him in Montreal while he's on leave.

His ship was scheduled to arrive tomorrow in the morning, leaving me with several hours to get some rest before the real hardship begins. I'm grateful I lack imagination, or else my mind would be in a terrible place.

I waited for everyone else to get off the train so I could avoid any unwanted touching. I felt if someone was to bump into me, they would feel the wrath of a grieving sister, and that was something unwarranted for anybody regardless of who they are. I shook the bricks out of my feet and walked out the exit. It was like seeing an ocean of people inside the station, none of them having a care about anything except for themselves. I resented it to an extent, of all the people lingering inside the station, not one of them is my older brother. I kept my head down and held my suitcase close for comfort, avoiding anybody that comes close to me. Anxiety clenched my chest like it was fitted by a corset two sizes too small. I've never known pain like this before. It isn't a flesh wound where all you need is a needle and thread to mend it. It's far deeper and more harrowing, something that I've never experienced and willing to bargain with the devil to never experience it again.

Outside of the station was even worse. After living in the countryside for so long I forgot what it was like to be surrounded by people. I hated it. I didn't want to be around other people. I wanted to be back home with Mindy and forget this ever took place. Or better yet, go back in time and have Billy and Dad back home with me. I didn't bother with taking the tram, I just walked down the street and pretended nobody else existed. That was until some arsehole in a uniform spotted me and thought it'd be cute to be friendly. "Bonjour mademoiselle, comment ça va?" I ignored him and continued to walk down the street. That wasn't enough to tell him he'd been rejected so he continued to follow me down the road. "Do you speak English?" he asked. I grunted in response.

"No disrespect sir, but I wish to be left alone."

"Well, how come? Could it be because you're a pretty little thing walking downtown by yourself?" I was NOT in the mood to be dealing with these pig-headed men! I pushed the pervert to the ground and laid down my authority.

"DON'T YOU EVER CALL ME A PRETTY LITTLE THING AGAIN! WHY IS IT THAT PIGS LIKE YOU ARE STILL ALIVE AND MY BROTHER IS DEAD?! TELL ME WHY MY BROTHER IS DEAD!" I screamed. A crowd swarmed around me in fright. I felt so embarrassed by my actions I checked myself into the closest hotel and cried myself to sleep.

* * *

I woke up in the early hours of the next morning with my undergarments drenched in sweat. My mouth was dry like sand and the nightmare that woke me up was playing repeatedly in my mind. I couldn't shake the terrors, so I went to the bathroom sink and splashed myself with cold water. After several splashes my heart slowed down to a comfortable pace and I got myself a glass of water to cool the rest of me off. While I savored my water, I looked out the window to the St. Lawrence River, trying to distract the pain by thinking how the saltwater air could cure my headache. I got on my shoes and walked alone while drunken soldiers and sailors roamed in packs looking for any delinquency they could find. I ignored them all and headed straight for the water. The closer I got; the less people were around. When I found sand, I sat down and stared at the lighthouse, listening to the tide coming ashore. The light beaming from the lighthouse was the only thing keeping the beach from being covered in darkness. Not even the stars could offer any illumination. It made me grow tired and yearning for sleep. Not just for a little, but for a long while. Not permanently, but long enough for the war to end. My thoughts were tantalizing; however, Dad wouldn't approve of it. He'd just say somethin' like "Oi! Quit being a Feardie and git yer arse back in the saddle yuh lassie!" His thick accent from the homeland always cheered me up, even in the darkest of times. If I could hear my father's voice again, I could sleep comfortably again. This was the only thing on my mind until the sun peeked through the clouds on the horizon. It reminded me of an old wives' tales I heard growing up, "red skies at night, sailor's delight. Red skies in the morning, sailor's take warning." Whatever warning it is, it can't be any worse than losing Billy. At least that's what I keep saying to myself. It helps me to my feet and dust myself off, but more care was needed by the time I was ready to see Dad. I resorted to singing a shanty on my way to the harbor.

My mother told me
Someday I would buy
Galleys with good oars
Sails to distant shores

Stand up on the prow
Noble barque I steer
Steady course to the haven
Hew many foe-men
Hew many foe-man

SOMEWHERE OVER THE ATLANTIC

OTTO

I'm not one to shed a tear over loss. I had never wept from heartache, never cried over spilled milk, always stoic as my mother would say. I once saw the side of a man's head explode while we were sharing some rum and conversation about loved ones back home. I turned my head left for a mere second when a sniper took out the poor lad in a clean swoop. It happened so fast; his blood was dripping down from my chin before I even knew he was gone. It gave me the shivers for a little, but I kept going and fulfilled my duty as a soldier. Before every battle, Conor and I shook hands and hugged each other goodbye in case one or either of us didn't come back. We started the tradition back in Gallipoli and it got us through that God awful mess. You wanna talk about lions led by donkeys b'ye? I tell ya spend two weeks under the command of a man named Winston Churchill and you'll understand Haig's a crumb in comparison. It wasn't Haig's fault the Germans were prepared for us. He wasn't aware the bastards intercepted our communications and decoded our plans weeks beforehand. Haig may be an old dog that's been around the calvary too long, but for once this slaughter was not his fault.

The Somme was a twelve-mile field full of crops and life, a beautiful change of scenery from the Dardanelles. There were no rotting bodies everywhere... at least in the beginning that is. With over two million shells fired on the enemy lines, our battleground went from a Monet to a desolate quagmire. For a week straight, the British and French pounded the hell out of that field, and with the

Newfoundland Regiment being positioned in the reserve trench, we got front row seats to the fireworks. Any man worth his salt would've assumed there were no Germans left after a barrage like that. It was a spectacle like no other. Day after day Whizz-bangs and Lemons made moon-sized craters, shockwaves rippled through our lines, moving massive pieces of rock effortlessly. The Brits saved the grand finale for Confederation Day, a mine under Hawthorn Ridge. My God what a sight, an explosion powerful enough to make the whole country shake. It lifted the spirits of the men, cheers and laughter in reinforcing the idea this was going to be easy. We waited for our signal to go over and waltz to the German trench without a scratch. General Rawlinson's plan was working... until the Bosch opened fire. The British were cut to ribbons, over the hills we saw men drop to the deck by the clusters. We couldn't believe it. How the Germans survived such a ferocious attack was nothing short of a despicable miracle. I knew it was a matter of time before it was our turn to fight.

We assembled at St John's Road at 8.45, taking as much ordnance as we could carry. With our Enfield's and our Mills, we were ready to support our allies in need. As time passed fear began to infect the men. Some prayed to their god, some held pictures of their loved ones, some went as far as taking a drink for courage. The poison of choice was the Screech, a diabolical rum that settled the nerves but brought out the devil in you. If a man were to have too much of the stuff his mind would break and he'd be reduced to an animal, forever searching for its prey. Once in a blue moon is fine, but I'd rather see the devil in my line of sight than in the mirror.

Our objective was to capture Beaumont Hamel, a quaint village decimated by two years of war. There were two problems we faced. First, there was over 700 meters between us and the Germans that's been under their control over the last two years. The second problem was the weight of our kits. Over sixty pounds strapped to our back, as ordered by some donkey from London. We were like turtles walking into a sea of sharks, and at 9.15 it was our turn for the grinder.

We went over the top and charged across the land as fast as we could. Conor was two meters ahead of me before he saw one of his buddies shot, then ran to his aid. I remember being angry with the boy because the first rule I taught him was that dead bodies attract dead bodies. When you see a comrade wounded you don't stop to tend to him, you keep going or else you'll be in the same grave. I took cover under a tree so I could yell for him to get back to the line. With all the gunfire and shells exploding around us, he was deaf to everything I had said. I kept calling his name repeatedly, "Conor! Conor! Conor!" But I was out of his sights. Might as well have been in another world. I couldn't focus on the mission until my boy was out of that crater and only two feet away from me. I ran across the field like an idiot and tackled the boy to the ground, shielding him from the bullets zipping above our heads. I smacked him up the back of his head, giving his brain the jumpstart it needed to get back to the mission.

We got to our feet and looked across the land. With each passing second our numbers got smaller and smaller. The wave of sea turtles became a splash in the pond. We had to move quickly before we would be the only ones left alive. The Danger Tree was in our sight, with a wall of smoke behind it. Looking around to see who's left was a crimson sight. We still had 500 meters to cross, and we lost half of the regiment. There's no sense in hiding when Valhalla was waiting on the other side, so I grabbed my boy and onward we went.

When we got into the smoke, Conor and I separated. I only looked forward with my rifle ready and focused on nothing else. The guns were silent, a painfully uneasy feeling that sent knots into my stomach. My feet treaded lightly across the mud, dreading what was waiting for us on the other side. The smoke was so thick I couldn't see two inches past my face. Conor could've been only ten feet away and I wouldn't have known. The closer I got, the easier it was to hear the Germans talking to each other. I couldn't be bothered learning the bloody language, it was pure gibberish to me. But, when I heard the clicks and clacks from their MG's being fed with ammo, their message was clear. I dropped to my stomach and aimed down sight. The guns remained silent; more gibberish was yelled instead. Were they waiting for the smoke to clear? Were they waiting for us to move closer to save bullets? I didn't know. I knew I was safe where I was, and that was enough. As each second passed my thoughts focused more on my son, "Conor!" I called out. It was a mistake on my part, the Germans opened fire, and I dropped to the ground. I returned fire hoping I'd get lucky, another mistake on my part. When I emptied my clip, they stopped firing and allowed the silence to flourish. I reloaded my weapon and prepared for a charge. No charge happened, instead the sound of a whip cracking echoed my ear drum then the ground exploded behind me. I was hit by a mortar. I was thrown off my feet and crashed into another body. I wasn't sure who it was, everything happened so fast my memory is foggy as a result. I couldn't hear anything either, it must've gotten damaged from the mortar. I remember asking myself how I am still alive. I didn't even get a blighty, not a scratch on me. I sat up and saw the smoke dissipate. My cover was going to vanish, so I desperately found a crater to hide myself. I grabbed the body without hesitation, dragging the poor sod into cover with me. I remember hesitating thinking it could've been a Hun, but the uniform was the same as mine, green khaki with beige suspenders. I didn't see his face until his body fell to the bottom of the crater. It was my boy; it was my Conor. I cannot say how he looked. It pains me even to think about the mess the Huns made of him. My heart felt like it was ripped out and thrown into the mud, waiting to be washed away by the rain. I couldn't look anywhere else but into my son's eyes. He must've been right beside me when I called for him, or maybe the Germans killed him when I called out his name. I mustn't succumb to wicked thoughts. It's not going to get me back home to Annie. She's all I got left. The fog was almost gone, and I needed to go but I couldn't leave Billy behind. It was only a matter of time before the Germans counter attacked and I needed to get back to the front lines so defend myself. I ditched the rucksack and carried only my rifle and my bombs to gain more speed, my only ally. I tightened my boots and my helmet, last I needed was to lose one or both. *By God, please let me live*, I thought. Deep breathes, control yourself, Otto. Come back home to your daughter. My thoughts weren't putting me at ease; I kept looking at Conor, thinking if I could have a piece of him with me, he would keep me safe. I went down and grabbed hold of his uniform and cut off his patch with his knife. His tags I took as well. They were going to rot like the rest of him out here and I couldn't bare anybody knowing he was here. I stuffed them both into my breast pocket over my heart, the best place I knew to put him. I grabbed four smoke bombs and pulled the pins on all of them, throwing them towards the Germans. A blanket of smoke laid down some cover for me, seconds were a luxury, and luxury was something I couldn't afford. I got to my feet and ran back to St. John's full steam ahead. The Germans fired into the smoke, their bullets missing me by inches. More mortars exploded behind me as I raced against time. I began to hear charges coming from the German lines. *fuck, this is where I'm going to die,* I thought. The main support trench was in sight, along with our machine guns pointed at the Germans. I waved my arms in the air to get their attention. They recognized me as one of their own with a few soldiers going over the top to help me. They grabbed me by the arms and brought me back to the trench, dusting me off and checking for wounds. One of the soldiers felt my breast pocket and pulled out the dog tags. "They belong to my boy," I uttered. The soldier's face went cold. He took the liberty of reading his name out loud.

"Conor Middaugh. That's a good name. I hope you're proud of it." I took the tags back and put them in my pocket, along with my fear and grief for the loss of my son.

"I'm something," was all I could say back. I stole a stogey from the man and walked down the line, searching for a spot to be silent and alone so I kept walking until I found a grassy spot to sit down. I it up my stogey and wondered what was next for me. Was I going to die tomorrow, or the day after? If my time was limited, I owed it to my daughter to tell her what happened here. My commanding officer Lieutenant MacDonald agreed with me and gave me a pass to go back home. I took the first ship out of England and was on my way back to Halifax. I kept Conor's memory in my pocket the whole time, dragging my thumb across his name. It reminded me of the days I would rock him to sleep when he was a baby. The wee lad was as big as Mindy back then, rowdier mind you, but he was a good boy. I'm ever so thankful both him and Annie inherited their mother's looks. Especially the eyes, all three share the same beautiful hazel-colored eyes that give peace to a man's soul. After the terrors of the front, it was a site seeing those eyes at the harbor waiting for me. When I saw Annie, the poor girl looked miserable. She did her best to smile, but when I gave her the dog tags and patch, she melted into my arms and wept. She apologized for crying but I just said nothing, I held her in my arms and started to cry with her. This isn't how life is supposed to be. The children are supposed to bury the parents, not the parents burying their children. God hoping I never lose Annie. She's all I got left until she finds a man and starts a family of her own. For that man's sake he better not be a soldier, or else I'm feeding him to the Germans.

Ladies of the evening.
1916

VII
OCTOBER

We are fighting Germany, Austria, and drink, and so far as I can see the greatest of these deadly foes is drink.

DAVID LOYD GEORGE

AMHERST, CANADA
TOMMY

The 147th had to be quarantined because of an outbreak of Diphtheria. It started with Alpin over in A company then spread like a plague across the battalion. Even Major Corrie was sent to the hospital to fight off the rotten bug. This caused us to miss the date for our voyage to war. Now we are stuck in camp until the shipment of serum arrives which for the time being has not been defined. Major Griffith keeps telling us sometime in the following week, but it has been almost two months' worth of waiting for a needle. Those not infected by the virus were expected to carry out their regular duties and training while the rest stayed in sick bay. The Holmes family may have strong genetics but the thought of Alpin being choked to death by his own mucus scared me into wearing my gas mask on sentry duty. All the boys laughed at me in the beginning but when more men got sick, they gave my idea a try. I am proud to say our unit was one of few that remain untouched.

There are many similarities between Amherst and Borden. Both camps are in the middle of nowhere, filled with brave young men full of pent-up patriotism and idealism. Both are headed by the same Battalion CO and everyone else directly below. If you take a hard total of differences between the two camps, the only thing Amherst has over Borden is the city of Halifax which has taverns and brothels. On the weekends we would have off most of the boys drive two hours to one if not multiple watering holes to drink themselves stupid then visit the girls to close out the evening. I never bothered to join in, as much as I enjoy the company of my fellow soldiers, I lacked interest in such adventures. I have nothing against any man that partakes, I just felt too uncomfortable being intimate with a stranger. That and I hate the taste of alcohol. I'm more inclined to enjoy my leisure time writing letters to my parents or reading a book. My current book of choice is The Strange Case of Dr. Jekyll & Mr. Hyde, a book recommended by Holloway. I was more accustomed to Rudyard Kipling's creativity and the way he told stories but for some reason I'm allured to the strife between science and morales. It was something new, something out of my comfort zone. I was able to read a quarter way through when the boys came back from the showers. They were laughing and having a sport with each other before Redfern found me on the bed.

"Eh, Tommy! Missed you in the showers," he said.

"Had mine in the morning," I retorted.

"You coming out with us?" Reekie asked.

"Well -" I tried to say no but I was cut off from Grieve.

"What was the name of that girl who spun the plates?" Holloway answered with his thick French accent.

"Yvonne." All the men chuckled.

"Do you think she'll be there tonight?" Grieve asked. Reekie gave a sarcastic answer.

"They all live together in the same house, Grieve. You think they work in shifts?"

"Reekie, you're just jealous that she looked at me first."

"The reason why she looked at you first is because she saves the best for last."

"I'll show you who's best for last!" Grieve and Reekie were two seconds away from fighting before Sergeant Broadhead stuck his head through our tent.

"When you women are finished bickering at each other, come get your serum at the medical tent." Broadhead closed the flap and walked away in the rain. While everyone struggled to get out of their wet clothes, I was already in the medical tent in line waiting for my shot. Captain Howes, the medical officer was having a cigarette while he filled the syringe.

"Private Holmes, have a seat." I did as he instructed, and he put out his smoke. "Where's the rest of your unit?" Coincidentally the rest of them barged through the door like a wild pack of hyenas. Reekie had a fresh cut above his eye and Grieve had a fat lip. Captain Howes was furious when he saw the fresh wounds. "You mind telling me what happened?" He asked Reekie.

"Oh, nothing bad, Sir. Just a friendly dispute over a friend." They giggled amongst each other while Howes gave me a stern look.

"Make sure you keep these imbeciles alive when we go over." Grieve overheard the last sentence and voiced his opinion.

"Captain, just when exactly are we going over? Need to add some Huns on my mantle."

"By the time I know Private Grieve we'll be on the boat going north on the St. Lawrence." Captain Howes jabbed me in the arm and put a piece of bandage to stop the bleeding. "If you wake up in the middle of night vomiting, come back to the medical tent," he instructed. I nodded in approval.

"Yes Sir, is there anything else I should be worried about?" I asked.

"Rash, fever, loss of appetite, worst you could have is seizures and if that happens just get one of your buddies to bring you in." He took the bandage off and threw it in the garbage. "Alright Private Holmes. You are free to go." I got up from the chair and Charlie went in. Before I left the tent Charlie stopped me.

"Tommy! Wait up for us."

"It's okay, I'll see you guys back at the tent," I retorted.

"You didn't think we would forget about your birthday, did you?" I was stopped in my tracks and felt terror grow up my spine. If Captain Dowes finds out I lied about my age, I'll be discharged.

"I didn't realize what day it was," I answered.

"Well, that's unfortunate for you, but we remembered. We got a surprise for you."

"What kind of a surprise?" I asked. Grieve spoke while the needle went into his arm.

"Don't worry about it. Just wear your best clothes and you'll be fine." I was scared to speak, unsure of whether to be happy or angry at the boys for giving me a birthday present. Captain Howes spoke as he sterilized his needle.

"No Brothels," he uttered. Holloway sat in the chair and lit up a cigarette while he waited for the doctor.

"Nah, don't you worry about that. Just gonna get the kid nice and plastered," he said.

"Oh, well if that's the case, better to get it out of your system now. You Don't know when you can do it again." I was in disbelief after hearing what the doctor said. Maybe I was being too uptight over not wanting to drink. It was time to relax and step out of my comfort zone like I did with the book. Getting drunk couldn't be that bad, right?

* * *

We arrived in Halifax early in the evening. The sky had a little bit of sun while the rain clouds cleared away, giving a beautiful view of the city at the bottom of the hill. It reminded me of home for a second, making me wonder how

Roy was doing. It feels like forever since I have heard from either him or Father. I'm sure Father told Roy I've enlisted. The army could just be withholding the letters to curb the espionage within the ranks. I'm hoping once we get to England, we could run into each other and could catch up. It's been far too long since I've seen my brother and not even sure if the bugger's been hurt or not.

The Billa Tent was on the far end of a series of rickety old log cabins built by the soldiers. It wasn't a cabin like the rest of them, this was a fully built two-story Victorian home with patrons gathered on both upper and lower decks. The fascinating thing about it is that the front windows bore paintings of each battalion that has frequented the establishment. The 147th wasn't there but the 58th was. The thought of Roy being here gave me enough courage to walk into the tavern and see all different types of soldiers filling the room full of cigarette smoke and entertainment. There was a group by the piano singing sea shanties while drinking large glasses of beer, another group was playing darts and gambling away their earnings. The one group that intimidated me was the Newfoundland Regiment sitting at the middle table, cheering on a soldier playing five finger fillet. It was a frightening sight to see a man risk his fingers over a pile of money, at least to me it was. To everyone else, they got great joy out of it like life was a gamble to them. While I was distracted by the game Grieve left the group to talk to a soldier sitting at the end of the bar. I couldn't make out what they said but money was exchanged between the two. After a few minutes of bantering Grieve comes back with a smile on his face.

"It's been taken care of," he said. Holloway cackled with joy and rubbed his hands together. He muttered something in French and then asked in English "So, when are they coming?"

"Sergeant Dickson said Madam Lucienne should be here any minute."

"Gah, that's a minute too long," Charlie grunted.

"Who's Madam Lucienne?" I asked.

"Oh, you'll see," Grieve answered. My eyes were drawn back to the game and this time the leader of the group looked back.

"Oi! Newbloods!" The man called out from across the room. We looked in his direction where he waved us over to have a seat. The Newfoundlanders grabbed extra chairs for us to sit comfortably amongst each other. The leader extended his hand to us first.

"Call me Otto," he said.

"Private Holmes, Sir," I said back. He grabbed a full beer glass on the table and handed it to me.

'Oh, cut out the formalities. We are amongst friends not soldiers. What's your first name?"

"It's Tommy, Sir," I answered.

"We'll work on it." We crashed our pints together and drank. I only had a few sips while Otto guzzled down his beer. His pint was half-gone when it touched the table. "So, what's your unit?" He asked us.

"We're the 147th. The Grey's," Charlie answered.

"Good on ya. Where are you all from?" We all said Owen sound in unison. "Aye, I know the place. Have a cousin that lives up that way."

"What's your cousin's name?" I asked.

"Nellie McClung, do you know her?" He asked me. The only Nellie I knew was the fish lady Nellie. Lucky for me, that was her. "Haha! Good. She's still alive, that old crazy bat." He changed the subject back to us. "You must've all gone to the same school together, right?" we nodded in unison except for Grieve.

"Not me, I'm American," he said, proudly.

"Oh, are ya now? My grandfather fought alongside General Brock at the Plains of Abraham. You guys don't plan on coming to our shores once this mess is done, do you?" Before Grieve could give an answer, the front door opens and in walks an old woman with orange curly hair and a rugged walk. Behind her is a group of women wearing simple garments of clothing. The old woman calls out to Sergeant Dickson.

"Norman! These girls need a minute!"

"Take as much time as you need Madam," he said back. The girls all rushed upstairs with Madam close behind them.

"Let's go, pits and cooches, on the double!" Cheers and whistles came from the men. All except for myself and Otto. Otto picked up on this observation as well, he looked at me intrigued by something.

"You alright there, b'ye?" He asked.

"Yes Sir, just a little nervous is all."

"Take a drink, it'll smooth out the edges." I looked down at the pint and had a few more sips. The hops and the sting of the beer hit the back of my throat, causing me to give a disgusted look. Otto laughed at my expense.

"Not a big drinker, are ya?"

"No, Sir. I am not."

"How old are ya?" I sat in my chair frozen with fear. Luckily for me, Reekie came to my rescue.

"He just turned nineteen on Monday," he said. Otto had a look of awe and confusion.

"Oh, did you now? Well, if that's the case then you need to drink up! Us Scotians have a tradition for every soldier that parties with us." The rest of the group got excited. I couldn't help but feel overwhelmed with joy. It has been a long time where I felt special and part of something bigger than my father's approval. I couldn't disappoint the lads and say no to the initiation. I grabbed hold of my beer and drank the rest down as fast as I could. The hops made me belch like a madman, but I got cheers and applause from everyone in the group. "Good job, Private Holmes." He walks over to the bar to grab a bottle of brown liquid along with two smaller glasses. He brought it all over and set up two more pints with one of the smaller glasses next to it. He popped the cork on the bottle and filled the smaller glasses to the rim.

"We call this a caper wedding. What you do is, you take a shot of screech and drop it into your pint. Not a second later you down your pint then kiss a cod fish." A soldier pulls out a large fish from a barrel, a hideous looking creature that was just as stuck as me in this deranged debacle. "If you can do that and not throw up, you've become a man." The crowd gathered around us, anticipating what I was going to do. "You can always back out, but Shirley here will be mighty offended if you did," Otto was persuasive and knew which string to pull on me.

"You're on, Sir!" I was about to grab the glass and drop it in before Otto interrupted.

"Slow down, bud. Wait until your commanding officer gives you the order." Otto grabbed his glass and was about to give the command before Madam Lucienne interrupted us again.

"Oh, boys," she said with a devilish grin. We turned around in sync and saw a long lineup of beautiful women wearing voluptuous dresses. The man at the piano was inspired to play a song as the ladies walked down the stairs and joined the men at the party. Men flocked to them like they were lost puppies searching for their favorite toy to play with. One girl approached Holloway and his eyes glistened.

"Good evening darling," the woman said softly.

"Valerie!" She did what she asked and straddled him like she was riding a horse. They started kissing and groping each other. I was in utter shock while the rest of the men cheered him on. Holloway's admiration for Valerie could be heard from across the room. "Mon Dieu, j'adore cette guerre!" Reekie comes back from the bar and taps me on the shoulder.

"You need to go upstairs with Madam," he said. I clued in to what my birthday present was, and my hands shook violently. I shifted down the couch and tried to escape without anyone noticing. Otto unfortunately has the eyes of a hawk.

"Hold on a second!" I was stopped dead in my tracks. Otto just laughed and pulled out a cigarette.

"Have some liquid courage to go," he said. My heart was racing with excitement. I could feel it pounding my bones, beating four times as fast as it should be. It wasn't ideal for what

I was about to do. I needed to take the edge off, and the gifts Otto laid in front of me was the only plausible solution. I grabbed the shot glass and hovered it above the pint, Otto followed suit. "On three, two--" I couldn't wait any longer and dropped the shot in. The liquor made the beer taste almost unbearable, but I upended that pint in a heroic fashion. Otto was shocked but laughed at my expense. "Atta boy! You feel more relaxed now?" All I could do was nod and belch. "Shirley will be here waiting for you when you come back." I shook Otto's hand and stood up from my chair. The alcohol hit me like a ton of bricks, and I almost stumbled to the ground. The bottom half of my body went numb, like my legs were made of spaghetti. I stumbled my way up the stairs to the bedroom, where a blonde woman was waiting for me.

MINUTES LATER
OTTO

I was expecting the kid to yak the second the shot hit the deck.

That screech is a mean tasting bastard and for first timers it always ends the same. They hit the bottle too hard to prove themselves worthy but instead they humiliate themselves by passing out in their own vomit. I liked the boy; I saw through his uniform and knew there was a good kid hiding underneath. Therein lies the problem: he's just a kid. If he was going to go over to fight the Germans at his present state, they would pick him off before breakfast. I felt it was best to encourage the boy to live a little, then wait outside for the fireworks. While I waited, I enjoyed a cigarette and stared up at the night sky and thought of Conor looking down on us. It's still difficult for me to talk about him but the visit with Annie helped ease the sorrow and grief from losing my boy. I remember our visit so vividly, most of our conversations were about George and how easy it was working for him compared to that pompous arse Cockburn. She told me how she almost choked the bastard with the measuring rope, and I laughed until my cheeks were sore. I relish the fact that Annie inherited my attitude. It gives me peace of mind knowing it will scare off all the men that are unworthy of her. It's a shame I won't get to spend any more time with her. I met up with George when he arrived in Halifax and requested to join the Canadian Corp. I was done with the Brits, just absolutely fed up. He did his best to get me into the 147th but something happened involving a captain and paperwork and I had to settle for the 58th. I'm sure whoever's in charge is a good man but I would rather serve somewhere closer to Annie so I can keep an eye on her. That, and the replacements for the 58th we're shipping out tomorrow and I was dreading going back to the front. I kept that intrusive thought locked away and focused on my cigarette instead. After a few minutes of concentration, I walked towards the front entrance. I was about to open the door before it burst open and an angry woman dressed in a vomit-colored dress ran out of the door yelling in a foreign language. By the sounds of it she's a Ruskie. Her dialect was sweeter, perhaps from the Southern parts of Belarus. I may not be able to read maps, but I've done my fair share of fighting to pick up other languages along the way. It's a natural gift I wear proudly on my sleeve. I couldn't tell you what the hen was saying but judging by her walk she was a raging dragon. I imagine it had something to do with the hollering and the yelling going on inside the bar. The doors opened and Private Holmes stumbled over himself, yelling obscenities loud enough to wake up the entire town.

"I didn't kiss the fish!" He collapsed onto the ground which made me laugh while I was picking him up.

"You alright there, sonny?" I asked him. His stare was blank, and his breath was foul.

"I didn't kiss the fish!"

"Well, that's alright son. We can go back inside and get it done. Only takes two seconds."

"No, Sir... I... don't think...I am using the... right words to say."

"Then what are you trying to say, private?"

"That... I... didn't... kiss... the fish!" I wasn't in the mood to argue with a drunk, so I just smiled and nodded.

"We'll talk about it when you're a wee bit sober, how's that?" Tommy nodded his head then fell to the ground. I stood over him thinking of how to get this boy back to base without the MP's finding out. I went back into the bar and looked for his unit only to see nobody in sight. The whole lot of them were upstairs with the girls. The only men left in the room were the bartender and an angry Brit captain with his back facing towards me doing something obscured. When the good captain turned around and saw us his face was blood red, and his crisp uniform tarnished.

"I WANT HIS NAME AND SERVICE NUMBER!" I was in a morale conundrum. Do I reveal the private's identity, or do I lie and risk insubordination? Ah, to hell with it. I could've used an extra few days in town.

"I just found the lad passed out on the grass," I answered.

"Well, then you will find out for me now, won't you?!" This limey's fixing to get 'imself a good right hook to the jaw.

"And how am I supposed to do that when the boy's unconscious?" The cheeky captain stood nose to nose with me, with his gin breath lurking underneath his chin.

"I am giving you a direct order to find out the identity of this pathetic excuse for a soldier and deliver it to me, Captain Alfred Winston Talbot, by 9.00. Is that clear, Lieutenant?" His tone was as cold-blooded as a rattlesnake. I felt genuine pity for the poor sods under his command. Nonetheless, an order's an order.

"Yes Sir," I uttered. He grunted then walked out of the bar leaving me alone with the boy. If I bring the boy back to the house and have Annie fix him up, we can have him back at the station before noon. I'll talk to George and tell him to take the heat off the boy and pretend this night never happened. Lord knows this wasn't the first time a soldier's been smuggled back into base.

EARLY IN THE MORNING

ANNIE

I got woken up in the early hours of the morning by the sounds of what I thought was a shrieking bird, turned out to be Dad carrying a drunken soldier. When I saw them in the street from my window, I rushed down to avoid waking the neighbors. Dad sighed when he saw me, "Wanna give me a hand, please and thank you." His head was buried in Dad's jacket, so I was unable to see his face. I'm over nursing drunk soldiers. I never signed up to be a maid either but here we are in the middle of the night looking after a boy courtesy of Dad's shenanigans. I'm unsure of what he got into, but he was so drunk Dad had to carry him up over his shoulders. He wasn't asleep either, the boy was slurring his words and made nonsensical statements. It's hard for me to describe as well because I haven't been able to get any sleep since.

We managed to get him inside the house without any complaints. The next challenge was to get food into his stomach. He needed to have solids, so I heated up some chili I cooked up the day before along with some buttered bread. While I made the food Dad got the boy wrapped in blankets and placed a bucket next at the edge of the boy's feet. "Alright son, if ya feel like yer gonna yak I kindly suggest ya do it in the bucket here." All the boy could do was groan.

"Okayyyyyyy." We assumed that the boy would be safe and secure being wrapped in blankets, but we were wrong. When Dad took his eyes off him for a second, the boy flopped to the ground, landing headfirst into the coffee table. It was a miracle his head didn't crack open. Dad built the table with his bare hands using solid maple and a few bolts to hold it together. If the boy was an inch to the left on impact he would've lost an eye.

Once we got the boy fed Dad got the boy to his feet. His legs were shaking, and he struggled to stay standing, so Dad lifted the boy over his soldiers and carried him into Danny's room with me close behind with blankets and the bucket. When I got a look at his face I recognized him from the recruitment office back in Owen Sound. I couldn't remember his name, so I asked Dad if he knew his name. "Tommy something, I didn't catch his last name." When we got Tommy into bed I called his name. He looked at me with the biggest puppy dog eyes you will ever see.

"You're so pretty. What's your name?" He asked me. I brushed his comment off as I laid him down on his side.

"There we go, you're all settled," I said. He smiled and laid his head down.

"This is...a really soft pillow. It feels really good," he said, then vomited into the bucket. I comforted the soldier while Dad went downstairs to find another bucket or bowl.

"That's it, let it all out, Tommy."

"THAT'S MY NAME!" I grew more annoyed but retained composure.

"Yes, Tommy. That is your name." Tommy looked at a photo of Conor and I together as children.

"Are these your children?" He asked me.

"No, that's my brother and I."

"Is your brother in the army?" I felt the grief festering in my heart, crippling my mind into giving a bleak answer.

"He was." Tommy didn't take the hint.

"Is he dead?" He asked. I didn't have the strength to give him an answer. Drunken vision be damned though, he picked up on the subtlety and understood what I meant. "Don't you worry about it, pretty lady. I'm gonna kill every German and avenge your brother. They'll pay for every war crime they committed. And THEN! I will have my father's respect!" All I could do was shake my head.

I just need to go back to sleep and pretend this whole event never occurred.

* * *

Dad woke me up the next morning to make breakfast for Tommy. He needed to report back to base before ten or else he would be punished. I'll admit, I woke up in a sour mood, but that sour mood dissipated after some breathing exercises.

I focused on my frustration and released it by cooking bacon and eggs while I hummed a shanty.

My mother told me
Someday I would buy
Galleys with good oars
Sail to distant shores
Stand up on the prow
Nobel barque I steer
Steady course to the haven
Hew many foe-men
Hew many foe-men

Unbeknownst to me, Dad was standing in the hallway sipping his coffee watching me cook in the kitchen.

"What is it?" I asked him.

"Nothing, I just miss your mother is all." I smiled and blushed. Dad always said I could've been her twin if she survived giving birth to me. He turned his attention back to Tommy upstairs. "Is it ready?"

"Just about."

"I'll go wake him then." He headed upstairs while I set the table. Moments later when they were coming down, I was pouring the coffee. The boy was as white as a ghost, with dark lips like he was dehydrated. I fixed the boy a small glass of water and watched him down the glass in a few gulps. I took the glass and refilled the cup while the men sat at the table. Once I gave him the cup, I brought the bacon and eggs over and plated the food. The boy's eyes were wide, and his mouth was drooling. Dad looked at him and winked at me. "We say grace at the table," he said to him. The boy reluctantly put the bacon back on the table and hung his head low. I felt Dad was being crude towards the boy, but the boy also puked all over my bed. He can afford a few extra minutes of punishment. Dad put his hands together and looked at me to do the same. "Dear heavenly father. We thank you for the food you have blessed us with and continue to love and cherish my family and my new friend, Tommy.

For he had a little too much fun last night and could use your strength today. I also ask in your name to bless my daughter for she is coming to the end of her journey in the army and will begin on a new path that brings her joy and independence in the factory. We say in Jesus' name, amen." We all grabbed our cutlery and dug in. The more I looked at the boy, the more I focused on his features. His pure blue eyes were the first to catch my attention. I'm under the belief that the eyes are the gateway to the soul, and with Tommy's it was like looking into an old soul trapped in a young man's body. It was more astonishing to see the color flourish when he bit into the bacon.

"This is a delicious meal miss, thank you," he said to me.

"You're welcome, you can call me Annie if you like," I said back. He smiled and continued to eat in silence. After he was done, he placed his head back on the table.

"Sorry sonny, but we got to head back to base before the MP's find out you're AWOL," Father said while getting Tommy to his feet. Tommy composed himself and stood tall without Dad's assistance.

"Yes sir," he said. He fixed his uniform and walked slowly to the front door. Before he walked out, he turned around to look at me. "I, uh, also want to extend my sincerest apologies for my atrocious actions last night. If you wish to never speak to me again, I will understand." Tommy put on his hat and walked out the door, leaving Dad behind in the front hallway. Dad walked up to me and gave me a bear bug.

"I'll write to you when I get to Shoreham." I nodded to stop the tears flowing.

"Okay, Dad. I'll miss you." I don't know why, but I thought of Tommy when I hugged Dad. I wondered if anyone was going to miss him if he got killed. "This isn't right," I said out loud. Dad looked at me confused.

"What do you mean?" He asked me. I couldn't give him an answer, just ran out the door to find Tommy. He was sitting the passenger seat of the automobile, wiping his tears away.

"Are you okay?" I asked him.

"Oh yeah, just have bad allergies is all," he answered. I looked at him, annoyed.

"Do you have anyone to write to?" I asked him.

"What do you mean?"

"Are you married? do you have a family? Do you have anyone to write home to?" He must've sobered up because his brain turned on after that.

"I have parents, and a brother, but nobody has really reached out."

"Do you have a pencil and paper?" I asked him. He reached into his pocket and pulled out a small dull pencil and a vomit-coated pad. The first page was salvaged enough for me to write on.

"I'm not a fan of soldiers or war, but if you ever wish to write to me. Write to this address." I wrote as clear as day on the paper:

ANNIE MIDDAUGH, 72 LUCKNOW STREET.

I gave the writing utensils back to Tommy and extended my hand. "Good luck, Private Holmes." Tommy reluctantly stuck out his hand in return.

"Thank you, Miss Middaugh." We shook hands, then I walked back inside. Dad looked at me weird.

"What's that smile for?" He asked. I quickly changed the subject.

"Oh, Dad, you're running late. You need to get going," I said while grabbing his bags. All he did was shake his head and agree.

"This conversation isn't over, missy." he said, annoyed.

"Yep, no problem, it'll be the first thing we talk about when you get back." I gave him one last big hug and kiss and wished him luck. I walked out with him and watched drive away. Wasn't exactly how I intended my last day with Dad, but romanticizing over a soldier wasn't on the agenda either. I wouldn't be surprised if he scowled Tommy on the way to the base.

Shoreham Camp
Sussex, England

VIII
DECEMBER

Beware of false prophets, which come to you in sheep's clothing, but inwardly they are ravenous wolves.

BOOK OF MATTHEW, 7:15

SHOREHAM, ENGLAND
TOMMY

When the outbreak was over, we were the first battalion shipped out on the Olympic.

At the docks there were no cheers of us leaving, no hero's goodbye of any sorts. Annie was there. She didn't blow me a kiss, but she tipped her hat to me. Might just have to take her up on the offer of being pen pals. The boys don't know anything about her and for now I would like to keep it that way. I'm afraid if I speak her name she will vanish into thin air. It's not like anyone ever inquired anyways. The boys were more concerned about the events that happened at The Billa Tent. I'm not sure if it is my mind or the liquor but I have vague memories from that night. I remember arriving there with Grieve, Redfern, Reekie, and Holloway. I remember having a drink with Otto, the Newfie Lieutenant. Correction: It was two drinks with Otto. One was a beer and the other a boilermaker I believe they're called. I remember walking up the stairs to meet Veronika, the Ukrainian hen waiting for me on the second floor. She was expecting us to be intimate, but I chickened out. I told her I didn't want my first time to be with someone I didn't know. To her, it didn't matter as she was paid in advance. We spent ten minutes talking until the liquor hit me like a ton of bricks. I know I made it down the stairs without puking, but the last thing I remember was going to the restroom to vomit. After that, there's nothing. From what I was told by Otto, I threw up on a British Captain almost got myself court-martialed. He said for the time being keep my head down and out of trouble until he talked to Colonel McFarland and explained the situation. I asked the boys about it, they verified his story and added that the captain was ready to crush skulls so the rest of them flocked away before they were discovered as co-conspirators. I threw up on poor Veronika too. I was hoping I would get the chance to apologize to her, but we shipped out two weeks later. We all agreed to keep quiet about it and pray we never encounter that British Captain again. We tried finding out who he was, but nobody knew. It was like he disappeared.

When we arrived in London, we loaded ourselves onto the trucks to which they drive us to Shoreham, our temporary base until we're given the orders to go to Paris. We kept up with our training and excelled beyond the British standards. At first, they didn't like our bantering, but as time passed, they learned to accept our customs as we're the most resilient army the Germans have ever seen. On our first leave from base, we went into the market square to buy supplies. The Merchants gave us a hero's welcome with all sorts of free food and supplies to spread amongst the men. Some were feeling the effects of the war and could only offer something as small as two apples. Two apples may not have been a lot to some, but it was more than enough to me.

Towards the end of the year, more rumblings emerged from "C" Company about where we will be going. It was all speculation of course, but there was logic behind some of the choices like The Somme but Major Corrie corrected that rumor by telling us we're heading north. He said: "When we are given the orders from HQ we will make an announcement," and left it at that. We changed the topic by focusing on our training and ironed out any kinks we missed back in Borden. Colonel McFarland often joined our marches and gave lectures when warranted. It made some of the Brits dumbfounded as most of their CO's kept their congregation close to either HQ or at the pubs. The whole battalion admired and respected McFarland and when rumors of him being transferred to another battalion circulated, fear and doubt pursued. When Corrie was asked about it, he either dismissed the soldier or walked away. It wasn't just him giving us the cold shoulder. Captain Mercer and Sergeant Broadhead contradicted themselves when asked about the Colonel. It was like some big open secret the higher ups refused to give up. That was until the 22nd when McFarland gathered the whole battalion in Hanger B.

"Everybody listen up," he said with a frown. "I know there's been talk amongst all of you over what's going to be happening over the next few months. There's a lot of confusion, a lot of frustration, and most importantly, doubt. And as your acting CO, I apologize for keeping you all in the dark, so this is where we currently stand. As of the first day of the new year, the 147th will be dismantled and we will merge into the 4th Canadian Mounted Rifles. From there on you all will gradually be transferred into different units and go your separate ways. This is unfortunately a direct order from General Byng. He said he needed the best soldiers Canada has to offer and well, I don't know about you gentlemen but, I can't see anyone else in the corps more qualified. Do you all agree?" Grieve spoke up on our behalf.

"We're the best in the world, Sir!" Colonel McFarland shook his head and laughed.

"Thanks, Private Yank." The room erupted into laughter for a moment, something to soften the blow. "Nothing would give me greater pleasure than to go over the top with you boys, but seeing as my skill sets are more prudent in Paris, I must do what's best for the corp. It is the only appropriate action your CO can do. There is just one last thing I need to share with you all. Would you all rise for me." We stood straight and proud of our CO. "As you leave this building, I wish to shake your hand and wish each and every one of you the best of luck." We followed his order and synchronized our exit. First "A" Company stood up, then "B", then us, "C" Company. I may not have agreed with the methods taken for me to enlist, but if I'm to be candid; he's a far better man to learn from than my father. Father made me distaste wearing the uniform whereas Colonel McFarland taught me to see integrity and honor when wearing my colors. I hope whoever replaces him is just as good.

When we got outside Sergeant Broadhead was waiting for "C" Company to finish before making an announcement. "When I call out your names, please step forward. Adair, Holloway, Grieve, Redfern, Holmes, Bowman, Kent, Rush, and Brown." We all filed in and stood at attention. "We are the first pick. Report back here at 0500 for the convoy. Congratulations, boys. We're going to the front." Lucky for us, we were so exhausted from the day we passed out the second our heads hit the pillows.

* * *

The next morning, we stuffed two years' worth of gear into our sacks and waited for the convoy to arrive. We were all anxious men, looking at the horizon hoping to see trucks in the distance. Minutes felt like hours. And once the trucks were spotted a roar of cheers echoed across the plains. Ten trucks in total drove up to the camp. When they came to a stop, the stretcher men dropped the back gate and carried out the wounded. They were covered in bandages and blankets so we couldn't make out who they were. The last man to step out of the Truck was holding a jar of blood upside down while a tube extended to his comrade's left-arm. He passed the jar along to a soldier and the soldier followed behind the stretcher men. He took out a cloth and wiped his hands clean. He was short in stature, with short hair that he looked around us and found a table to stand on. While he stood above us, he did a small head count then hopped back down and started walking amongst the men. "For those of you who have not had the privilege to meet me, listen carefully because you are only going to hear this once. My name is Charles Winston Talbot the third, but you are going to address me as Captain. You are going to address me as such out of respect for my army. Yes, my army. An army that is conditioned and battle ready at any time I choose. You see lads -" His eyes locked with mine. For reasons unbeknownst to me, he grew a large smile then continued speaking. "You see lads, unlike the lot of you who came from a dirty womb across the pond, I have a certain level of expectations that I must live up to. And those expectations involve my company having the most daring and bravest of soldiers and if there was an individual amongst my company not performing at my level, they will be punished. For instance, there is a soldier amongst us who disrespected his king and country by regurgitating on a Captain's uniform-" Out of the corner of my eye I could see Holloway looking at me with concern. He looked long enough for Captain Talbot to spot it out. "What's your name, Corporal?" He asked.

"Holloway, Sir. Frederick Clarence Holloway."

"By the look on your face I suspect you know the individual I am talking about. Would you be kind and point him out to the rest of us?" Holloway was unable to fulfil the Captain's request so Talbot approached him with calm and precision. He didn't say a word, just looked at him with a cold expression. Instead of asking Holloway again the Captain slapped him so hard he hit the deck. "That's unfortunate. The King expects us to have his unwavering loyalty and here you are protecting a peasant. I'll save you another backhand by revealing the soldier myself." He turned around and walked towards me, slowly. My heart raced with panic knowing I'm about to be publicly humiliated.

"Tell me your name, peasant." I was so scared my words were skipping.

"Pr-pr-pr-private Ho-Holmes, sir."

"Are you such a coward that you struggle with your own name?" I corrected my breathing and posture to appease the captain.

"No, Sir."

"So, you're saying I am incorrect then?"

"Yes Sir. Er, no Sir." Talbot was inches away from my face, ready to lash out.

"Which one is it, Private Holmes?" I hesitated for a second too long. The captain slapped me so hard his ring busted up my lip. "ANSWER!" He screamed.

"No Sir. You are correct," I said in a panic.

"I don't allow cowards in my company, private. You best ask my god for mercy because I won't give it. I am going to make every second of your time with me a living nightmare. I will degrade you and treat you like the vermin that you are because you thought it'd be funny to regurgitate on a Captain. Do you think you deserve this form of treatment, Private Holmes?" I looked over to Sergeant Broadhead for wisdom, only to see him look on with a disgraceful look.

"Yes Sir," I said. Talbot chuckled and crossed his arms behind his back.

"That's the answer I was looking for, peasant. You might just live long enough to wipe the blood off my boots. Congratulations." Talbot walked back over to the truck and climbed up the tailgate. He then placed a small metal pole along with two Lewis drums on the tip of the gate then instructed me to jump onto the truck.

"Lift up your arms," the bastard commanded. I did what I was told with a humiliated heart. He then placed the rod in between my neck and shoulder blades then hung the Lewis drums off the parallel hooks at the end. I tried to fight him off when he was strapping my hands in but his response was deafening. "YOU SAID YOU DESERVED TO BE PUNISHED PRIVATE!"

THWACK!

The Captain hit me again and I conceded. He strapped my hands into place and sat down in the corner like he instructed. "Whoever steps foot into this truck is specifically ordered to not speak to the peasant. Is that understood?" The crowd was silent. Captain Talbot was annoyed with the lack of reaction. "I said; whoever steps foot into this truck is specifically ordered not to speak with Private Holmes. Is that understood?" The company spoke in unison, like how we did it with McFarland.

"Yes Sir!" It was enough to satisfy the captain's ego. "I will see all of you in Belgium. Carry on." He hopped down from the truck and walked away with the other officers. I remember sitting in the corner with no ally except for misery and agony. It was the most humiliating thing I had ever endured. The soldiers that sat in the same truck as me followed the captain's orders and stayed silent throughout the whole trip. Not even Holloway said a word, but at least he was sitting beside me.

The 4th Canadian Mountain Rifles
1914

1917

IX
JANUARY

Never think that war, no matter how necessary, nor how justified, is not a crime.

ERNEST HEMINGWAY
FOR WHOM THE BELL TOLLS

ARRAS, FRANCE
TOMMY

We've been at the front well over a week and I have been reduced to Captain Howes' errand boy.

I've been feeling resentful for not fighting alongside my friends and all the blame was directed towards that wretched man Talbot. Captain Howes understood my resentment, but he wasn't tolerating it for a second. On quite a few occasions he heard me speak ill of the Captain and he put a hard stop to it. "Private Holmes do not blame him for your own decisions. It's not his fault you can't handle liquor." There was one instance where I compared Talbot to a dog, and I was sent to latrine duty for two days. From then on, I kept my thoughts to myself and nobody else.

When the boys came back from the front, they looked tired and weary. What haunted me more was the amount that showed up. Went sent fifty of our guys to help the 4th and when I finished counting there were only thirty. I was thankful to see Grieve and Holloway come up over the ridge. They looked tired like the rest but had a look of anger more than exhaustion. When Grieve saw me he nudged Holloway, and they walked in my direction. I met them in the middle with concern.

"What happened?" I asked them. They struggled speaking until Captain Talbot looked at us with disdain.

"We'll meet you behind the kitchen," Grieve uttered. The two men walked away and left me alone with Talbot who gazed into my soul with his black eyes.

"You got something to say, peasant?" He asked me.

"No Sir," I answered with a quivering heart. He walked away and said nothing else. Something awful happened. What did Fritz do? When I walked behind the kitchen, I found Holloway and Grieve staring at the ground smoking cigarettes and sharing a flask. They offered me a drink, but I declined, after the last time I got drunk I think alcohol would be the worst thing for me. "What happened?" I asked them. Holloway threw away his cigarette then pulled out another.

"Rush is dead, and Kent is wounded." Grieve continued the story.

"And we have that fucking bastard Talbot to thank for it." Holloway finished a drag then carried on.

"Gets us to go on a trench raid at 0900 while the sun's coming up and Fritz cuts us to pieces." There was a pause in between the two, with Grieve taking a swig from the flask.

"Rush got it in the neck and bled out."

"Did you see it?" I asked him.

"I was six feet away from the bastard, Tommy. My granddaddy told me stories from Gettysburg. This ain't the trench warfare he fought." Holloway put down his cigarette and grabbed the flask from Grieve.

"We're going back to the front in two days with replacements from the 58th, including a new sergeant."

"Which one did we lose?" I asked him.

"Bradley," Grieve uttered. Holloway intervened before Grieve lost his cool.

"Don't be surprised if you're called up. There's too many wounded back there." They gave each other a look and decided to reconnect back at the tents where we're more secluded. They said Redfern and Charlie would be there as well.

* * *

The air was brisk and cut through our skin like it was butter. Redfern was stoking the fire with kindle and wood while the rest of us sat silently with coffee and cigarettes in our hands. The mood was low, with nobody feeling the need to improve. It was an uncomfortable feeling being the outsider not knowing what they had seen on the battlefield. I thought about writing to Annie, but after Otto's warning I decided against it. "Ye touch a single hair on my daughter's head and there'll be nothin' left of ya but tenderized meat." I chuckled at the thought and felt it was best to take his advice. Even though thinking about her radiant smile made me grin from ear to ear. The boys caught on to my happiness and probed.

"Whatcha thinkin' 'bout, Tommy?" He asked me.

"Nothin'," I answered.

"Gotta call malarky on that, buddy," Charlie said. Grieve chimed in his opinion as well.

"What's her name?" He asked, sarcastically. My ears shot up and panic ran down my side, allowing the boys to cheer and laugh at my expense. "I knew it! Only a woman can make a man smile without cause. Spill the beans, Holmes." I was put into a corner with the only way out is to reveal her name.

"It's Annie," I said. The boys whistled and cheered then asked for more.

"What's she like? Is she blonde?" Redfern asked.

"Or is she a redhead?" Bowman added.

"Is she tall or short?" Charlie asked.

"How big are her tits?" Holloway asked. I answered the questions with a bashful tone.

"She's neither, she's brunette. I couldn't tell you how tall she was, nor do I wish to tell you how busty she is." The boys continued to probe until Sergeant Broadhead came into the tent.

"Ev'nin' boys, you holding up okay?" He asked us.

"Tommy's got a girlfriend!" Grieve answered. Broadhead was too focused on the mission to care.

"Is that right? Well, I hate to break up the party, but Captain Talbot wants us front and center of the camp to meet the replacements."

"How many?" Holloway asked.

"Whatever's left of the 58th," Broadhead answered. Redfern looked to me and asked;

"Roy's from the 58th, right?"

"Last I heard from Father he was," I answered.

"Well, don't get too fancy on the family reunion because we're heading out tomorrow." The good sergeant was agitated by what he said but hid it as best as he could by leaving the tent. The rest of us grunted and groaned as we got on our gear.

We stepped out of the tent and some of the guys from the 58th walked past us disheveled. Their faces were pale and riddled with debris. "Where did they come from?" I asked the Sergeant.

"The Somme," he answered. I gazed amongst the men walking past, searching for Roy like he was a needle in a haystack. What made it more difficult is seeing the same facial expression in every soldier I saw, the expression of the walking dead. I heard no news from anybody back home and thought the worst. I began asking some of the men if they had seen my brother. "Excuse me, have you seen someone by the name of Roy Holmes?" I must've asked that question over twenty times, not a single soul could give me an answer until Captain Dowes approached me.

"Private Holmes?" He called out.

"Yes, Sir!"

"Latrine duty, ten minutes." Dowes left the room, and I grunted. Holloway shook his head in annoyance.

"Wasn't even your fault," he said. I looked at Holloway confused. "The night at the Billa Tent. Yes, you were drunk, but he was the one who picked the fight." Even Grieve looked confused, and he was there.

"You were upstairs with Valerie by the time it went down," he said.

"I was, Private Yank, I happened to spend the entire night with Valerie into the late morning when Miss Veronika came back. According to her, Captain Talbot grabbed her by the arm and tried to have his way with her. You Sir, had the liquid courage to step in but once he hit you in the stomach, you were done." My jaw was on the ground along with everyone else. Grieve was the first to speak up.

"You know, Stokes Bombs tend to miss fire if not properly maintained. It'd be a shame if the good Captain was near one if it explodes." Charlie laughed at the concept.

"If he had the sand to even be near the front, sure. It's possible." The men grunted and moaned at the logic. Myself I felt it didn't matter because knowing my luck the bomb wouldn't go off to begin with. I focused on the task at hand, so I stood up and grabbed my rifle.

"I'll catch you guys later," I said, then walked away to fulfil my duty. I wrapped my scarf tight around my neck as I walked through the rain, reminiscing over Roy. The latrines were ten feet away and I couldn't have been any happier to see them. As awful as it smelled, the fire's kept me warm. I recited the Chronicles prayer as I grabbed the Kerosene and matches from the supply tent. "Stand firm, hold your position, and see the salvation of the Lord on your behalf, O Judah and Jerusalem. Do not be afraid and do not be dismayed. Today go out against them, and the Lord will be with you. In our Lord's name I pray; Amen." There are three rows of stalls with 7 on each side. Each one has a small trap door underneath with a drum filled with excrement. It was wiser to do one row at a time then all at once, so I started with the first row on the right. I saw a soldier walk into the last stall and I groaned. I couldn't see his face so I couldn't have asked him to go to another stall. I stayed focused and pulled the first bucket out from underneath. The door was made up of wood salvaged from a destroyed barn then bolted together by lead. The door was heavy, and it made an awfully loud bang if you let it drop. I did this intentionally to signal any of the men inside it was time to finish. The first door scared nobody; it was the second door that angered somebody. The soldier that was sitting on the toilet was yelling at me to put the barrel back. "Hey! I'm using this! Put it back!" I ignored his call and let the door drop. "WHEN I GET MY HANDS ON YOU!" The soldier put on his pants and charged out the door but stopped abruptly. He stood still long enough for me to look in his direction. And who I saw standing before me, all five feet and four inches of him was Roy. His hair was clean shaven with fresh cuts on his cheeks. His eyes were so dark it was almost as if you were staring into the eyes of a demon. The brother I knew would've given me a hug and said, 'I miss you'. Instead, he greeted me with his fist and his helmet.

MOMENTS LATER
OTTO

I was wandering around basecamp enjoying my ev'nin' smoke enjoying a moment of silence after a week of hell.

Between the two sides it was amazing any of us are left. Half the rifles in our company jammed from the frost so we had to strategically time our attacks to be on the defensive, so our guys weren't cut down by the MG's. Credit for that goes to Sergeant Holmes, an angry lad but so methodical with his tactics. I knew him only a few months and took him as my closest ally. The way he observes and handles himself under impossible conditions is impeccable. It's a shame really. He'd be the perfect soldier if the war didn't break his spirit. Poor lad lost his entire unit in the Somme from a gas attack. According to those who were close he became a different person. He never speaks of it, nor will I ever ask. As long as the man's fit for duty, I couldn't care less.

He was yards away from me when we passed the forest. He was eager to shower and shave as he was living in filth planting mines. I don't like to rush if I don't have to, so I enjoyed strolling into camp. I saw Thomas from a distance, but my wounded were more important. I was promoted back to Captain when our CO Captain Cavangh was killed. Sergeant Holmes' behavior drastically improved once I took over. Perhaps the root cause of his anger was incompetent leadership. Again, I am unsure of the truth as rumblings of sabotage were at play without evidence to confirm. He was doing good until this morning when I heard from Lieutenant Shier that he got into a scrap with one of the guys from the 8th reserve. I couldn't make out what the lieutenant said with his froggy accent, so I followed him to the latrines where I found multiple men holding back Sergeant Holmes while the poor victim was buried in snow. I dissipated the chaos and put Holmes in his place. Not in an aggressive way, but with a look of authority that got him to calm down. Once the situation was under control I walked towards the lad and helped him to his feet. When he was raised from the snow his face was revealed as Tommy.

Just what in God's name did this boy do, now?

"Ye seem to be living under a black cloud, private." I wasn't sure if he was surprised to see me, or Holmes gave him one too many blows to the head. He looked at me and chuckled.

"Only when you're around, Sir," he said. I laughed and turned my attention to Sergeant Holmes. "Ye mind explaining this to me, Sergeant?"

"HE ISN'T SUPPOSED TO BE HERE!" I looked at him ready to kill.

"Oh really? Since when did you get promoted to general?!"

"Our father told him to stay back in Canada, but he lied about his age and betrayed my family." My eyes widened.

"Sergeant Holmes, I will speak to you about this matter after I tend to your misfortune." I grabbed Tommy by the shoulder and walked him to the aid station. Throughout our walk my mind kept reverting to what Sergeant Holmes said. I knew he was a boy, but I didn't think he was that young. Maybe I was a bit harsh on him when we first met. Eh, never mind. Him being seventeen makes him the same age as Annie. If anything, I need to be more formidable if he plans on writing to her.

"So, did ya write to Annie yet?" I asked him while blood poured from his nose. Tommy looked confused.

"Aren't you going to ask me what happened?" He asked back.

"Well, I hate to break your ego but there's a graveyard in Flanders filled with young souls like yourselves, so don't be thinkin' that you're the only one to do it." Tommy looked at me and sighed in relief. "So, did ya write to her?" I asked again.

"No Sir," he answered.

"Good." The doctor walked over and looked at Tommy's nose.

"What'd you do now, Tommy?" He asked him. I found his tone condescending and intervened.

"One of my guys attacked him, unprovoked." The doctor was almost in disbelief.

"Who attacked him?" He asked.

"My brother," Tommy answered. The doctor scoffed at his response.

"Must've been an interesting reunion," he said, then placed his hands over Tommy's nose. "This is going to hurt."

CRACK!

Tommy's scream could be heard all the way to Dunkirk.

"AARRRGGGGHHHH!" I laughed then lit up a smoke. As the doctor left Tommy looked over to me with a sinister tone.

"You'll be fine, lad," I said.

"Why do you find this amusing, sir?"

"Scars build character, and characters tell the best stories. Just wait till your grandkids hear about this." I offered him a smoke and he declined. "Suit yourself." We were silent for a moment, then Tommy asked me a question.

"Did something happen to him?" I looked at him and gave him the truth.

"I've only known the man for a few months, hasn't said a peep about you. In fact, I was heading over as soon as I knew you were good. Are ya good?" He looked at me then nodded.

"I'll be fine, sir," he answered.

"I'll see you around, then." I waved him off then walked over to the Officer's Tent where Roy was waiting for me. He had a few swigs from his flask judging by his breath. He didn't say a word, just kept his head down. I took the flask and held it in my hands, contemplating if a drink would help me find the right questions to ask. I screwed the cap back on and put it in my pocket.

"I'll give it back when you answer some questions."

"Yes Sir," he said.

"Is it true what you said back there?" He gave me a look of regret.

"I don't know, Captain. It's what our father said."

"When did he tell you this?"

"In the last letter he wrote."

"Do you still have it?" He never said a word, just shook his head back and forth. "Aye, that puts us in a bit of an issue then, eh?" He had a faint smile. I looked at him and thought of a solution that was best for both siblings. "You know what I think? I think you should spend more time with him. Maybe something got lost in translation over what yer dad said." Roy looked at me with rage in his eyes.

"What are you asking of me, Otto?"

"Let me get back to you on that," I answered, then walked out the tent. Roy called out from behind.

"Can I have my flask back?"

"No," I answered. If memory serves me correctly, Wilson was supposed to be the new A company Sergeant. I feel a change will be the remedy we're looking for.

TRENCH RAID
TOMMY

The six of us were in a tent ready for a trench raid.

It was a last-minute order given to us by Talbot, and one he was pleased with. That was until Roy interjected himself into the mess. While Talbot was giving us the instructions Roy waltzed into the room and re-designed the attack to suit his ego. The original plan was for us to go over at sunrise, but Roy felt the blanket of darkness was better suited. The idea was to shoot a single flare across no man's land to determine our distance then use the cover of darkness to infiltrate the other trench without anybody getting killed. The lads were happy with the changes while I resented it. I may hate Talbot for being a cruel, insensitive human being, but it doesn't give Roy the right to change mission tactics and embarrass an officer the way he did.

As we sat around the campfire Roy was giving us bleak instructions on how to live in the trenches. "Hang your boats upside down over the fire to kill the lice. You see a rat, you kill it - even if it wears a uniform. Keep your bayonets dry and well-greased or else the frost will eat it, a shovel is more useful than the Ross, never lose it. And lastly, if you start seeing things that don't belong, you're shell shocked. Any questions?" Nobody said a word, not even me. I kept my head down and did what I was told. Roy didn't look at me the entire time. He wasn't a talker like he used to be. He only spoke when it was necessary and when he did it was with a violent tone.

I was getting nervous as the time for the mission was nigh. My breathing intensified with each step we took towards the front line. On our way Roy approached a corpse with a scope in his hand. "Thank you," Roy said to the dead soldier. Grieve looked at him puzzled.

"Why did you do that?" He asked.

"He isn't going to need it," Roy retorted. Grieve went silent while we continued to follow Roy. We walked past Otto as he was standing at attention with binoculars in his hands.

"Good luck Sergeant," Otto said while shaking Roy's hand. Otto did that for all of us participating in the raid. It was comforting compared to Talbot. He said one last thing to Roy as he shook Charlie's hand. "Make sure you teach them the song, eh?" That was the first time in two years I saw my brother smile. The smile went away when we saw Talbot try to imitate Otto by wishing us all good luck. Roy walked past without saying a word.

The closer we got to the front, the quieter we became. Fear seeped into our bones as the cloud of smoke thickened with our breath. Men stood at their posts with their guns drawn on no man' land. One of them fired a shot and killed a German. Cheers can be heard down the line. "That's how it's done, boys!" Bowman threw up after hearing that. Roy looked at him and scoffed.

"Come on, keep up," he said. He took a clip from his bag and loaded his weapon as we walked. I followed suit as did the rest of the patrol. The clicking and clacking from the bullets being loaded into the chamber felt like little pieces of glass cutting into me. *This is what war really is,* I thought. I hardened my skin, and I prepared myself for the worst as we got to the end. Roy looked at us then threw his rifle on his back then took out his shovel. "Keep under the wire, do NOT stick your head above the deck. Just feel the ground and listen to everyone else." My hands were shaky, and I couldn't control my breathing. I started whispering the Chronicles prayer.

"Stand firm, hold your position, and see the salvation of the Lord on your -" Roy pushed my shoulder and whispered;

"Shut up!" I gave Roy the nastiest look I could muster then went quiet. He pulled out a flare from his belt and fired across No Man's Land. The flare illuminated the battlefield, and the bodies scattered around. Sons, fathers, brothers, countrymen, all lay waste across a seven-mile patch of land, and it was my turn to go over. Roy waited for the flare to die before he made the advance. One by one our unit climbed the ladders and crawled under the wire. We were like snakes in the grass hunting for our prey. My heart was racing, my breathing amplified. The cold pierced my wool jacket, but my hands were sweaty. Roy looked back at me as if he knew what I was feeling. He gave me a nod to move forward to be closer to him. As he was waving me over, a second flare shot out of our trench across the battlefield, making Roy incredibly angry. He was the only one to see the culprit because when we turned our heads back Fritz was hammering us with machineguns. Roy was shot in the shoulder and went down. Blood was pouring from his back, but he mustered the strength to grab his rifle and returned fire.

"Fire!" He commanded. We took aim and gave Fritz a taste of his own medicine.

TAT! TAT! TAT!

We fired in unison towards our target, just like we were trained while Roy kept us encouraged. "KEEP SHOOTING! KEEP SHOOTING!" Another flare shot out of our trenches across the line, allowing a sniper enough time to find Roy and shoot him in the head. The back of his head exploded causing blood and bone to spray everywhere. My heart stopped cold, unable to process what happened. Both Holloway and Grieve grabbed me by the shoulders and dragged me back to our trench with the others close behind. Bowman was the second to be killed, he was shot in the chest and dropped to his death. Once the guns stopped and I had the seconds to breathe, I dropped to my knees, and I wailed from grief. It was an indescribable feeling, and no one knew how to handle it, especially that monster Talbot. He walked up to us disgusted.

"WHAT HAPPENED?!" He barked.

"Fritz caught sight of us after someone shot a flare. Sergeant Holmes and Private Bowman are dead," Holloway answered. Talbot didn't find that answer suitable enough.

"Your orders were to infiltrate the other trench and find intelligence, Corporal!" Holloway looked at him with rage.

"Our Sergeant was killed, Captain!"

"This is war, Corporal. It is unfortunate but when a soldier isn't prepared for battle, he is doomed to be killed." I looked at the captain with shock and horror.

"What did you just say?" I asked. He walked close to me and brought his head down to my level.

"I am saying your brother was a terrible soldier and got himself killed." Without thought or emotion, I punched the Captain in the face. One right hook to the jaw and he was on the ground. I gave him a second to breathe before I got the mount and fed him every ounce of anger I had. Grieve pulled me off the Captain and tears rained down my face. The Captain didn't say a word, just got to his feet and brushed himself off. He walked back over to me and spat in my face.

"Congratulations Private Holmes. You got yourself field punishment for a month." A month living underground was worth the right hook to Talbot.

Underground Tunnel
ARRAS, FRANCE

X

FEBRUARY

The old self must die. He had always known it, but had so seldom acted it.

HENRY WILLIAMSON
LOVE AND LOVELESS: A SOLDIER'S TALE

SOMEWHERE IN FRANCE
TOMMY

I never believed hell existed until Roy died.

There is no heaven, no god, no angels, not even a holy saint looking over my shoulder. The only thing I know to be true was hell was real. It wasn't like what the bible said, no fire or demons coming from the ground to punish you for your sins. Hell is on a cold battlefield where all my friend's lay dead in the frost. When I sit here alone in the tunnel with my essentials, my mind is festered with visions of Elvidge's lifeless eyes as he foamed in the mouth. He fought so hard against Captain Talbot. He was the first to spot the gas shell but... I don't know what else I can say. It is impossible for me to describe how I'm feeling. All I know is pain and suffering, like being stabbed by bayonets all over. When I am not in fear of my life for being taken, I am being belittled and berated by Captain Talbot. Every day for three hours he had his goons tie me to a wheel, where they would throw random objects at me and called me 'peasant' repeatedly until the three hours were finished. Every stick or rock or piece of dirt they found they threw it at me, making me more bitter as time progressed. I never felt so humiliated in my life before then, and I have nobody here with me to help. Not even Grieve or Holloway. They were killed during the midday attack on Fritz.

They hit us with artillery first. Whiz-bangs, Jack's, plum puddings, and bouncing Bertha all simultaneously. The gas shells were next. One exploded behind our lines and we thought we were safe...until a gust of wind blew the mustard smoke towards us. After it was done Talbot ordered us to charge the Germans hoping to catch them off guard. We went over the top and walked into a turkey shoot. Carnage and mayhem was all around us. In training we are told to never look in any other direction but forward, and of course, I made that mistake. I tripped over a corpse and fell to the ground. I looked into the dead man's eyes to see flesh sagging off the bone with his jaw frozen open. It was a look of absolute horror, violent enough to make me lose sleep. When I think of it I think of Roy laying dead in a field, rotting away like the spoiled meat we used to toss out back at Mr. Boyd's shop. They say only some of the men are given proper burial while the rest are tossed into a pit. I don't wish to think of Roy in that light but it is wreaking havoc on my soul. It makes me look at Redfern's bottle of whiskey sitting across from me. The constant artillery shortened a screw in Redfern and he was sent down into the mines with me. They hoped it would help but it only made matters worse. He spiralled down into a deep despair, numbing his pain with alcohol. Unfortunately alcohol didn't help either because three days ago he snapped and walked across no man's land, shooting any target he saw. All he had for a weapon was a pistol but miraculously he made it all the way to the German trench before somebody saw him. Back at the Billa Tent when I was drunk I felt the same feeling of blind courage as Redfern. Maybe a little whiskey is all I need to get me through this pain. This thought had festered and had me inches away from grabbing the bottle before a soldier approached me. "Private Holmes?" He asked me.

"Yes?"

"Report to Company CP as soon as possible. Sergeant Broadhead wants to see you."

"Thank you," I uttered. I looked at the bottle and felt grateful I didn't give in. At least not at that moment.

* * *

I found Sergeant Broadhead in a makeshift office inside of a tent. He was taking notes of something before he saw me. "Private Holmes, Welcome," he said then closed his book. I sat in the chair next to him as he closed the tent flap. "I want you to know that everything you say in this tent will be strictly confidential. Your name will be stricken from the records as if this conversation never happened. Do you understand?" I looked at the Sergeant confused.

"I'm sorry, sir, but what is this regarding?" I asked. He looked at me almost dumbfounded.

"Did Redfern talk to you?" I looked at him more confused.

"Sir, Redfern's dead," I answered. The Sergeant put his head down and nodded to himself.

"That explains a bit," he said while kissing his teeth. "I'm filing an official complaint against Captain Talbot over endangerment of his troops. Colonel McFarland is asking me to provide testimony from his troops and since you've gotten the worst of it, your word is gold." I looked at him puzzled and scared.

"I'm not sure anything I say holds value, sir. I'm just a private." Sergeant Broadhead wasn't accepting that answer and tried a different method.

"You don't have to go into explicit detail over it. I have all the dates and names of the deceased. What I need from you is confirmation as you witnessed the events firsthand. Just a series of questions, nothing else." I took a deep breath to calm myself and I gave him an answer.

"Okay."

"First question. Is it true that during the morning of February 9th Captain Talbot stole Corporal Elvidge's gas mask during an attack?" I looked at him and nodded yes. "I'm sorry, private Holmes. But I need more than just a nod." I took another deep breath then used my voice.

"Yes, sir. On the morning of February 9th. Captain Talbot had stolen the corporal's gas mask."

"Is it true the captain used a flare during a trench raid?"

"I don't know. My brother was the only one who saw the individual." The Sergeant sighed.

"Okay. Let me rephrase. Would it be safe to say Captain Talbot struggles with his eyesight at night?"

"I wouldn't know, sir. I don't have his eyes."

"Okay, fair enough. Who organised the trench raid originally?"

"It was Talbot's plan originally, but my brother re-designed it."

"Do you remember what the original plan was?"

"Yes, sir. The plan was supposed to be a morning raid."

"Do you know why it was changed to night?"

"It was so we had the cover of darkness for protection."

"Good." He wrote down all my answers in a tattered notebook. "Have you witnessed any erratic behaviour from Captain Talbot?"

"That would depend on what you define as erratic, Sir."

"Violent outbursts, near-sighted decisions?"

"Everyday, Sir. Or at least everyday when I was with his unit."

"You sound unsure of yourself, Private Holmes. Is there anything that casts doubt?"

"No, Sir. It's just that whenever it happens people seem to deny it or tell me I've mistaken." Sergeant Broadhead stopped writing and took a deep breath before continuing.

"Are you willing to give names of those you told?" I looked at him and sighed.

"No, Sir. They are just as fearful as I."

"I understand," he uttered. "We'll stick with your testimony alone, then."

"Is there anything else you care to share? Any other incidents that involved you and the captain?"

"Are you aware of the incident that happened at the Billa Tent?"

"That's a vague statement, private. Can you be a little more specific?"

"The night I threw up on the captain?" Sergeant Broadhead's eyes widened.

"Elaborate, private."

"Back in Halifax we were at the Billa Tent one night and I was inebriated to the point of regurgitation. When I spoke to privates Grieve and Holloway, they said he was the aggressor as well. I just happened to use vomit as a defense."

"Do you feel the captain has a vendetta against you over this event?"

"I have strong suspicions, Sir, but nothing to prove it."

"Okay. We will have to strike this from the report, but I'll keep it in mind when I speak with the Colonel." He wrote down his final notes then closed his notebook. "I have one more thing for you," he said while grabbing an envelope from his breast pocket. When he handed it to me I held it tight in my hands. It had been a long time since someone from home had reached out.

"Thank you, sir," I said.

"I need you to go now. The less suspicion the better." I nodded then left.

When I got back to the mine I put some oil in a lamp and lit the wick with a match. When the tight corridor was illuminated I opened the letter and smiled.

Dear Tommy

How are you? My father told me what happened to your brother and I wanted to extend any love and support I can offer. We lost my older brother Conor at Beaumont Hamel, so we understand the grief you are going through. I am upset with your tardiness in writing to me, though. We had made an agreement that you would write to me when you made it over to England and I am still waiting for your letter. Soldier boy for us to correspond you gotta start reaching out more. Even if it is only a paragraph, write to me. My work is rather repetitive at the munitions factory so any story you can share will give me something to look forward to.

Take care of yourself, Tommy.

Annie

Canary Girls
1917

XI
MARCH

No lack of time, strength or money shall prevent me from anything what I want to do.

SARAH MacNAUGHTON
A WOMAN'S DIARY OF THE WAR

MONTREAL, CANADA
ANNIE

My hands are tarnished, callused, and fail to grip something as simple as a doorknob. I've only had the job for a week, and an awkward week at best. Colonel McFarland referred me to the defense minister Mr. Hughes. Mr. Hughes had a friend who operated a munitions plant and offered my name along with other English-speaking women to work in Montreal. It was a terrible idea if you ask me. When we got there, we were greeted with shuns from the Francophones because we couldn't speak a word of French. The plant manager Monsieur Chevalier on the contrary not only spoke English beautifully but was also polite, sophisticated, and caring. His dark hair and blue eyes also made him easy to look at. There were only women that worked at the plant, not a single man on site. Mr. Chevalier said men disturbed the workflow by berating and unwanted advances. He even solved the francophone problem by separating us. He said it was best if we were segregated to ensure maximum results. I disagreed with this logic as the Franco's outnumbered us two to one, it meant we had to work twice as hard. The foreman of the floor was a short French woman everyone called Napoleon. She's a real piece of work. She only spoke to us in French, never acknowledging the language barrier. It frustrated the hell out of me and almost made me walk off the job my first day. When she was showing me the in's and out's of the machines, I asked her to slow down, and her rebuttal was scathing. "vous n'avez aucune autorité, Madame Middaugh. Je fais! Si tu me manques encore de respect comme ça, je ferai de toi un fantôme. Est-ce clair?!" I looked at her afraid and confused. When she left, one of the factory girls approached me and offered comfort.

"Don't mind Napoleon. I'll show you how everything works." The woman was named Joey. Amongst all the women there she had been there the longest and it showed poorly in her complexion. Her skin was yellow, and her face had more wrinkles than a used bed sheet. Her vocabulary was limited but she conveyed her instructions incredibly well. "This here you push it does the do-hickey thing to clamp the shell. This valve controls the jobby thing down here that pours the powder into the shell. Be careful you don't overload it. Any loose powder could blow up the factory and kill us all." She was so cheerful it was disturbing. I couldn't imagine the sights she would've seen over the years.

Joey was from Charlottetown but moved to Montreal when her son enlisted two years before. He's still alive as yesterday she read his letter out loud during our lunch hour. She read his administrative tales with such pride while Mildred and Agnes, the two girls Joey talks to grumbled and groaned the entire time.

"For the love of mercy, Joey. We get it! Your son is the Colonel's errand boy! Now shut up already, we're trying to eat!" Mildred would yell from across the room to Joey whenever she went on her tangents, startling everybody else in the process. It was hypocritical if you ask me. She pulled the same amount of weight as everyone else but did so with such misery and disdain it was nauseating. Agnes wasn't as bad as Mildred, but she had a resting face that resembled a bulldog. I am ashamed to admit that her jowls made her equally annoying.

The thing I am envious about is the letter. I mailed out the letter to Dad two weeks ago and still no answer from Tommy. I know he isn't dead. Dad would've told me. I know he wasn't captured or else there would be a report. I try not to let his absence get the best of me and concentrate on my work... but he had an infectious smile I couldn't shake. I cannot deny I was beginning to wonder if he was worth hanging on to. Those feelings subsided three hours ago when I walked into the dormitory and found his letter in my mailbox.

Dear Annie

It was swell hearing from you. Sincerest apologies for not writing you back sooner. I wish I could tell you what all has happened but we're under orders not to disclose any information that could fall into enemy hands. What I can say is ever since I got your letter my mood has improved and given me strength to make it another day through this war. If it is not too much to ask, would you write to me again? I would love to know more about you and what home is like. I find myself missing it dreadfully.

Take Care,
Tommy

Tommy sounded lonely and it broke my heart. The death of his brother must've wounded him deeply. I had the urge to pick up a pen and paper, but my hands were too weary to write. I tucked myself into bed feeling ashamed of my physical limitations.

* * *

The next morning, I made it a point to write Tommy a letter while on my lunch break. Throughout the morning, I visualized what I was going to say to him, even dwelling on particular words to use. It kept me distracted from the aches and pains I got from the machine's vibrations. The six of us were working our tails off while the 12 French worked more comfortably. It made me more resentful by the hour to where I wouldn't even look at them. There was one girl who kept looking at me while she worked. She was short, olive-skinned and wore her hair in a black bun. She kept trying to take on tasks that were closer to our side. She saw an opportunity when she picked up a fallen wrench by my feet.

"Bonjour," she said. I said nothing in return. "Hello," she said. I stopped what I was doing and looked at her.

"Can I help you?" I asked.

"May I ask you a question?" she asked, politely.

"You may," I uttered, dreading what was about to come next.

"Do you know Nellie McClung?" I looked at the woman startled. How would she know my cousin?

"Yes. We are related." She had a look of great joy.

"C'est magnifique! This Saturday we have a meeting. Can you attend?"

"No," I said, coldly.

"It is for your cousin, though."

"My cousin is coming to visit?"

"Yes! In the summer. Do you guys even talk?" I gave her a blank stare, debating whether or not to slap her. "Oh, I am sorry. I didn't mean to offend. It is a great time for you to catch up."

"I have a fair bit to do around the house that night," I said to avoid going. A look of desperation formed in the girl's eyes.

"Please come. We can't speak English well enough to talk to Madame McClung." I looked at the girls who were looking at me with tired eyes.

"What's your name?" I asked the girl.

"Helena," she answered softly.

"Well Helena, I have a request first. You help us with the quota, and I will attend your meeting." The look on Helena's face was dismal.

"Would you please excuse me?" She asked, then walked to Napoleon who stared at her clipboard in the back corner of the floor. Mildred comes up to me in a panic.

"What did she say?" She asked.

"She said 'would you please excuse me?'" I answered.

"That's it?!" I turned my head the other way and shook off the stupidity. Helena came back with her head down.

"She said 'no'." I looked over to Napoleon and we exchanged grim looks to each other. While we were being petty Monsieur Chevalier walked onto the factory floor with General Currie. Once Napoleon saw the medals on his chest, she instructed all the girls to stop.

"Attention!" She yelled. The girls dropped everything that they were doing to address the general. The general is amazed by our discipline and smiles.

"Good morning, everyone. Just ignore the elephant in the room. I'm only here for an inspection." Napoleon instructed us all to resume our work in English.

"Back to work!" She yelled. In unison we resumed our work. While I poured the TNT into the shell, I reminisced over Napoleon speaking fluent English.

"She speaks English?!" I shouted. Agnes overheard me and laughed.

"You're alright, Caper!" she said. The other girls laughed while they worked, increasing our morale as we left the floor for lunch. I hope Tommy gets a laugh out of it when he gets the letter.

A CANADIAN CRUCIFIED.

A lieutenant-colonel serving with the Expeditionary Force, whose letter is quoted by the "Morning Post," says:—

The Canadians have done splendidly. They are mad with rage because they say they found one of their men crucified. This is not mere camp gossip. A general vouches for the fact.

War Propaganda
1917

XII
APRIL

In time of war, truth is always replaced by propaganda.

CHARLES LINDBERGH

PARIS, FRANCE
GEORGE

All eyes were focused on Vimy Ridge.

From Monday to Sunday, dusk until dawn we analyzed and hypothesized every strategic angle on an upward hill battle. The battlefield is riddled with bones and shell holes after three years of attrition and failure. Underground is a subway system that's two mines away from annihilation. To use a metaphor for the preparation. It's like walking into the lion's den every morning. Vimy is the first major assault from the Canadian Corp and the expectations are high as the entire Triple Entente is looking down at us.

We built miniature versions of the battlefield out of heavy cardboard that took two men to carry. We upgraded to digging mock trenches over ten yards when it was time to instruct the troops. Those are the days I enjoyed the most. While my time of war has been more pleasant than others, I feel compelled to join the boys in the fight. I miss the action and the deeper we go into Vimy, my thirst grows. I've kept myself distracted by tending to Corrie who is suffering from Typhoid. The stubborn ass refused treatment when it was just a cough, and it flourished into a nearly fatal fever. We took him to the hospital early this morning where he will most likely stay until his tenure is up. It feels like my right hand has been taken from me over something that could've received treatment if willing to accept help. Tom's a good man, just infuriating when good men are taken from the fight.

I walked towards my car from the hospital staring down an empty side street wishing I was still a barrister in Markdale. Before I started up the car, I sat for an unknown length of time just overthinking the situation. My sanity was saved by a young private knocking on the door. "Colonel McFarland?" The young private asked.

"Who's asking?" I asked back.

"Private White Sir, I have a message from Major Lipsett."

"What's the message?" The private hands me a note then leaves. As I open the paper my hands tremble with stress.

`Lt-Col McFarland, sir.`

`Your presence is required in my office. Be here ASAP.`

My first thought was more requisitions for uniforms or something equally mundane. I was expecting to walk into a room filled with pencil pushers and bureaucrats. When I got there, there was an ominous vibration in the air. Soldiers were standing outside the building talking amongst themselves. I ignored them and walked into HQ to find Major Lipsett in his office on the third floor. When I opened the door, I found a room full of people. Alongside Major Lipsett sat General Byng, General Currie, Otto Middaugh, and a young private I have never met before.

"Good afternoon, everyone," I said.

"It's good to see you, George," Currie said with a smile.

"Likewise, General. May I ask what this meeting is about?" General Byng looked down at the young private.

"I want you to tell Colonel McFarland everything you have shared with us. He was the former Battalion commander and knew the troops." The young private took off his helmet and played with it as he told us a horrifying story. The story he told is one that involves Sergeant Broadhead. I remembered him vividly as a strong leader and waiting ever so patiently on the promotion to Lieutenant. Remembering him made it even more traumatic as the private told us he and another runner found Sergeant Broadhead crucified onto a barn door. According to the private, Broadhead was pinned by bayonets and wore decayed wounds on his face. I asked him if he saw this happen personally and he said no as they were already on their way to Paris.

"We couldn't find his CO so that's why I told the major, Sir." His voice was soft and weak like he had seen a ghost.

"Who's company CO?" General Currie asked. Major Lipsett spoke up to answer.

"Captain Talbot, Sir. He was originally from the 58th but was made company CO after Christmas." General Currie looked at me with sadness.

"That was when Major Griffith had you transferred." I kissed my teeth in disgust when I heard that name. I am still ever so sore from that. The man made a petty political move because he got caught gambling with army funds. The man was a weasel and when I heard a grenade took him out, I was not ashamed to smile. The more I thought about Captain Talbot, the more I remembered him back at camp Borden handing out the rifles. I remember thinking there was something about that man I did not trust, and the feelings were amplified upon hearing the news of Sergeant Broadhead.

"What do you want me to do?" I asked. General Byng looked directly into my eyes as he gave me the order.

"I want you to investigate this further and find the individual responsible. Be thorough with your sources and report back to me when you have a solid case."

"Yes Sir!" I answered. I walked towards the door before Arthur stopped me.

"And George. When you find the culprit, see to it the punishment be severe." I looked at the man and understood the gravity of his tone. This war is too convoluted as it is. We can't add another scandal on top of it.

BURBURE, FRANCE
THE NEXT DAY

Burbure is a small haven for soldiers on the outskirts of Arras. I had my new orderly Private White come with me to dictate and deliver messages. A strong wind would've knocked him over if given the chance. Respectfully the boy's got a lot of heart. It speaks more volume in comparison to Charles Winston Talbot. The fucking coward has had a series of events involving unusually cruel punishment of his soldiers. Back when he was in the 58th he was scheduled for court martial but somehow evaded it. Well, he sure as hell won't be receiving any leniency from me.

Otto met up with us in front of the morticians with a cigarette and a flask most likely filled with screech. The previous times we spent together he was in a more joyous mood. I guess he's seen the body. "Mornin' Colonel," Otto said softly.

"Good morning. Have you seen the body?" I asked him.

"I saw him being loaded into the truck, but I hadn't seen him this morning. Figured you'd want that liberty."

"What do you know?"

"Nothing relevant to the case at hand." Otto offered me a sip from his flask, but I declined.

"Are you sure?" Otto knew where I was going with this. He knows I know about Talbot.

"For a scrawny stump, that Captain is a very cruel bastard."

"Tell me about it." Before Otto spoke the door opened and the mortician came out. The man was young for a mortician. I was expecting someone older.

We walked down a narrow doorway towards the autopsy room. The further we walked, the more horrific the stench was. On the battlefield the winds take it anywhere it choses. In this building the smell has lingered for far too long. I put plugs up my nose and put vaseline underneath for further protection. I instructed Private White to follow suit. The mortician opened the doors and, on the lay, laid a very dead Sergeant Oscar Broadhead. When I first met him, he was 32 and had a young family. He was always calm and uplifted, a great personality to have around the men. It was heartbreaking to see a man of his character decomposed and humiliated by his peers. I examined is body thoroughly and saw no wounds that would support the theory the man was crucified. There was a hole the size of a pancake in where his sternum should've been. Along the arms and legs there's signs of shrapnel, and a compound fracture at the ankle. Otto stood back and sat in the corner so he could enjoy his cigarettes. "He wasn't crucified," I uttered out loud.

"My theory is he was launched into the air by a Big Bertha and got himself impaled on a flagpole."

"Was it painless?" Otto asked. The mortician gave him a grim look.

"I don't know. Minutes, hours. I calculated the time of death to be the morning of the third. That's all I can really give."

"The two runners found him in the evening," Otto added.

"Why did the men think he was crucified? Were they the ones who took him down?" Otto gave me a blank look.

"I'm afraid you're asking the wrong man, Colonel."

"Fair enough. Do you happen to know the whereabouts of our friend?"

"He's quartered with a family in town. Couldn't say their names if yuh held a gun to my head.." I looked at him puzzled.

"Why isn't he bunked with the rest of his men?" I asked.

"Because he's a senator's son," Otto answered. My heart sank with frustration. I needed to be extra cautious for this matter or else the backlash will cost the lives of thousands. I figured it was best to have a one-on-one conversation with the man, so I sent Private White to go find him and relay that he is ordered to report to me at the officer's barracks. To make it even easier I took the liberty of building a tent next to the barracks, so I'd have a place to sleep. The only thing I asked was for a second blanket and a lamp.

I woke up the next morning tired and yearning for coffee. The ground was a bit rough but manageable throughout the night as silence draped across the land. As peaceful as it was, I was furious. The man still had a few hours to go to report, but I had expected him to have the courtesy to move quickly and efficiently. After Private White handed me a hot cup we sat on a pile of rubble and talked about life as a soldier while I waited for Talbot to arrive. Private said he found the Captain and gave him the message so I am unsure of why the man feels the need to disobey a direct order. I paced around the tent with my hands in my pocket, encouraging myself to remain calm and not lose my temper. A real soldier would rather die than to show disrespect to his commanding officer. I will not tolerate such insolence when we are so close to having a united Canadian front. The man better have a god forgiving miracle of a reason for his actions. As I was repeating my lap, I saw a runner approach Private White and hand him a note. I walked in a straight line to read it.

Colonel McFarland. Your presence is required for an immediate court martial hearing.

For crying out loud, now what?!

MOMENTS LATER
TOMMY

I'm sitting on a bench across from Talbot awaiting my future in the army. I guess it's what I deserve. According to Talbot if I washed out It would do everyone in the army a favor. His authority is just too powerful. It happened because of my new friend Abe. I found Abe on the ground next to a dead soldier, covered in mud. When I picked him up and cleaned him off, I mistook him for water and downed the bottle without hesitation. The taste was far more bitter but I felt numb to the despair and found solace amongst the chaos. To Talbot, Abe was just another excuse for him to get rid of me.

As I stare at the clock, counting down the minutes I saw my judge approach us from down the hall. It was Lt. Colonel McFarland with an orderly close behind. I feel so humiliated I can't look him in the eye. I kept my head down as he walked past. To make it worse, he stopped walking when he saw us, making my heart race with fear. He didn't say anything to me, but he exchanged a look with Talbot and said: "We will start the proceeds in two minutes. I hope you're prepared, Captain." Talbot smiled and replied:

"Yes, Sir. I have everything you need."

"I'm sure you do," was all the Colonel said before he walked into his office.

A few minutes went by, and the orderly told us to come in. I was instructed to sit on the right as Talbot was to the left. He had a grin so villainous it made me nauseous. McFarland walked out of the room holding a file in his hands reading it tentatively. We stood at attention while he sat in his chair and got comfortable.

"You may be seated." We sat down in unison. "Due to your Battalion CO no longer in action I am your interim commanding officer who will be conducting this hearing. I want to remind both parties now that this is just a preliminary and not an actual court martial. I am unsure of who dreamt this concept but regardless, there's no sense in crying over spilled milk. Captain Talbot, if you would please give your argument for the government to hear." The Captain stood up from his chair and took out a folded piece of paper. Inside were lies that he spewed to the colonel.

"Since his transfer from the 147th Battalion, Private Thomas William Holmes has disobeyed direct orders time and time again and this time it has resulted in the death of a Sergeant. I have strong evidence and eyewitness statements that connect Private Holmes to the heinous crime of the crucified soldier and should be publicly condemned." The colonel looked at Talbot and raised his eyebrow.

"That's a bold statement, Captain. Wouldn't you agree?"

"I do, but my word as Captain is unbreakable." The colonel kissed his teeth and asked to see the paperwork. My heart was filled with hate when I saw the exchange. It was all lies. The real evidence rests in a dead man's footlocker.

"Well, I just can't take your word for it. I'm going to deliberate over this over a one-hour recess." Talbot shortened his breath and protested.

"Uh, Sir, is that really necessary?" The Colonel raised his eyebrow.

"I beg your pardon?" The cowardly Captain changed his tone.

"Apologies, Sir. Take as much time as you need." The Colonel put a pipe in his mouth and sat in his chair.

"You know something, Captain. That's the best idea I've heard all morning. Let's give it a two-hour recess and be back by noon." The Colonel looked at Private White and asked for a sandwich. When we sat on the bench Talbot was furious and gave me a cold stare.

"If it wasn't for you, I'd be on the first ride out." I absorbed his comment and looked at the floor. It brought back pleasant memories of Annie working for the man who not only lied for me to enlist but is now determining whether I should face the firing squad. I wish I had a say in court, but as the Captain said it's best if I just kept my mouth shut. Nobody's going to believe my story anyway.

When the two hours were finished, we walked back into Colonel McFarland's office where I expected a grim fate. As we sat in our respective chairs, he was holding up one of Talbot's written statements. The Colonel placed the document down then rubbed his eyes, airing out his frustration with a loud sigh.

"So, after careful consideration I feel it is in the army's best interest if I dismiss this case entirely. I see no clear evidence that connects Private Holmes to any illegal killing." Captain Talbot's face went blood red.

"I object! Colonel, you must look over the evidence again. On the night in question there are two eyewitnesses that state Private Holmes abandoned his post to act like a drunken buffoon. He deliberately disobeyed a direct order and should be exemplified!" The Colonel had a look of confusion mixed in with rage.

"Tell me, Captain Talbot. When A Colonel sends a dispatch to a Captain and that Captain disobeys that order. Should that Captain be subject to the same level of treatment?" Talbot looked at the colonel confused.

"I'm not sure I follow, Sir."

"Well, based on your testimony you are saying not reporting to your commanding officer when requested justifies a firing Squad?"

"Well, yes Sir. It is a soldier's duty to follow the chain of command and obey his army commands." The colonel rose from his chair and locked the door. He turned around slowly and approached Talbot like a coyote hunting its prey.

"I'm just trying to understand why I am wasting my time and energy on this ridiculous hearing when you were given specific instructions yesterday by my orderly." The Colonel was nose to nose with Talbot who was now dripping with sweat. I hoped he at least pretended to have some honor and confess to his sins, but he remained a narcissist.

"I apologize, Sir, but no runner had come to see me so therefore I was unaware of such an order."

"Oh really? Is that a fact? Maybe you just need to give your head a good shake!" The colonel lifted Captain Talbot off the floor by the scruff of his jacket and pinned him against the wall. "CAPTAIN TALBOT, DO YOU HAVE A BETTER MEMORY NOW?!" Talbot's answers were screams of terror.

"YES SIR!"

"Good! Now I will ask you again! Did you or did you not receive a message from Private White to report to your commanding officer?!"

"I RECEIVED THE MESSAGE, SIR!!"

"What did Private White say to you?!"

"He said for me to report to Colonel McFarland as soon as possible."

"Good! So, I will ask you again. Why am I wasting time and resources on a single soldier when his commanding officer cannot follow even the simplest of commands. Do you enjoy making a mockery out of my army?!" The captain was too scared to answer with full sentences so only syllables left his mouth.

"Aye-aye-aye–" The Captain threw him back into the wall.

"Aye-aye-aye is not English, Captain! I need a competent answer!" The Captain coughed and wheezed, grabbing the colonel's hands and pleading for his life. The colonel saw the blue forming in the coward's lips and dropped him to the ground. "Once we handle our business in Vimy you will be next on my list. It is painfully clear you cannot handle any form of leadership, so you are hereby demoted to Private. And your first duty as Private is to relieve Private White as my personal assistant. Make no mistake Private Talbot if you go AWOL on ANY order, I give I will have you shot on sight. Is that understood?" The demoted private regains his composure and fixes his tie.

"Yes, Sir." Talbot nodded his head pitifully then left the room with his head low. When it was just me and the enraged colonel I panicked. *What was he going to do to me?* The colonel took a second to sit in his chair to breathe before acknowledging me.

"Private Holmes." I stood at attention with pride. "Just because you're still in the army that doesn't mean you're off the hook. Considering Private Talbot's repulsive leadership, I have no choice but to keep you in the rear with the engineers. Once Vimy is captured you will be called as an eyewitness for what I already anticipate being a ludicrous trial and you will give the full truth and nothing less. After that, we'll see if we can get you back into the fourth for the next advance. Is that clear?" If I'm to be honest with myself, I'm relieved I'm no longer going to the front. I know If I took one step onto the frozen ground I would surely parish in minutes.

"Yes, Sir. Crystal clear."

"Good. I never want to hear any nonsense over this again. Dismissed." I gave the colonel the warmest salute I could muster, then walked out of the building. My heart was racing the entire time. Lucky for me Abe was on my bunk when I returned to my barracks.

LATER THAT AFTERNOON
OTTO

I had a very peculiar and eventful day today. I was in camp enjoying my afternoon smoke and coffee when Captain Talbot approached me. He was delivering a message from George, requesting my presence in his office. I found it odd that a captain was doing a runner's work. I took the liberty of making small talk along the way. "So, how's the morning going?" The coward said nothing. George must've given the boy a good licking. For a moment I felt sympathy... until I saw his Captain's pin was gone. "So, did it hurt?" I asked him. Talbot gave me a confused look.

"Did what hurt?" He asked, annoyed.

"When you fell down the ranks." Sadly, the boy did not share my sense of humor. "Oh, come on. You don't have to be so private about it." The boy grunted and I smiled. We had a entertaining hour-long walk back to HQ. At least from my perspective that is.

When the private and I walked into HQ we were given an escort to George's office. Talbot gleefully waited outside while the men talked business. At first, we shared a laugh over the boy then got down to nitty gritty. The Colonel wanted me to take Talbot's place as Captain of A Company. It meant that I could be closer to Tommy Boy and keep his arse out of getting shot. That is one plus I will give to the former CO. I may strongly disagree with the tactics used, especially during the incident with the deceased sergeant, but the pipsqueak is still alive, so I am obligated to be grateful.

* * *

The first day of training for Vimy was a rough one. They knew how to present themselves, but when it came time to do the work, they all fell in the cracks. Some even forgot the simplest of tasks like cleaning their rifle. When I gave my initial report to George, I made sure the eejit Private Talbot was within range of hearing my grievances. On the second day of training, I changed tactics. I instructed the men to list everything they struggle with and give the notes to their company Sergeants. From there the ones who struggled were grouped together to concentrate on the areas of improvement. They were tentative about my teachings in the beginning. The best morale boost I've come to terms with is to sing an old sea shanty on our morning hikes.

My mother told me
Someday I will buy
Galley with good oars
Sail to distant shores
Stand up on the prow
Noble barque I steer
Steady course to the haven
Hew many foe-men

My father was a fisherman off Ireland's shores and used to sing to me sister and I when we were young. It was a nice soother to the soul for the men. By the end of the third day every company in the 8th brigade was singing loud for King George to hear.

After two weeks of endless drills, they were ready for the creeping barrage. The Ruskies were the first to use the technique and wiped out their own troops. When the Brits tried at The Somme there were too many cooks in the kitchen and thousands died as a result. God bless the French for they perfected the technique during their time in Verdun. When General Pétain paid us a visit in January, he stressed the importance of timing by having his soldiers demonstrate their movement with live artillery. The way it works is instead of the artillery focusing their guns on the enemy trench they fire their rounds a hundred yards downrange to create a shield of smoke for our boys. It is a brilliant but bold tactic to say the least. The few men Pétain had at his disposal were fearless as they walked into the smoke. My Sergeants on the contrary were shivering with fear. I can't blame the man for having such a cold approach, by the time Falkenhayn withdrew his forces there was an ocean of corpses left behind., We don't have 300 days nor half a million casualties to spare. We needed a solution quickly, and a young man by the name of Billy Bishop rose to the call. The man was a pilot and an exceptional one to be humble. The man's been shot down three times and a certified ace. The man was still good looking, that part surprised me the most. He took me non-com's and educated them vividly on aerial reconnaissance and navigation. Hell, he even took them up into the air and pointed out their respective objectives. That was of course after I got to take a ride up first. Captain privileges ya know.

By April 3rd the boys were ready to unleash hell. They were focused and lean, like a wolf hunting its prey. The mood was somber while we walked to the front line. The winter clouds concealed the sun, and the frost crisped the ground. It didn't feel like April, perhaps more along the lines of February or early March. I was ahead of the troops with my new colt and a fresh uniform with my captain stripe freshly sown. It was interesting wearing Canadian colors for the first time. It didn't come with predisposed judgement from the Brits, far from it. The Brits looked at us with hope and respect. Vimy is deemed impossible by many yet here we are walking over the frozen bones of our allies into the gates of hell armed to the teeth with tools of death and destruction. It'd be a magnificent sight if I knew we would all survive

VIMY RIDGE

GEORGE

I was sleep-deprived yet adrenalized by the awesome power of the artillery. Our new 106 shells decimated the German lines, most impressively taking out their communications and logistics trench. The morale in our trench was high as fresh coffee and bread was passed around the officers. We ignored the stench of death as best we could by using a concoction of vaseline under our noses and burning coffee grounds. Runners came and went silently into our trench, bringing us confirmation of the troops getting into position for the attack. It was a blissful feeling not letting politics get in the way of combat. It would only lead to self-destruction.

It was close to zero hour and General Byng had his eyes set to his pocket watch. The goal was a hundred metres per three minutes. We found through training the boys wouldn't survive the hundred yards per minute so Byng slowed the boys down to a more measurable pace. If the assault stays on schedule we anticipate taking the ridge by early afternoon. Byng was calm and collected, fixated on the map while he stirred his tea in a calm manner. The majority of men had a cigarette hanging from their mouths with sweat staining their collars. As the time grew closer General Byng had requested someone fetch his vintage bottle of gin so I left the task to Private Talbot. He showed some improvement. A task of meaningless importance would be an extension of gratitude and could demonstrate what real leadership is. It was a dismal failure when he came back as the 100-year old bottle was broken by shrapnel. That was the only disappointment in Byng's eyes. Lucky for him he always carried a backup and had a different private fetch it for him. We finished our coffees and held our mugs out while the private rationed out the bottle. Each officer and their orderly held their cups high while Byng made a toast. “Alright lads, let's bring this home for Canada.” All of us repeated in synchronicity.

"For Canada." We emptied our glasses on the edge of the table, with the miniature statue of the ridge in the centre. The room went silent, so silent we could hear echoes of footsteps coming from the tunnels. It was 5:15am when the sound of footsteps faded, a signal telling us they're ready to go.

At 5.20 Byng picked up the phone and gave the order. These next ten minutes are the longest I've endured since I took over as CO. My neck feels tight and my chest compressed but for the sake of the men, I remained stoic like Arthur as he sat in his chair drinking his morning coffee.

"You squared away, Colonel?" He asked me.

"Yes sir," I answered. He nodded his head and went back to his coffee while the rest of the officers got to work. The room was filled with noise and chaos as each officer delegated the orders to their respective battalions. It was until General Lippsett gave a harrowing order to make every man in the trench silent.

"Set off the mine." The men embraced different pieces of the wall, bracing for impact. The exception was Arthur as his body was too big to fit into a trench with 10 other men. Lippsett's assistant counted down from ten to zero, then the trench erupted like a volcano. Muffled screams are heard and the shaking subsides. Arthur held his cup in the air to rally us back together.

"Eyes forward, gentlemen."

Our grips on the wall were released and more orders were given. Our voices grew louder as the artillery increased. Each minute was documented and monitored as the boys advanced. Arthur's boys were the first to reach the Black Line while the fourth was pinned down by enemy machine guns. Our guns failed to take out the pimple and it caused a bottleneck in our assault. Byng instinctively had the answer.

"Colonel McFarland; send in the 8th reserve to support General Watson." I relayed that message to Private Talbot and he left the room to deliver the message. He thought he had some freedom but as soon as he left I grabbed my scope and observed from the small gap in the sandbags. The boy bowed his head below enemy fire as he ran down the line. Machine guns offered him as much support as possible until the Germans launched a counter attack with their artillery. The more time I wasted looking for Talbot the less focus I had on the mission. I returned to the mission as a runner entered the trench.

"Sir! The third division has reached the Black Line!" I rushed over to the other side and peaked with my scope. The boys were giving Fritz a run for their money, and my heart was filled with pride. General Lipsett asked to borrow my scope to see for himself.

"Colonel, I must say you've done a majestic job training the men." He returned the scope for me to see. On the battlefield I zeroed in on a Canadian soldier beating a German soldier to death with their own helmet. It was difficult to see who the soldier was as half his face was covered in blood.

"Don't count on the training too much, sir. Canadians are born to fight." I handed the scope back to the general and he resumed looking.

"Beautiful," was all Lipsett said as he watched the battle with a smile. Minutes later General Byng gave Lipsett the order to detonate the secondary mines. Once again we hugged the walls and prayed the ceiling didn't collapse on top of us. Halfway through the tremors another runner entered the trench.

"Colonel McFarland! Your attention is needed at the aid station!" I rushed out of the hut and staggered my way to the medical camp. Along the way I encountered a sight rare to be old. Private Talbot was hit in the chest with a large piece of shrapnel. The boy was coughing up large amounts of blood while six feet away Private Holmes laid faced down in the trench with blood soaking the snow underneath. I assessed the victims and felt Holmes was expected to survive so I carried the boy the rest of the way. When we arrived, I found out our medical officer Captain Howes was killed. I took over as CO and spent the rest of the attack assisting the nurses as they treated the wounded. In the following days, more wounded flooded the tents which fed our hearts full of fear. We were scared the attack had failed. You could only imagine the feeling of relief when we heard the truth.

Vimy Ridge
04.12.1917

Canada	Germany
3,598 - K.I.A	EST. 20,000 CASUALTIES
7,004 - WOUNDED	4,000 PRISONERS

XIII

MAY

I can calculate the motion of heavenly bodies, but not the madness of people.

SIR ISAAC NEWTON

SHORNCLIFFE, ENGLAND

TOMMY

I am alive, but I feel dead.

When I wake up, I am disturbed by the lights. When I am asleep, I am disturbed by nightmares. Nightmares of myself being shot, or my friends being shot, or Roy being shot. Bullets zig-zagging down our lines behind a wall of guns fill my mind with terror, and my heart with pain. Every time I look down at my forearm, I see the bandage covering the wound. I keep looking at it in wonder, almost like I am in a trance. *Did it really happen?* I remember bringing the spool of copper to fix the phone lines. I remember seeing Talbot, then hearing incoming artillery fire. When I came to, I thought it was a shrapnel wound and feared the worst. The nurse said I was shot, "a clean through & through," she said. She vanished the day after she told me. Her replacement got overwhelmed at the sight of blood. I have no trust in a nurse who gets squeamish over blood, so I am a mute as far as she's concerned. There's a part of me that should care more about what she says. Because of my silence I was placed in a ward where the insane go to heal.

In the ward there's twelve bunks with only six taken. I gave them all aliases because I choose to forget their names. There's Mr. Waddle, a man with a crooked spine and walks up and down the isles muttering to himself. Mr. No jaw spent his time in his chair looking out the windows. Mr. Pinky only talks about killing himself but cannot accomplish his goal because he only has one finger. Mr. Deaf couldn't hear you if you were yelling in his face but would drop to the deck and hide under his bunk if anyone said the word “bomb”. Mr. Tears laid in his bunk all day and cried. He'd weep all day and night while holding a letter. I stayed in the corner and away from the crazies as best I could. I didn't want to look at any of them. They all reminded me of something I chose to forget. If I was at the front, I wouldn't have time to reminisce painful memories. I needed to get out.

Lunch was served to us, and it was pork and beans, and it was dreadful. Mr. Pinky started complaining like a wild hyena. “What the hell am I supposed to do with a damn spoon?!” He slammed his hand on the table and the nurse took it away as punishment.

“Fine. You want to act like a child, I'll treat you like a child!” Mr. Pinky did not approve.

“Fine! When I blow my brains out, you'll remember the fork!” I grunted and ate my food in silence. The pork was so overcooked the constant chewing ripped the stitches in my cheek. I felt a warm sensation trickle down my face like a tear. The nurse didn't notice until my white pillow was crimson.

“Oh, my goodness!” She gasped. Instead of grabbing gauze she hesitated and didn't know what to do. She raced to the supply closet and grabbed a roll of bandages, then came back over to me in a panic. “Please forgive me. I do not know how to change a wound.” I looked at the woman dumbfounded.

"You're not a real nurse, are you?" I asked. The girl panicked and blurted out the truth.

"No, I'm not. I apologise if I misled you. I will be leaving now." The girl walked slowly towards the exit but stopped and realised she never gave me the bandages. She turned around and handed them to me. My heart warmed with empathy, and I moved to the side of the bed to let her sit down.

"Let me show you what to do," I said. She sat next to me, and I told her to watch closely as I peeled off the bloody bandage from my face. I asked her if there was blood crusted around the wound. She said 'yes' so, I asked her to grab me a wet cloth and bucket of water and gently clean the wound. "Thank you," I told her. She nodded and patted my face down as softly as she could.

"May I ask a question?" She asked me. I nodded 'yes' to answer. "Have you ever met the man in that corner before coming to hospital?" I She looked over to Mr. No Jaw, the quiet man in the corner of the room.

"Why do you ask?" I asked her. The woman bowed her head in shame.

"He's my son's father." She hid her tears and ringed her cloth out in the bucket. I sighed in sadness and shared my grief. "We only shared a night together, but I saw his face every night in my dreams." She puts the cloth down. "It's clean."

"Put this one over my cut then wrap my head with the other." She did what I asked and placed the bandage over my clean wound.

"Does he remember you?" She sighed and shook her head 'no'. "Where is he from?"

"He only told me he was a Lieutenant and that I'm beautiful...but he was listed as a corporal and doesn't speak." He reminded me of Talbot, the snake he is. I wish I remembered what happened to him.

"You said his name was Talbot?" I asked.

"No, it was Livingstone." I changed the subject to avoid further embarrassment.

"Are you from around here?" She wrapped the bandage around my head and wrapped it tight.

"Anatolia. I am a refugee."

"Where's that?" Mr. Tears called out to the nurse like he was gasping his last breath.

"NUURRRSSSEEEEEEE!" It was loud enough for the doctor to run frantically into the room.

"What's going on?!" We turned our heads collectively and were horrified to see Mr. Tears sitting upright cutting himself with a metal spoon. Both the doctor and another nurse ran to his aid.

"I must go. Thank you again." She rushed over to help Mr. Tears as the screaming continued. It went on well over a minute before the doctor gave him morphine to calm down. Once he was dead asleep everyone breathed a sigh of relief. If he was smart, he'd stop the whining and act like a man. It would've gotten him out and evaded a pointless scene. And now he is gone, and I'm still here, watching these pathetic men carry on with their daily insanity. If I had needle and thread, I would stitch up his lips so I wouldn't have to hear his annoying voice. While I was at it, I'd grab a gun and put Mr. Pinky out of his misery as well. *I was never like this before the war. It has done something I cannot understand. I am not weak, I am strong.*

"Liar!" A voice called from abroad. It was raspy and bitter. It echoed without a mouth and scared the daylight out of me. I gave my head a good shake and focused on anything else.

* * *

I woke up from a slumber and saw Mr. Tears back in his bunk sedated with fresh sheets. It was quiet. So quiet I can hear a pin drop. I had to use the water closet, by some miracle my bladder was full. I hardly touched food or water all week. I looked around for any signs but wandered around the hospital without knowing where to go. I walked down numerous hallways looking into the rooms and seeing only wounded soldiers. They all slept peacefully in their cots with empty bladders. The last room on the left had a water closet at the far end of the room. I walked as slowly as I could to avoid disturbing the others. The door to the water closet had a loud creek when you swung the door, so I took both hands and pried it open as slowly as possible. I went inside, did my business and felt a minor relief. It wasn't enough to take the pain away, but my bladder is relieved. I flushed the toilet then washed my hands in the sink. I avoided the mirror because every time I looked at it, I saw myself in full gear. I didn't have a weapon, but my uniform was tattered and torn, and my face covered in someone else's blood. I hate what I see, and I hate the noise that comes with it. I tried to fix my brain by turning the light off and on, hoping it remedies my ailment. After several flicks of the switch, I gave up and walked out of the bathroom. I saw the others sleeping peacefully and felt it's best to forget the whole ordeal. I am tired and have been cooped up in this hospital for too long.

"Kill him." A voice says out loud. I look around the room and see no one there. I looked around the room frantically until I came across a pair of eyes. Eyes I had recognised. The rest of the face and body attached was covered in bandages, but I knew those eyes. And those eyes were staring into my soul. They knew my flaws and they knew what I was capable of. They were tormenting me by flooding my mind with memories, memories I choose to forget. A cold breeze brushed past my neck as I heard the voice become more distinctive. It was Roy's. "What are you waiting for?" He asked.

MONTREAL, CANADA
ANNIE

"Je," Helena said slowly.

"Je," I answered back.

"Suis."

"Suis."

"Une femme."

"Une femme."

"Je suis une femme!"

"Je suis une Femme!" Helena and I clapped our hands together with joy.

"C'est magnifique! Vous pourrez l'apprendre à vos amis très bientôt!"

"Oui," I said while smiling. In the beginning I struggled with the language immensely. Changing the words to accommodate the context, adding accents on certain words, even the silly rolls off the tongue, I despised it all. Helena, bless her heart, was more than patient with me. Her young soul was humble and broke down each syllable and stressed the importance of being fluid with the language. To go from that to being able to understand the French girls belittling us has been very rewarding. One prime example was when a lady by the name of Marie tried to tell Helena I was poisoning her mind in my presence. She thought she could get away with it by talking French but when I snapped back in her native tongue she hid in her corner for the rest of her shift. I would be lying if I said I didn't enjoy her walk of shame.

I started learning after Helena and I had the interaction back in February. We began meeting in a church and tucked ourselves in a quiet spot and proceeded with her teachings. Everyone became aware of our escapades, so we felt it was best suited to stay in my room while everyone was away at the taverns. To be frank Helena was more fun to be around then the English girls as all they did was smoke, drink, and complain about anything and everything. That is not fun to me. Fun is learning a new skill with someone you can connect with, and when it comes to Helena and I we are one and the same. Our only difference is our age gap. Helena is only fourteen years old and has been with the plant since she was twelve. She astonishes me, I tell you. For a soul as young as hers, she is quite mature for her age. She started working here shadowing Napoleon, who protects her like a mother lion. Napoleon LOATHED the idea of Helena teaching me French. That woman has made my life almost unbearable with her constant scolding. If I were to hold a hammer wrong, she yelled in French. If I were to fill the black powder in a 'different' way, she would yell in French. If I'm to be candid my motivation to learn French is to tell Napoleon off in her own language. Helena Enjoys her company after the factory hours. Helena says Napoleon is like a different person. She is more kind and caring when she isn't being watched by dogs who claim to be men.

Monsieur Chevalier and I lost respect for each other when he told us men were working in the plant. He went back on his promise and the French girls never batted an eye. They were too accustomed to the treatment and resented us for not putting up with it. Like a snowball that resentment grew into daily yelling matches on the factory floor. It's become so toxic Monsieur Chevalier had to leave his office twice a week to kick two employees off the lot. It is an unbearable work environment.

One morning I had enough of Napoleon. She grabbed a casing and shoved it in my face, barking like the dog she is. I was at my wit's end, and she deserved to be told off. "Fermez-la!" Everyone on the factory floor heard me, including Monsieur Chevalier.

"Is there a problem?" He asked Napoleon. She gave me a grim look then told a lie.

"No problem here, Sir!" He shrugged it off and went back into his office. She turned to me and spoke with a scathing tone.

"Go back to your dorm. And don't ever let him catch you speaking in our tongues again." I was confused but didn't say no to the command. I was over the politics. I missed home. More so I miss Mindy. I miss her fuzzy little mittens making biscuits on my lap. The thought of her eased my sorrow on the walk back to the dorm. I expected to remain alone for the rest of the night, but that wasn't the case.

Late in the evening I was awakened by a knock at the door. The room was without a candle or lamp, so I walked slowly with my arms waved out, expecting to be arrested. Once I found the handle, I opened it to see Napoleon with a candle glaring at me. She stood there stoic and timid, "I request an audience," she whispered. I brought her in to avoid detection and closed the door softly.

"What brings the almighty to my sleeping quarters?" I asked her. She struggled to speak so she set the candle on the ground and sat comfortably. Her words were so quiet the neighbors muffling drowned her out.

"I understand your odious tone. I understand if you wish to see my head on a platter. I accept that fate. I accepted that fate a long time ago. But I must beseech you to end these "lessons" with Helena. You are an outsider, you have no quarrel with Monsieur Chevalier, you do not know what it's like for us." I looked at her frustrated. I sat across from her inches away from her face.

"Explain it to me," I said. "Allow me the chance to try. What is the harm in that?"

"Everything. The more you know, the more you get curious, the more pain it will cause."

"What pain do you speak of?"

"The kind of pain you will never know."

"Try me." Napoleon was at her wits end. She breathed heavily to control her emotions.

"You and I are nothing alike, Miss Middaugh. When there isn't a need for bombs, where will you be? You will be back in your life of leisure while the rest of us steal scraps of bread. How does an opinionated girl like you benefit from knowing our struggles? Struggles you don't deserve to understand?" Napoleon hit me hard with her words. She was right. I know nothing of their world, but that wasn't going to stop me from expressing my frustration.

"You're right. You and I are nothing alike. I am young without wisdom, and you are old without empathy. But we are both born in a world where our voices are silenced by war, raised off the tainted soil of our fallen ancestors, and taxed by men who profit from murder. I may not deserve a lot of things like your respect, but it is only through drastic change where resolve is found. You can sit there and say I don't understand your pain, and, in your defense, you have validity. But it is my generation who will suffer. And not just my generation, but our children and our children's children will also suffer unless we give ourselves a voice and teach our children to learn from our mistakes. Is that something you can benefit from?" Napoleon sat in silence, lacking the words needed to rebuttal. Seconds felt like hours before she answered.

"I will see you at work, Miss Middaugh." She got to her feet slowly, groaning at the aches in her body. She stands up and walks to the door with a limp. It was a sad sight to see. The 'old woman' comment may have been a bit harsh. She's only 10 years older by estimate yet walks like my grandma. She's nothing like that on the factory floor. It's almost heartbreaking.

"Hey Napoleon," I said. She turned around slowly and gave me a look with tears in her eyes.

"Yes, Miss Middaugh."

"Comment vous appelez-vous?" I said as best I could. She opened the door but hesitated to walk out.

"Amelie," she uttered, then closed the door behind, taking the source of light with her. I sat in the darkness and pondered over our conversation. I barely got a wink of sleep that night.

* * *

The next morning, we were working on the main line together. It was unusual for all of us to see. Normally Napoleon would be walking around inspecting all the munitions instead she is filling the casings with black powder.

Her back was turned to the French girls the whole time. She tried to hide her mood, but I could tell something was off about her. I tried to seek answers from Mildred but even Mildred refused to speak of it. "It's a French problem. Not mine," she uttered. I focused on my work and forgot about it. I was sleep deprived as it was, and Monsieur Chevalier was on the factory floor talking to a young, ugly looking rich man smoking a pipe. He walked up and down the line examining the women. As he walked past a lady of interest he said; "En Francais?" in such an eerie tone it made my stomach curdle. Every single speaking girl all said no, while the French had the same soft, bleak tone. "Oui," they would say. For each French girl he found he gave a tap on the shoulder, five of them in total went upstairs into Chevalier's office, with the two men following close behind. Napoleon spoke English and caught us off guard.

"He only picks the French girls because they're submissive." Our close circle looked at Napoleon confused.

"What do you mean?" Mildred asked. Napoleon put on her mask and went back into boss mode.

"I mean you English girls talk too much. BACK TO WORK!" Everyone grunted and went back to work. While everyone distracted themselves, I looked over to Helena who was mounting the fuses.

"Hey Helena," I said to her.

"Yes?" She answered.

"When did you say my aunty was arriving?"

"End of June, miss Middaugh." I looked at the other girls to speak on their behalf. They in return gave me a look of fear. Fearful of what I am about to say next.

"My conditions still stand," I said. Napoleon lifted her head and looked me in the eye.

"Give me the weekend and I will have an answer." Our talk last night must've kept her awake too. The following morning when we all showed up, she added three girls into our rotation. They even volunteered, imagine that. We didn't ask what she did or what she said. We accepted at face value. It was funny, when the French girls came into our line, they all said “bonjour,” to us. All the English girls gave it their best to answer, even Mildred the old bat that she is.

“Barn-gerr.”

Emily Murphy
Author and member of activist group
“THE FAMOUS FIVE”
03.14.1868 - 10.27.1933

XIV
JULY

Show respect to all people, but grovel to none.
TECUMSEH

FORTIERVILLE, CANADA
ANNIE

The movement began on a warm Saturday morning outside of Fortierville. Napoleon knew of this spot from a friend and assured me she could be trusted. Her name was Marie Anne, a young housewife Napoleon had been friends with for years. Marie was a sickly housewife of two adorable little girls that spent the morning pushing each other on the swing. It was warming to see innocence still existed.

When the girls saw us, they offered their assistance with bringing the displays into the barn. Well, more so they made a good effort. The eldest Marie-Jeanne was fine bringing one at a time, but the youngest Aurore dragged the cross across the mud. Bless her heart as she was able to keep up the pace. Their father's who's name I couldn't pronounce, stayed in the back chopping wood as some women sat next to him enjoying a beverage. Napoleon told me to ignore them and continue with our work. It was quite easy when the girls distracted us with their silly antics.

We only had two hours to set everything up before Aunty Nellie arrived. Our intentions were to unite all women workers and march on City Hall, and with her voice leading the way. Her and her friends succeeded in both Alberta & Manitoba, inches away from success in Ontario, and had her eyes set on Quebec being next. Napoleon has stressed the men in Quebec are not like the men out west. They are vastly more stubborn and stuff their backbones in their front pockets. According to her, a massive demonstration will humiliate them enough to give in and adhere to our demands.

The other girls arrived shortly after to help us finish with the stage. Mildred by some miracle got an army truck and filled it full of anyone interested in joining the cause. We didn't count heads, but we ran out of chairs as the room filled with fresh eyes and new optimism. They enjoyed the refreshments distributed by Helena, who was the most excited out of us all. Her energy was infectious and amplified the atmosphere. When me aunty arrived, the women were so exhilarated they were chanting her name as she approached the podium.

"Thank you all. You can settle down now." Napoleon & I Napoleon stood behind Nellie as she spoke with the utmost passion. "Ladies of Kabeck, thank you from the bottom of my heart for joining me here today. We both travelled far and wide in hopes to gain our right to vote." I looked amongst the crowd and some of the French-speaking women gave Nellie blank looks. They didn't understand what she was saying. We had been struggling with the language barrier still, so I approached Nellie by tapping her shoulder. She turned around and I suggested she have Napoleon translate. Nellie agreed reluctantly and allowed Napoleon to translate. Once Napoleon was finished Nellie continued. "Manhood suffrage has plunged our fair country into a perfect debauchery of extravagance, a perfect nightmare of expense. Think of all our young men sent off to die because of its customary hot-headedness. Does the price of handling scorched lead cover the expense?" All the English women shook their heads no, with Napoleon leading the French close behind. "Man was made for something higher and holier than voting. Men were made to support families and homes which are the bulwark of the nation. What is home without a father? What is home when you are a widow? A widow can't even have a bank account!" The women cheered and applauded Nellie's words, drowning out Napoleon's voice forcing her to wait until they were finished. Nellie saw this and settled the girls down. "I know my words carry very strongly across our country. If it were not for this fatal modesty which on more than one occasion has almost blighted my career, I would stand before you just as you are standing right now. For the sake of our cause, I must not dwell on such an overwhelming calamity but go forward in the strong hope that I may live to see the day this war comes to an end. For I say no more bloodshed! Get the women into power and bring an end to man's tyranny across this ball of soil and stone we call our home!" Napoleon gave up translating and had everyone applauding and cheering. Out of the corner of my eye I saw the husband and woman standing behind Nellie's eye line giving us judgmental looks. I gave them a wink in return. As I brought my focus back to Nellie as she continued to rally the women.

Later, when the rally was finished and the girls were done with asking questions, Nellie and I had some time to catch up as a family. She asked how Dad was doing, then I told her what happened to Conor. She felt saddened by the news, but it was like her anger made her determined. "No boy should die before his father." She asked if I was married or engaged, and I said neither. She could tell I was hiding Tommy, so she continued to pester. "What's his name?"

"Aunty Nellie, I'm far too busy with the movement to be worrying about marriage."

"But you're at the perfect age, darlin'. We just need you out of that factory and into a man's arms. At least one that knows his place."

"I hate to disturb your ego Aunt Nellie, but the type of men you see around here don't offer the comfort I seek."

"He's overseas then?" I got so frustrated with her interrogation I conceded to shut her up.

"Yes," I grunted.

"What's he like?"

"Average height, dark hair, quiet and shy personality."

"And he's a soldier?"

"Undoubtedly."

"British?"

"Canadian."

"Oh, thank God!" I was treading on thin ice if I gave any more information.

"If I tell you more, will you tell Dad?"

"Annie, I haven't spoken to your father in years. Whatever you say will stay in Kabeck."

"Well, Father already met him. The night before he left, he got drunk with Dad and slept in my bed." Nellie shook her head in annoyance.

"Of course, your father would do something childish like that. The lad survived, I take it?"

"He has been at the front for some time now. I'm not sure if he has gotten any of my letters."

"Do you check the casualty list?"

"Every Tuesday. His name is never on it."

"Good. For his sake he better come home alive because he's got a pretty bride waiting for him."

"Aunty Nellie, stop!"

"Oh, come now. I'm just bugging you. Does mystery man have a name?" I changed the subject.

"So, about the march on City Hall." She laughed and went along.

"Alright, alright, alright. I uh, appreciated you bringing me out here and rallying all the workers and all, but there is no money in this. We need to spend to add value to the cause. If you were all housewives, it would be different, but because you are munitions workers your spirits are not enough. We are going to need a stronger hand, and I have the right woman in mind, but she isn't cheap. We also need more recruits. Tall, small, fat, skinny, anyone that produces estrogen, bring them on board. Because Hunny, if the premier were to walk in and see this abysmal turnout he would laugh at us, then rip us to pieces. Do you understand what I'm saying?"

"I do. Who's the woman that you will be contacting?" Aunt Nellie laughed.

"I'll give you her name in exchange for soldier boy, how's that?" I looked at the woman, annoyed. "Trust me, it's better if you don't know. We don't want to get our hopes high in case the French don't come through." I swallowed my ego and agreed.

"Will I at least get to meet her?"

"In time. We have to build a case for it first to have validity." She pauses for a moment, then formulates a plan. "Meet me at the St. Gabriel hotel in two weeks. My friend's got some business coming up and I think I can give you a couple of hours alone with her. Bring your translator with you as well. It'll show her we have an in." We walked from the barn to her motorcade where a woman driver was waiting for her. Before Nellie got into her seat we shared one last moment together. "It was wonderful to see you, Annie."

"And you as well, Aunty Nellie."

"Oh, stop with the Aunty you'll make me feel old." We laughed and she sat in her seat while the driver started the car. We waved each other goodbye, and they drove away into the sunset. Once Napoleon knew they were out of sight she approached me.

"What did she say?"

"She said: "We need more money and women. Tall, small, fat, anyone with estrogen bring them on board." Napoleon looked dumbfounded.

"What's estrogen?" All I could do was laugh.

MONTREAL, CANADA
THE NEXT DAY

We arrived back in Montreal and gave the girls the update. We met up at the church in a private corridor. The girls were excited and nervous at the same time. Joey had her arms crossed and her hands tucked in. She tried hard to be a positive sport, but she kept quiet and listened. It was an unusual characteristic. We had a few minutes to chat alone, and she told me her concerns for not being able to recruit. "What Mrs. McClung wants cannot be done." I reassured her that we have a greater chance of success by trying than sitting back and doing nothing at all.

"Joey, you let Napoleon and I handle the stress of worry. You just focus on the tasks you can control, ok?" She nodded then shared a hug. I understood her worry as I was fearful of the same outcome. Make matters worse, half the women are too fearful of being discovered to recruit off the streets. But Aunty Nellie was right. For the sake of the cause, we must dwell on the things we can control. "Tell me, Joey. Do you have any hobbies?" Her tears subsided instantly.

"Why, yes. I knit."

"What do you knit?"

"I make birds," she said with a smile. I gave her a look of confusion in return. She opened her bag and pulled out a small, knitted canary that looked like a child's toy.

"Oh," was all I could say. I held the bird in my hand, feeling the cotton stuffed inside.

"I was on my way to the hospital to see an old worker. Her favorite bird is the canary."

"Can you make more of these?" I asked her. She nodded her head and smiled.

"And other colors," she answered. "I have a blue jay and a cardinal on my nightstand."

"Is it expensive to make?"

"For something this size, yes. The pins I make cost a fraction worth." The stuffed toy gave me an idea. It's not entirely ethical, but perhaps we can sell these items to women like us. Women who work hard for pennies who want to surprise their young ones with a gift. The funds will go to Nellie's mystery friend, and God willing someone interested enough to join the march.

I pitched the idea, and all the girls loved it. Some volunteered to assist Joey in making more while others volunteered to sell them. The francophones went door to door while the anglophones roamed the streets. We knocked and talked to as many people as we could, trying every attempt we thought could make a profit. The first day was a failure but recoupable. We just needed a clear vision to guide us to victory. With that came an idea from Mildred. The idea was formed during an early morning meeting in the munitions cellar with coffee and cigarettes. We talked over the first day and what areas we can improve. The biggest challenge was nobody was interested in the toys because we sounded like cheap salesmen. A couple of girls even came back with broken baskets claiming some kids got the jump on them. Every story the girls told was like a knife piercing my heart. Napoleon had the idea of saying the money goes to an orphanage, Helena said she almost got taken away by the cops for roaming parentless. Joey thought of saying the money was for grieving war brides, Agnes said "I'd rather lie about orphans than grieving brides," in return. Mildred threw her hands in a fit of rage.

"Well, why don't we just say it's part of the war effort." Napoleon cut her off.

"We can't say that either, Mildred."

"How is it not helping the war effort? The proceeds go to a political figure who makes a paid appearance to tell us what to do and how to feel. It is no different than a king telling a jester to send his peasants to their death because a different king has a bigger castle." Napoleon's face went blood red. Mildred might've faced a painful death if I hadn't said anything first.

"Why do you speak like you're convicted of treason?" Mildred realized what she just said and abruptly changed her tone.

"Oh, sincerest apologies Miss Middaugh. I expect to face a gruesome death if I leave or snitch. I'm just saying it's another way to end the war so yes, it's helping the war effort."

Napoleon spat on the ground and spoke in French when she sat back down.

"Dieu me donne la force de ne pas la frapper." I looked at Napoleon and spoke up.

"Anyone want to vote?" I asked. Napoleon grunted.

"Don't bother. We'll do it the hag's way."

"Thanks for your love and support, Napoleon." I gave Mildred a grim look.

"From now on, you will address her by her proper name." Mildred gave me a confused look.

"I don't know her real name!"

"Well, with all due respect Mildred. That a mute issue." We adjourned the meeting, and she stormed out of the cellar. Napoleon and I were the last two in the room, standing across from each other exchanging grim looks. "You got something to say?" I asked her. Napoleon took a deep breath and exhaled.

"It's not words I feel, it's emotions. I feel conflicted."

"Why do you feel conflicted?"

"I feel conflicted because even though this ordeal has aged me horribly... to see it for once being obtainable is... surreal. Don't mind how I'm feeling, we just need to stay focused on the tasks at hand."

"Are you sure?" I asked, concerned.

"Quebec women are more resilient than you think, Miss Middaugh. I am just in uncharted waters for the time being."

"I understand," I uttered. "We'll get some rest and come back with fresh minds in the morning."

"Agreed." The workers finished the day with a solemn tone.

After the day was finished, I decided to take a stroll to clear my head from the stress. From the top of Sherbrooke I walked south on St. Laurent not paying any attention to the world around me. I was lost in myself and struggled to find a distraction. The distraction found me instead. While I was waiting to cross the street, I saw a young soldier surprise his love with a bouquet of flowers. The young woman screamed in joy and kissed the soldier like he was the center of her world. She threw the flowers on the ground and dragged the soldier away with intense passion. I had feelings of envy as I watched them disappear and wondered how Tommy was doing. It would be good to see him and be able to share my woes with him, but on second thought I mustn't let Aunty Nellie's fantasies project on my own. They got a strong hold on me as I fell into another woman because I wasn't paying attention to where I was walking. I felt so embarrassed I helped the woman to her feet and dusted her off.

"Oh, I am so sorry, Miss. Forgive me for I am not of sound mind," I said to her. She held my hands with kindness and revealed herself to be Dakota, Angeni's daughter. Her smile lit up my world and I gave her a sisterly hug.

"Always wonderful to see you, Annie," Dakota said back.

"What are you doing here?" I asked her.

"On a task from Prime Minister Borden. And you?"

"I work in a bomb factory. One of Dad's friends knows the plant manager."

"As long as you are safe and happy."

"What task does the Prime Minister ask of you?"

"I uh, am currently unable to answer that question. I must be going. It's good to see you, Annie." I looked at Dakota oddly. It was out of character for her to disregard me like this.

"Let's catch up tomorrow," I offered. Dakota was hesitant but agreed. We met on the following Saturday at a park where no one could see us. It was Dakota's idea as she seemed cautious around those she didn't know. We passed the time reminiscing over our families and mourned over Conor. It has been rather painful discussing him over and over, but it was also easier to accept what happened. I found solace in acceptance, and it helped ease the conversation with Dakota. That was until she told me her reason for being in Montreal.

"I am not supposed to tell you this, but there's a new law being passed."

"A new law?" Dakota held her head down as she told me.

"Volunteers are no longer enough. King George demanded we pass conscription, and the Prime Minister gave in." My heart sank like the Titanic.

"When?"

"Sometime next month. Minister Kemp is scheduled to meet with the Premier on Monday and it's my duty to translate."

"How do you think it will go?" I asked her. All she could do was shake her head.

"Both sides are too stubborn to listen. Somedays I feel it'd be more applicable to translate a brick wall than a debate amongst men." My heart spoke out with an idea.

"What if there was a way for them to listen?" Dakota looked at me oddly.

"I don't understand," she uttered.

"I have some friends I want you to meet." If What Dakota says is true it is a cause that the French can support.

On Monday before roll call I pulled Napoleon to a private corridor and told her about the new law.

"Are you sure she can be trusted?" Napoleon asked me.

"She's extended family. She has no reason to abuse my trust."

"What kind of white woman is named Dakota?"

"She's not white. She's Indian." Napoleon's face white pale.

"You're joking," she muttered.

"Why is that an issue?" I asked her. "Nellie didn't specify race." Chevalier blew his whistle to initiate the roll call.

"We'll discuss it later," Napoleon grunted. That later became another late-night visit with candlelight. She was feeling trepidation over the idea. She said Indian women get treated worse than French women. She didn't understand that Dakota was not only fluent in English and French but also spoke German and Russian. Her skill set gives her the ability to have front row insight into how men think, or more importantly how men behave. "Nobody has to know it was an Indian who told us. All we need to say is 'end the conscription' and leave her name out of it." Napoleon wouldn't give in on Dakota's heritage. She asked to meet with Dakota first before she made her decision.

The two got together the day before Nellie's arrival. It was awkward to say the least. Napoleon questioned her relentlessly, switching between English and French. Napoleon even spoke German to add more confusion into the mix. Dakota didn't bat an eye and retorted with a firm tone. Napoleon's judgemental demeanour subsided and began to listen to Dakota's story. The two realized they share an equal level of passion and concern for our country with different approaches.

"There's an update that I need to share with you." Dakota said to me. "Emily Murphy is expected to be in attendance." My heart skipped a beat upon hearing that name.

"Emily Murphy as in the first female magistrate Emily Murphy?" I asked.

"Yes," Dakota answered. She must be the woman Nellie was referring to. If that's the case it's not a matter of if Quebec allows women to vote, but a matter of when.

* * *

We arrived at the hotel early in the morning. We took the liberty of booking our own room for the night using the money we collected from the stuffed birds. If George were here, he would be complaining about staying in a hotel as luxurious as the St. Gabriel. The hotel we stayed at in Ottawa was miniscule by comparison. I hope Emily is worth it.

As we checked, in minutes felt like hours while the young clerk looked for my name. He found it at the bottom of the list and gave us a key to the room. Before we went up, I instructed the clerk to notify Aunty Nellie where we were while Dakota and Napoleon loaded the bags onto the trolleys. Dakota was a bundle of nerves while Napoleon stayed quiet, to where she only said one word when we got to the room, "merci." Dakota felt at ease. While she sat on the edge of the bed her breathing subsided and was able to take her shoes off. "What's got you agitated?"

"If the Prime Minister discovers I'm converting with Emily Murphy, he will have me fired," Dakota answered. Somebody knocked on our door and startled us.

KNOCK! KNOCK! KNOCK!

Napoleon and Dakota fell silent while I approached the door slowly.

"Who is it?" I called out.

"It's your Aunt," Nellie said back. My heart grew with excitement, and I opened the door frantically. When I saw Nellie with another woman, they didn't seem pleased to see us.

"May we come in?" Nellie asked.

"Yes, of course!" I ushered them into our room as the others stood with admiration.

"Annie, I want you to meet Emily Murphy. She had just told me something disturbing." Emily cut in and gave a condescending remark.

"There's no need to elaborate, Nellie. She's standing right in front of us." Both Napoleon and I looked at Dakota who stood frozen in fear.

"What is the issue?" I asked.

"The issue is you have a spy amongst you. That is Dakota Smith. She works for the war minister and is corroding the movement." I looked at Emily dumbfounded.

"Well, yes Madam, we are aware. She has been transparent about her business in Montreal. In fact, she was the one who told us you would be in attendance. She wants to help us. She has valuable information about a new law coming into -" The woman had enough and got inches away from my nose.

"I will not tolerate such ludicrous language. The truth of the matter is savages don't have the spine to stand as a pillar for freedom. That is finality." Her magistrate had the audacity to leave before I could say or do anything in return. I was crushed. Nellie looked down at me but never said a word. She left the room shortly afterwards where the rest of us sat quietly for hours on end, unable to grasp the heartache that transpired.

Francis "Peggy" Pegahmagabow
03.09.1891 08.05.1952

378 confirmed kills
...over 300 prisoners captured.

XV
SEPTEMBER

Treat your men as you would your own beloved sons. And they will follow you into the deepest valley.

SUN TZU
THE ART OF WAR

MÈRICOURT, FRANCE
OTTO

If I wanted to be bogged down with rain I would've stayed in Nova Scotia. For over a month we've been dealing with this God forsaken wasteland without any relief. Damn that Haig. Only a butcher would think to send us into his mess.

Before Méricourt we were at Hill 70. Fritz was a miserable old sod and brought out everything from tanks to flamethrowers to aerial bombing to kill us. In fact, just yesterday we were hit with gas shells, killing over a hundred men. The need for fresh faces is becoming an issue and even though George is working vigilantly to give us reinforcements, the men just aren't coming in quick enough. The word from home says the government began their conscription process, any able-bodied man between 20-45 years of age is up for enlistment, they say. Well damn, if I wasn't a patriot I'd say I'm five years too old for the war.

George and I had a laugh about it this morning at our daily meeting. It was a nice ice breaker for the gloomy news under a wet tent.

"We got orders from the butcher," he said. I sighed and took a drag from my smoke.

"Where we goin'?" I uttered. George took a sip of his coffee and gave a grim answer.

"Think of the worst place you've ever been."

"Rhodesia," I said, jokingly.

"Wrong war," he said. I thought about it for a second and sighed.

"Flanders," I said. George nods his head before he speaks.

"You're close." He handed me a map of the area. A large black circle was around the town of Passchendaele. I couldn't get past the P without cursing the name.

"Why?" I asked.

"For King and country, Otto," he answered grimly. George handed some aerial photographs to offer a better visual. Fritz doesn't just have trenches; he has concrete bunkers.

"How many casualties ye expectin'?"

"Sixteen-thousand, triple for the wounded."

"Enemy strength?"

"Two-hundred thousand. Reservists excluded."

"Haig expectin' us to kill 'em all, eh?"

"No more than what I'm willing to do, Otto." I pitied the shoes the good man had to fill. Then again, I'm only responsible for 200 and his is 2,000. I count my blessings where I can.

"Well, that's good. You tagging along?"

"After my business in Shorncliffe is finished, yes. I should arrive at the front no later than the fifth."

"What business ye got in Shorncliffe."

"Private Talbot. His father is making an inquiry into his death." I looked puzzled.

"That's why I haven't heard a follow-up on Sergeant Broadhead." I asked him.

"If it offers any consolation, I just found out on Monday the man's been dead for three months."

"How'd he die?" I asked.

"The telegram said suicide, but I have yet to see the autopsy."

"You lemme know how that works out, eh?" I stood up from my chair and put on my helmet. "Will there be anything else from me Colonel?"

"Yes, actually. I have a list of your replacements." George handed me a document with a list of names. "They should be waiting for you at the Captain's tent. Send a runner if you need any further assistance."

"Will do, George." We shook hands and I left. While I savored my walk in the rain, I thought about the fancy private. The thought of the man killing himself didn't sit right with me. He was too vain to try something as daring as suicide. I remember opening the man's foot locker and found a bunch of records that paint the private black as night. Seems good ol' Talbot was a bit friendly with Fritzy and kept a record of it. From food rations to troop positions, he bartered for goldmarks. Whoever killed him did him a **favor** as far as I was concerned. George was going to crucify the boy if he recovered from his wounds.

I sat on a stump to take a break from the hike. I took the list out of my pocket and looked them over. Every name on here is from a different colony. It might be a mistake on HQ. I wondered whether to go back to George and question the list or head over to their camp and see for myself. Seeing it was easier on the leg to continue I peeked to see them when I got back to camp. The boys were on their cots in their own little bubbles. The Indian boy was praying alongside the mick. The other Indian was cleaning his rifle, and the other lad was reading a book. I felt Mr. Reader would be the first one to approach.

"Good afternoon," I said.

"G'day!" The Aussie said back.

"What's your name?" I asked.

"Jesus Christ, and yourself?" He answered. I chuckled at his attitude. *I'm gonna like this one.*

"Captain Middaugh, your commanding officer."

"Ah hell! I'm sorry, Captain. Sonny Jones, Sir."

"I'll punish you later over a deck of cards. Wanna introduce me to the rest?" Mr. Jones got up from his seat and gathered everyone's attention.

"Oi! It's the CO!" The men stopped what they were doing and stood at attention. They were lean killing machines the whole lot of them. Their eyes told the story. Especially the Canadian Indian fella. He was next on my list.

"What's your name?"

"Peggy, Sir," he answered.

"Peggy short for somethin'?"

"Pegahmagabow." I was flustered by the name and stuck with Peggy.

"Where you from?"

"A barn," he said with a straight face.

"A barn?"

"Yes, Sir."

"Was the barn built on Canadian soil?" My comment struck a nerve.

"Ojibwe... Sir."

Got another good one, excellent.

It was time for the other two. The Indian fella stood next to a statue while the mick held his prayer beads in his hands.

"Who you prayin' too, son?" I asked the Irishman.

"The motherland, Sir," he said with pride. I looked at the Indian and asked him the same question.

"Dhanvantari, Sir. He keeps me calm at night."

"I like that," I retorted, then asked them for their names.

"Cormac Boland."

"Vikas Singh."

"Good. Are ya both complacent praying beside each other?" Boland looked me dead in my eye to show his character.

"As long as ye aren't the Germans, you're kinship." Singh followed suit.

"Agreed." They seemed too tame to be in the Canadian Corp. I was blunt to ask what makes them tick.

"So, how do ya feel about the Brits then?" Singh's smile vanished.

"My apologies, Sir, but that is a topic I must resist talking about," he said. Boland didn't have to say a word. I could tell by his accent he was from the dark parts of the old country. I choose not to imagine the horror he must've seen on Easter Sunday. Why was he here though?

"Boland, how does an Irishman find himself in a Canuck outfit?"

"Punishment," he answered.

"Punishment?" I asked him. Peggy answered on Boland's behalf.

"We're all here because we hate our bosses." The others giggled in unison, sending chills up my spine. I loved it, absolutely loved it.

"Well, I guess I'll just have to be on me best behavior now, won't I?" Jones jumped back into the conversation.

"If ya don't mind me asking, Captain. How do YOU feel about the Limeys?" I let my heart speak for me.

"Let's put a picture of King George on the target board and find out?" They all cheered and laughed. George, that old bugger knows me so well.

* * *

Over the next few days, the boys and I got to know each other through various games and exercises. Our favorite is poker. The way we played it was simple. Each of us places a bet on what kind of hand we'll get, then Peggy heads out into no man's land to hunt. If Peggy tags three Sergeants and two captains, you get a full house, he takes out five lieutenants, it's a royal flush, if he's bored and takes out a few privates it's a three of a kind. It's mesmerizing seeing that man behind the scope of a rifle. He'd first scout the area with a pair of binoculars to spot the enemy positions then crawl under the wire and shoot from a concealed spot. He used some sort of makeshift device to silence his rifle during trench raids, enhancing his lethality by tenfold. I have heavy brass, but not to that extent, my god Nova Scotia would sink from the weight.

One day we were playing a round of poker when we got a surprise visitor, Tommy. The boy was fully healed from his wounds and had a different look in his eyes. He was no longer the innocent boy who couldn't handle his liquor. The boy had the look of a killer. Boland was the first to greet him who sent him my way to report for duty. "Aye, Tommy Boy! Good to see you!"

"It's good to see you too, Sir."

"What brings ya out to these bunch of misfits?"

"This is my new unit, Sir," he said with his traditional shy self.

"Oh really? Well then welcome. I'll have the good Sergeant Boland show you around."

BANG!

Poor Tommy dropped headfirst into the mud while everyone else laughed. The kid still didn't know the difference between outgoing and incoming. "Let me teach you somethin'," I said to the lad as I helped him to his feet. Peggy had two rounds left so we waited until he fired.

BANG!

"That's outgoing." I counted from ten down to three when I heard Fritz return fire.

WHIZZZ!

BOOM!

The explosion was further down the line. Much to my delight it was a short round.

"That's incoming." Tommy was tense, yet calm.

"Thank you, Sir," he said, softly. The rest of the lads began asking him questions, starting with Jones.

"Where ya from?"

"Owen Sound, Ontario."

"Are you close to Toronto?" Singh asked.

"I don't know. I've never been."

"You're not missing much," Peggy uttered. "If you've seen London, you've seen Toronto." Jones cut back in.

"Can't be any bigger than Sydney." He looked at the boy and offered him a drink from his flask. To my surprise Tommy took it without hesitation but only had a single swig.

"Thank you," he said. He felt the aftertaste of the tequila and his face went sour. We all laughed at the boy's expense.

"Yeah, Tequila will do that to yuh!" Jones said while taking a swig for himself.

"I've never had tequila before," Tommy retorted. Boland killed the humor to ask the million-dollar question.

"Ya kill anybody before?" We waited patiently for the boy to answer.

"No, not directly at least." Boland gave the boy a wicked grin.

"We can fix that," he said, then gave me a look. "Shall we bring him in tonight?" He asked me. I thought for a minute of the repercussions. Annie would kill me if I got the boy killed, but I can't let the boy hide from the war.

"Peggy, he's with you," I answered. Peggy nodded. The lads got run over to Fritz' trench to get more Intel. It'll be good practice to bring him along.

CALIFORNIA TRENCH
TOMMY

I walked into no man's land expecting death, but instead we all got back alive. Through the rain and mud, we crawled across no man's land without the need of flares or cover fire. Peggy got himself two privates, a sergeant, and a lieutenant, while the rest of us went hand to hand. There was a captain we left alive long enough for Singh to come and translate. Once we got intel Peggy finished him off and gave me the Captain's stripes. He said it was for good luck.

We turned in for the night and enjoyed some rest and relaxation. Jones, Otto, Boland, and Peggy were playing cards while Singh read his book in the corner. We had some newcomers join us from C company as their trench was destroyed from the rain. Much to my delight one of them was Reekie, my old friend from home. It was damned good seeing him again. We shook hands and hugged while another soldier walked in soaked from the rain and whispered something into Otto's ear. He sighed then got to his feet. "Duty calls, boys. Sonny, make sure the young blood gets a turn to lose, eh?"

"Aye, Otto," Jones answered, then looked at us with a devilish grin. "Ya ever play euchre?" Reekie shook his head up and down while I shook mine side to side. "Holmes, you're with me." Peggy got out of his seat so the both of us could squeeze in. Reekie sat across from Boland while I sat across from Jones. Jones shuffled the cards while Boland grabbed a bottle from his bunk.

"Any you gents fancy some esh-kha?" He asked. We both said 'yes', and he placed the bottle on the table. "Help ya-selves." Sonny sorted the decks while Reekie and I took a swig from the bottle. Reekie grabbed the bottle first, holding the bottle in a way where the tip is an inch away from his lips while the whiskey falls freely down his throat. He hands the bottle to me, and I repeat the same movement. I set the bottle back in the center while Jones dealt the cards. Each of us were given five cards to play with the last card face up on the deck. It was a jack of spades. Sonny whistled and said; "Oh Boland, you lucky mick. Whaddaya say?" Boland looked at his cards, then to Reekie, then to me. When he looked at me, he said;

"Trump." I looked down at my hand, wondering what that meant. Jones asked him;

"Clubs or Spades?" Boland took a long second to answer.

"Clubs."

"You going in alone?" Boland looks at Reekie with a trusting face.

"Nah, he can tag along."

"Fair enough. Clubs are trump. Your move." We all looked at Boland to see what card he'd play first. When I looked down at my hand I had the jack of clubs, queen of spades, ace of hearts. Nine of diamonds, and jack of diamonds. If clubs are trump, then I have a losing hand. I felt Boland could see right through me as the first card he laid down was the same jack.

"Your move, Tommy," Boland said to me. Otto walked through the curtain-soaked head to toe with a lit smoke hanging from his lips.

"Did I miss anything?" He asked us.

"Tommy's about to make his first move," Boland answered.

"Is that a fact?" Otto approached me from behind to look at my hand. "Far left," he said with pride. He was pointing at my jack of clubs. I placed the card on the table and the table grew mixed reactions. Reekie threw away a queen of hearts and Jones threw away a ten of clubs.

"Trick's yours, Tommy." Boland said to me. I gleefully took the hand and set the trick by my right.

"Your move," Jones said to me. I looked at my hand and played the queen of spades. Reekie played a King of spades while Jones played an ace of diamonds. Boland only played a ten of clubs, but he won the trick. He ended up winning the round as he held only one suit. Once the game was done Jones killed the negativity with a joke.

"Hey Tommy, what does euchre, and sex have in common?" I gave him a blank look. "If ye don't have a good partner, ye better have a good hand." All the boys except for Singh laughed. He remained lost in his book. Jones was about to deal another hand until Otto grabbed his shoulder.

"I hate to interrupt this, but it's official. We're moving out." The room fell silent.

"When?" Boland asked.

"Sunrise," Otto answered. Boland took his pocket watch out of his jacket pocket to check the time.

"I don't know about the rest of you lads, but I rather sleep when I'm dead. You up for another round?" Reekie and I looked at him and nodded 'yes' in unison. We played for another three rounds until Otto drowned the candle and forced us to sleep. I'll be honest, I thought of the joke more than my friend abe during my post. Even though I was cold and shivering from the rain, I felt warm inside.

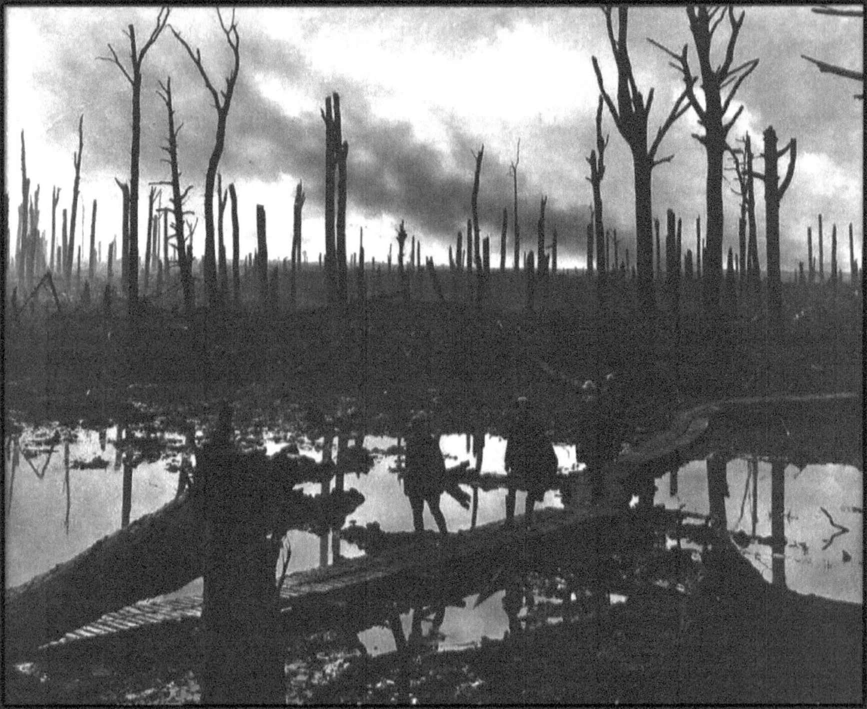

Chateau Wood
10.29.1917

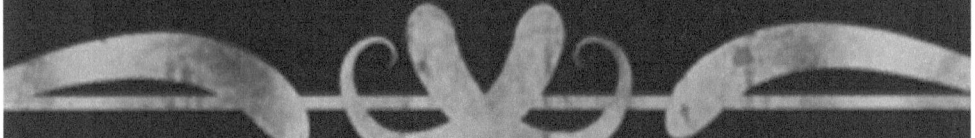

XVI

OCTOBER

Mankind has ten-thousand years of experience at fighting and if we must fight, we have no excuse for not doing it well

T.E. LAWRENCE

SEVEN PILLARS OF WISDOM

PASSCHENDAELE, BELGIUM

DAY 1 - TOMMY

A thousand of us were crammed into a train heading east. We were docked at Caestre waiting for the train of refugees to depart. We were dressed in dry gear and sheltered from the rain. None of us complained.

The refugees looked frail from across the road. Their skin tone is tan like the nurse from the hospital, he said they were Armenians. The conductor took his time starting up their train, enjoying one last smoke before we head east. Once the butt was flicked out of his hands, the engine's roared and pumped out the blackest of smoke from the caboose's chimney. The whistle echoed in the air, and the little faces staring across from us faded away in the distance. The boys were impatiently waiting for the train to leave until we heard a cry from outside.

"GOTHAS!"

The air raid siren screamed across the land and troops were giving it all to the sky. None of us could see what was happening but Machine gun fire and planes roared all around us. The train started to move but Fritz had us in his sights and dropped a bomb on top of us. It didn't hit our car, but the blast was powerful enough to derail the train onto its side. Bodies crash into each other like fish in a barrel, ready for fritz to feast. More gun fire persisted until silence deafened the car. Otto gave us the order to leave the train. "EVERYBODY OUT!" One of the boys climbed out of the window and opened the double doors. Another soldier got out and helped the soldiers get to their feet and off the train. After a few minutes we recuperated and proceeded to march to Ypres. I reserved a bullet for the next time I see that wretched plane.

DAY 2 - TOMMY

It took us a full day of walking to reach Ypres. Our boots were soaked in muddy water. Our uniforms were tethered to our skin and left blisters behind. We may have looked abysmal, but it was nothing compared to the horror we found at Ypres. Our maps told us there would be several small villages in the area. But, as far as we could see under the blackened clouds, only craters and death remained. Jones asked anyone if they had the pleasure of being here before. Only Otto and Peggy said yes. "It's only gotten worse," Peggy uttered. Once we got to base camp we huddled under as many fires as we could to stay warm. Only God knows when we will be dry again.

DAY 3 - TOMMY

We had beans and wet bread for lunch, a meal fitted for machine gun fodder. The mood was low, so low men debated over which way to die was the least painful. I chose to write to Annie instead. Seeing her piercing blue eyes would surely be a heavenly sight to behold right now.

DAY 4 - OTTO

We just experienced the worst attempt to relief in military history. My heavens the whole damn area is a quagmire filled with corpses. My executive officer got himself lost mid-way through the trek just to deliver a message to B Company. How the hell does Haig expect us to fight in such horrid conditions? There was no sense sending us in the dead of night when the rain was blocking everyone's vision, including the horses pulling the wagons through the mud. Some of the horses were so stuck, we were forced to put them down to ease their suffering. As far as I saw it. The only animals who deserved death were humans. This caused major delays in rations arriving at the front in time. I'm not sure if Fritz got lucky or spotted us from a distance but they sent a couple of shells our way and killed two officers: Captain Woods, and Lieutenant Campbell. The taste of the texture of blood and mud mixed will never leave my senses. It's as repulsive as you can imagine.

DAY 5 - TOMMY

I was standing at sentry duty looking over the landscape. We finally got some sun, so the boys changed into fresh kits. I was envious as they were all dry while I was still soaked. Seemed to be part of the process I guess, or my mood for the time being. It flourished into optimism after my conversation with Otto. We talked about life at home and some of the better parts of Roy. I was collected until Otto asked how he died, then I fell silent. It was too painful to express, too infuriating to believe, too horrid to envision. All I could tell Otto was it was too dark for me to get a full picture. It wasn't a lie, but it wasn't the truth either. He countered it by telling me the story of his son at Beaumont Hamel. It sounded like a terrible ordeal for him. Losing a brother is one thing, losing a son is another. It brought light to the matter when we reminisced over the night at the Billa Tent. He said I slept in his son's bed when I was too drunk to walk. I couldn't help but laugh at the irony. I remember thinking I would never drink again after a measly two shots. Now I need a bottle to help me sleep. I needed to keep Abe away until the assault was over. I need to be a soldier for the sake of the men, not a drunken buffoon that'll get everyone killed.

DAY 6 - OTTO

We were moments away from the attack and the bloody skies unleashed another storm. Soldiers from down the line cussed and cursed the rain as minutes went by. It was nice knowing the men's nerves were wearier of the weather than the violence that awaits us. Peggy had his eye looking down at his scope at the enemy across the road. The distance between us is only 500 yards, but the terrain will make it a nightmare. The boys didn't have much hope in the mission, we collectively felt this was a shame to satisfy Haig's ego.

Nevertheless, a job needed to be done, and it was up to us to do it.

At 5.40 the guns fired. Hundreds of Howitzers, heavies, and gas pulverized the German line, with our vickers picking Fritz apart by the triplets. In the rear we had sniping vickers moving half-speed. If any of us poke our heads up during our advance, we'd be dead. There were a few who didn't listen and were picked off at the start. One wasn't killed from the bullet; he drowned in the mud waiting for a stretcher. No fault on medics by any means. It wasn't their decision to have a battle in the middle of a swamp.

The ground began to tremble. The sounds of gears grinding together grew louder from behind. I looked and saw a tank rolling at a snail's pace. It moved only sixty yards before the mud infected the tracks. What a bloody waste. The men inside were trapped there for days if we failed to take the high ground. Biggest challenge we faced were the pill boxes in the dugouts. We were down Peggy as he was called to guide D Company on the right flank, and none of us were close enough to take out the guns.

They had us pinned down for hours. Unable to advance up the middle, I sent a runner over to D Company to find Peggy and bring him back. I prayed the private was able to find him in time. Fritz wasn't letting up any time soon, and with each yard we gained we paid for with men. I felt an indescribable anger boiling inside me. Heaven, deny me entrance as I do not wish to die in such a repulsive state of being.

It was 10.00 and no advance had been made. A runner came to inform me a reserve company was sent in to help. When they would arrive was undetermined. I told the runner to scrounge up more ammo but only got thirty meters before he was killed. Fritz had us wedged in the middle with an attack force on the left and right flanks. The only way we could move further is if we took out the pillbox. It looked hopeless as hopeless can be.

An hour had passed and still no relief. Us and Fritz took turns throwing grenades at each other while yelling obscenities like: "Yer mother should have killed you at conception you hun bastard!" They would say something back in German that Singh would translate.

"Go back to your colony you... hurensohn?" Singh was too educated in his vocabulary to know that was an insult to our mothers. Jones knew, and to put it bluntly, Jones went on a rampage. He emptied two clips at the pillbox and got lucky with two kills. The effort was minimal as two replacements fell in line and killed Jones. Jones, that stubborn Ausie was wounded several times over yet managed to tag one more before he was put out of his misery. It was strange. The man was smiling as he fell into the mud. I thought maybe he was ecstatic to die, but he saw what we all missed, and what we missed was somebody throwing a grenade into the German trench so pristine it destroyed their secondary guns. Screams and agony were heard and gunfire erupted. Out of the corner of my eye I saw a soldier running towards our line. The closer the man got, the easier it was to see who it was. If yuh wouldn't believe it, it was that little blue noser Tommy asking for bombs.

"Just what in the hell do ye think ya doin' boy?!" I yelled.

"Sir! Do you have any bombs to spare?!" I looked at him with shock and awe.

"You can't get lucky twice, Tommy."

"With all due respect, sir. If you don't have any bombs, then can you please get out of my way so I can find somebody that does?" I was speechless. The man had a death wish. I stepped aside and respected his wishes...while giving him a stern warning simultaneously...

"Don't you dare get yourself hurt out there, Private Holmes. Or you'll be facing the wrath of –" The bugger ran off before I could finish my sentence. I sent Singh and Boland to provide cover. My gut told me that wasn't enough, so I devised a diversion. I had the rest of the men in the trench draw Fritz's fire and encouraged the boys to be as belittling as possible. Do anything they can to lead them away from Tommy. Hell, I even forced Singh to learn a new word.

"Don't shoot at my comrade, you arsehole!" Tommy rushed to the pillbox with another Stokes bomb with him. With impeccable accuracy he threw the bomb into the hole and reduced everyone to charred meat. Without a second to spare we charged across the field to reinforce the hero. The man seemed unphased as he was waving a rifle at German soldiers who were waving a white flag. From afar he seemed to be saying something to the prisoners but as we got close to him, we saw he was rattled by own actions. I slapped Tommy across the face to wake him out of his daydream. There was little time to celebrate the victory as we had five-hundred yards to go.

"Thank you, Sir," was all he said to me.

DAY 7 - GEORGE

I had not slept for a week and my mind was wearing thin. I was smoking heavily and, on a few occasions, accepted rum from Major Lisbett. I was reading the battle reports from yesterday and almost all seemed too grim for my mood. I was drinking my third coffee when I got to A Company, Otto's outfit, and my hands shook upon reading. The shakes were not out of malice or fear. The shakes were from joy. One of our boys from the 4th single-handedly took out a pillbox. When I read the name of the soldier responsible, I damn near fell out of my seat. Haig was going to have a field day when he saw this report.

DAY 8 - TOMMY

I was treated like royalty when we were away from the front. Soldiers would ask my name and shake my hand to say thanks for taking out the pillbox. It was so bizarre. None of the boys complained as they got equal share. There was no movement either. We were able to relax and enjoy a brief moment of clear skies before the rain returned. We were still huddled in the trench, but it was a calm day. There was a point where a soldier dropped off letters to us along with a personalized note from General Haig.

The success gained by your troops yesterday under such conditions is deserving of the highest praise. While all the troops did well and contributed materially to the results achieved, the performance of the 3rd Canadian Division in particular was remarkably fine. The ground gained is of high importance and I congratulate you and all under you on the results of the great effort made.

Field Marshall Sir Douglas Haig,

The boys listened to Otto read the letter out loud while they stuck to their daily routines. Boland was taking swigs from the bottle, Singh was reading his book, Reekie was cleaning his rifle, and Peggy sat on the ground and did nothing. He sat there like he was frozen, or waiting for the next fight. When Otto was finished Boland spat on the ground and uttered a subtle cheer.

"Woot." Reekie had an unusual reaction.

"Captain, has Haig even been to the front line?" He asked. Otto looked at him with a cigarette and said;

"That's a good question, Reekie. Next time I see Colonel McFarland, I'll ask him." Reekie nodded his head, then thought for a second on what to say next.

"It's never the important people who are pulling the trigger." Boland looked at Reekie and handed him the bottle.

"I've taken dumps more important than Haig. The Butcher is no different than the scummy cops who killed my sister." Reekie handed the bottle back to Boland, who then handed it to Singh. Singh took a swig and offered his two cents.

"No different than the men who burned down my village. They take away everything from you and expect you to lie down like a dog. Not me, sir. No way." Peggy asked for the bottle and Singh gave it to him. Peggy took a long swig and spoke his mind.

"He's the same as the men who are raising my boy. He's going to grow up without any Ojibwe in him and be hated for it. I would take a bullet any day over enduring that." Otto put his cigarette out and changed the conversation.

"I got an idea. Instead of pondering over our illustrious leaders. Tommy, why don't yuh give us a distraction and read your letter to us?" I looked down at my letter and saw it was from Annie. Otto must've seen it as well or else he wouldn't have suggested it. I opened the envelope and read to the men.

Tommy

I hope you are doing well. As each day passes my I pray I get to see you again. It's wonderful to know Dad has your back. I hope he isn't too much of a heckler. If he gets too much just give him a kick in the arse and he'll get over it. I need you to hurry up and beat the Germans so you both can come home in one piece. For all our sakes. Life back home has become very complicated and I'm beginning to think Montreal is no longer a place I fancy so once I save up enough money, I'll be on the first boat back to Halifax. I hope to see you there soon.

Take care of yourself soldier boy,
With love, Annie

The boy of course had their fun until Otto smacked Boland upside the head for making a shrewd comment.

"THAT'S ME FREAKIN' DAUGHTER, YA KNOW!"

DAY 9 - OTTO

Another day in the woodshed. George gave us the order to return to California Trench, and the boys were dreading every second. Yesterday we were cracking jokes and enjoying the sunshine. Today, we're in the middle of a monsoon hiking our way into hell at a snail's pace. As we marched into the trench the rats were running in between our feet in the opposite direction. The bloody cowards they are. They steal our food and gives the boys typhoid, yet when the going gets tough, the critters vanish. I thought about it the entire way, I don't understand why but it infuriated me, but it put me into a better mood for entering combat. I made sure the boys stocked up on ammo before we left. As a joke we gave tommy extra grenades in case he felt the urge to go in alone.

Over the horizon we could see our guns beating the hell out of Fritz. Clouds of mud and German soldiers formed with the aftershock moving the earth around us. "The world is shifting in our direction, lads," I said to the men. The boys just smiled and continued our trek until we got back into position where we awaited orders to go over the top. Let us hope there aren't any men left to kill.

DAY 10 - TOMMY

We were woken up by Otto screaming a terrifying word. "GAS!" The lot of us got our masks on and charged out of our hideout. Machine guns and men were firing in all different directions. Reekie was on point while Otto was in the rear. Singh said a prayer while Peggy loaded his weapon. Boland did nothing. The man remained stoic and focused. My hands were shaking. I wasn't sure if it was from the fear of battle or Abe not being close by. Whichever reason it was irrelevant. I needed it to stop so I smacked my hand over and over until my nerves subsided. Otto made a comment. "You alright there, Tommy?" He asked me.

"Yes, Sir. Just warming up my hands," I said. He gave me a look of doubt but carried on with the mission.

When we arrived, we were knee-deep in muddy water. I could feel the grime seeping into my boots and filling my socks with dysentery. It was either die by a bullet or die by the trench, I thought. The same sentiment could've been said for the rest of the men. Colonel McFarland dissipated the despair as he walked alongside us and gave each of us a handshake and wished us good luck. One by one he went down the line being the true leader that he was. When it was my turn, he said something ever so flattering. "Private Holmes. Next time you take out a pillbox on your own can you grab a German flag for me? I ran out of toilet paper this morning." I blushed and laughed as a rebuttal.

"I'll do my best, Sir." He shook my hand and continued down the line.

Otto was glued to his watch until it was zero hour, then blew a frantic whistle. We went over the top with limited vision in the middle of a firefight, running over rotting carcasses that were meshed in with the earth. The gas sank low to the ground and covered the area. Every time I looked down, I prayed to God I wouldn't trip and fall over. Fritz was waiting for us with whatever type of weapon they had. Clubs, axes, shovels, knives, you name it they had it. We weren't any slouches about it either. Boland had his own melee weapon. On one end, you had the blade of a shovel, sharpened and narrowed to cut through flesh like butter. On the opposite end was a large club. It had a defense mechanism as well; the middle of the wood was wrapped in barbed wire so other soldiers wouldn't be able to take it from him. He called the weapon Ed. The way Boland wielded Ed, it was like Fritz was facing the wrath of mankind every time we went over the top. It was unfortunate but today was Boland's turn to meet his maker. In the middle of the fighting, he was impaled by a German bayonet. I couldn't leave Ed for the Huns, so I grabbed it and killed the first German I saw. I felt nothing as I cracked his skull with the club. The soldier looked as young as me, but I didn't care. It was either him or me, and I wasn't going to stop until I knew he wasn't getting up. It took five blows to do it. After the fifth I sat down to catch my breath while everyone continued to fight. As I looked, up to observe the battlefield, I began to feel useless. I found whatever reserve strength I had in the tank and charged back into battle. By the end of the day, I actually felt sorry for the Germans for the ell we put them through.

DAY 11 - TOMMY

Today we needed to clean the bodies off the field to advance to the next attack. The weather was dry, but cold. November was around the corner, and frost was expected. We started the day at dawn and didn't finish until sunset. It was harrowing seeing the blank faces of each man as we carried them to the mass graves. Reekie vomited on a few occasions, the stench of decayed flesh got the best of most men. There was no shame in it either, no one felt the need to complain when they're carrying their friend's bodies off the battlefield.

As the day progressed, the more numbed we became. We only looked at the dog tags and ignored the faces, out of our own perseverance. We called out the name of the soldiers we lost while somebody wrote them down on a scrap of paper. "Cameron, Alexander. Gundy, William. McNabb, William. J." Each name carried a harrowing tone as the mass graves filled with men. It reminded me of when I lost my friends... for a moment at least.

The day ended with the arrival of a German General. He arrived on horseback along with his own personal security. One of them was waving a white flag so none of us fired. The German on point had spoken to us in English.

"Can zai ask 'ou is zin charge?" Otto approached the Germans cautiously.

"I'm the man you're looking for," he answered. The German soldier was about to read from scripture until the general approached Otto and had a private conversation. No one knew what was said, but Otto guided him to where we buried their comrades. The old man stood silent and stared down at the mass grave. He moved his head from left to right as if he was looking for something. After a few minutes he shook Otto's hand and left with his men. Otto told us later that it was the almighty General Ludendorff searching for his son.

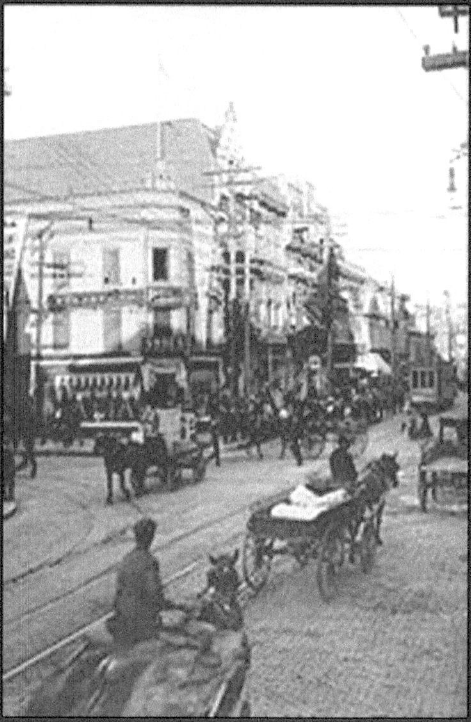

St. Laurent Bouvelard
Montreal, Quebec

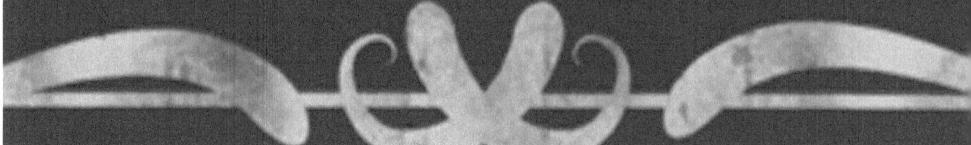

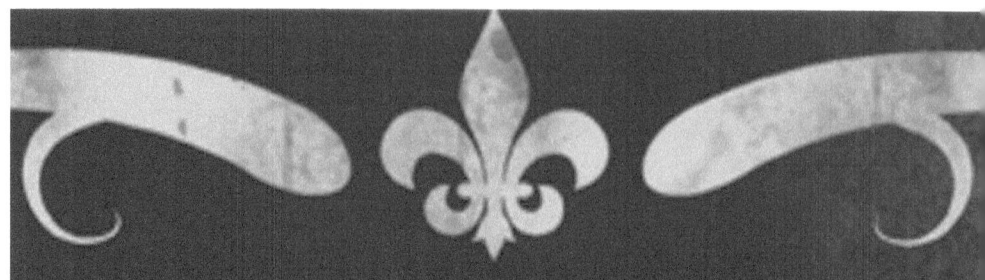

XVII
NOVEMBER

I know nothing of man's right, or woman's rights; human rights are all that I recognise.

SARA MOORE GRIMKE

MONTREAL, CANADA
ANNIE

The chemicals from the factory have damaged my body and the system had broken my soul. It has broken the souls of many women to whom only utter subtle hello's during work hours. We continued to keep things segregated at work but held private gatherings outside the city. We lost the farm at Fortierville, but found a cabin in Saint-Liboire. It was a quarter of the distance isolated from the world we lived in, where we must cover our yellow skin with foundation, and dye our hair to conceal the rustic roots.

During the times at the cabin the girls would enjoy some wine and good laughs. The only girl that didn't drink was Helena and Napoleon made it adamantly clear nobody made her try. Helena instead was our server and looked after the girls if they ever had too much to drink. Throughout this journey she has been the glue of our movement, and nothing would've happened if it hadn't been for her courage. The morning we discovered she had not been seen, we panicked and went to her room. We found it in shambles with drops of blood trailing from the bed to the door. Napoleon was found unconscious on the bed with blood dripping from her forehead. Mildred shook the woman violently until she woke up. We gave her some water as she struggled to speak. She mixed her words in two languages but the more cognitive she became, the clearer she spoke. "There were two men with black bags over their heads. One had a gun." She emptied the glass and coughed violently. "They must've taken her." She struggled to get to her feet but the wheels in her head were turning. She was plotting retaliation. In a fit of rage, she moved her bed to the other side and opened a secret compartment full of small weapons.

"Do I ask how you acquired these?" I asked her.

"I've seen many things at the factory, miss Middaugh. I'd rather be over prepared." She summoned all the girls and gave them all guns. "Au diable les hommes!"

We left the compound and went to the factory, holding every man at gunpoint. Napoleon struck the first man in the face to establish dominance, then interrogated him over any knowledge he had. Napoleon said she knew one of the voices as Marcel Dumont, a man with a grizzly beard, pudgy waist, and had a pocket watch tucked on his vest. After a few minutes the man wouldn't shut up about him. "He lives by Pascal and Rolland with several others. I don't know their names but I'm sure I can find –" Napoleon tossed the man down like a rag doll and left the building with everyone trailing behind.

Napoleon was mad with rage; so mad, she stole a truck from the parking lot and forced us all aboard. From Notre-Dame to Pascal the woman was only focused on one thing - find Helena alive. We pulled up to the intersection and went door to door looking for Monsieur Dumont. Out of the dozen houses there was only one that didn't open. Napoleon wasted no time and shot the doorknob to bits then opened the door. The house was empty - barely even furnished. The girls initial search turned up nothing except for a blood trail to the bathroom. The sink had bloody fingerprints and dirty bandages lying around. The man looked like he was cleaning a wound. Perhaps Helena gave him a taste of his own medicine.

The deeper we looked, the more clues we found. The motherload was a broom closet in the bedroom. The man had a telegram from Monsieur Chevalier with a port number and time.

PORT 7 - 23.00

"That girl is NOT getting on that boat!" Napoleon was so enraged she kicked the chair closest to the door. The chair legs broke under pressure and splinters of wood went flying.

"What do we do now?" Mildred asked. The girls started brainstorming different ideas. We couldn't waste time driving around town. We can't keep interrogating witnesses as much as Napoleon would like to. We needed to focus on Helena and the telegram was better than no information at all. We came to a collective agreement that Napoleon and I would drop the girls off at the pier then go look for Helena. The best chance we had was the men running into an ambush, unless one of us had a rabbit's foot tucked in our knickers.

We drove around city blocks as the fuel in our truck bled into the streets. The truck was almost empty and needed to figure out another solution. Napoleon didn't say a word when I inquired. “Amelie. What do you want to do?” No words were spoken so I tried again. “Amelie. We can’t keep driving around like this.” Napoleon’s thoughts were on another planet. I had to resort to yelling. “NAPOLEON!”

“QESQUE C’EST?!”

“WE CAN'T DRIVE IN CIRCLES!” Napoleon took a breather and asked which street we were on. “Rachel,” I answered.

“Did we pass Laurent?”

“No.”

“Good. We go left there.”

“Why?”

“We need leverage.” Napoleon sped up the truck and turned a hard left.

Napoleon was looking down every house, muttering descriptions of the houses. “Picket fence. Black door. Missing number. Where is it?!”

“What are you looking for?” I asked.

“White house with red shingles.”

“Who lives there?” Napoleon grunted and spoke in her native tongue.

“je te dirai quand nous y arriverons.” I felt my heart race from fright. I really hate it when she does that. We stopped at an intersection and the truck stalled. We're out of fuel. “TABERNAC!” Napoleon hits the steering wheel furiously. With a last headbutt she gave herself a second to breathe. I felt helpless seeing this woman's anguish and had to find an answer.

“Stay here. I'll be right back.” I got out of the truck and walked across the street. The sun was setting, and time was running out. I kept walking down the road until I spotted a little boy playing hockey with an empty net. He was playing out front of a white house with red shingles. I rushed back to Napoleon and told her what I saw.

"How old did the boy look?" She asked.

"Couldn't be older than eight," I answered. Napoleon went mad with energy and damn near broke the door off it's hinges when she got out. She ran past me and up to the front door, banging on the wood with frantic emotion. The door opened and a maid greeted her like they've known each other for a long time. I couldn't hear what they were saying but whatever Napoleon said the maid was in full compliance. The maid closed the door along with the window curtains to their living room. Napoleon in turn walked over to the little boy and grabbed him by his hand. They walked with haste to the car as I got the car to start. "What's with the boy?" I asked.

"I'll tell you when we get to Port," she answered. She got behind the wheel while I sat with the child who remained silent the entire time.

* * *

At the dock Napoleon and I waited at the dock alone with the boy. We instructed the girls to reveal themselves after we had Helena, so they stayed hidden amongst the shadows. Under no circumstances was there to be any shooting. Napoleon had instructed the maid to tell Chevalier to meet us alone by the dock. My hopes were low to think he would abide by our wishes. This entire year has been nothing but broken promises and neglect, and we aimed to end the nonsense. The girls agreed with me, but Napoleon was forceful. We kept our guns tucked in our backsides and faced the road without turning. I can't speak on Napoleon's behalf, but my heart felt like it was going to come out of my chest. I was so afraid but refused to show it. I distracted myself by talking to the boy. "What's your name?" I asked. Napoleon spoke on his behalf.

"He doesn't speak English."

"Quel est ton nom?" The boy looked at me with shy eyes.

"Felipe," he said.

"Je m'appelle Annie. It is nice to meet you." The boy stared at me as if he was too scared to say anything else. Napoleon tapped on his shoulder lightly and whispered something into his ear.

"Merci," he uttered. Napoleon was fighting back tears. I wasn't sure if it was anxiety or personal pain, but she had her arms around the boy as if to protect him. I looked at both of their faces and realized they had similar features. My suspicions were dissipated when Napoleon nudged me.

"They're here," she said. Her breathing intensified. Her eyes fixated on Chevalier behind the wheel of the truck. Also sitting in the truck was another man in the passenger seat with Helena in between. They kept the engine running while the three exited the vehicle. Chevalier retained his "innocent" facade as he tried to talk to Napoleon.

"Amelie! c'est fou! Que penses-tu faire ?!" Napoleon spoke English instead of French.

"He is not injured. He is okay. I wish to make a trade."

"Have you gone mad, Amelie?! What makes you think you hold any ground?"

"She does not deserve the same fate as I, Monsieur Chevalier!" Chevalier sighed. He rubbed his nose out of frustration, then chose his next words very carefully.

"Amelie. Whether you like it or not. This is the way our world works. If I had not made the agreement to let you work, you would still be living in a broom cupboard begging for a handout. I did that for all of you and this is how you return the favor. You steal my son and make a mockery out of my factory?! You only wish for equality because you are entitled. All you women are nothing more than entitled hens." He crossed his arms and moved in close. "There is only one way out of this, Amelie. And that is for you to give me my son back. He was not yours to take." Napoleon fought back every emotion not to shoot the man.

"Yes. He. Is." A single tear flowed down her cheek. My heart shattered for Napoleon, and I gripped her hand tight to give her support. "Bottom line, Monsieur Chevalier. There is nobody here except for us. I beseech you to be a competent man and give us Helena without violence. Because we are not leaving here without her, and I have grown tired of being diplomatic." Chevalier took a deep breath, then made a loud whistle. Four more men exited from the back of the truck, armed with pistols.

"There's one thing we can finally agree on, Amelie. I've also grown tired. The way I see it, you only have two options. Give me the boy or be shot in the streets while he watches. What is it going to be?" Out of the corner of my eye I saw Mildred looking at me, begging to give her the signal. I kept my focus on the men to not arouse suspicion. My heart was pounding so hard I could feel it coming out of my chest. Something had to give. I whispered into Napoleon's ear:

"Don't let him see this. He's just a boy." Napoleon screamed in anger and gave in. She loosened his grip on Felipe and whispered into his ear. The boy reluctantly went with Chevalier's stooges back to the truck while the adults looked on. Once Felipe was inside, we all took a breath of relief. "Good. It was the best decision you could have made." Chevalier then pulled out a pistol and shot Napoleon. The other men had their guns drawn at me while the coward lectured me. "Miss Middaugh if you had any sense of intelligence, you would leave Montreal and forget this ever happened. You are culpable of filling my worker's heads with the foolish idea that you are equal to men. Amelie getting shot was not my fault. We had a unique and efficient system running in our factory until you came along and ruined it all. Her screaming in agony is because you all refuse to learn your place in this world and it's sad that it had to come to this. I hope you find peace with yourself." Chevalier got only five steps to the car before he heard guns cocking from every woman that witnessed this man's atrocious crime. From the shadows the women revealed themselves with their pistols aimed at the men's heads. All six men had fear in their eyes and dropped their guns. The women moved in close so Mildred could tend to Napoleon. She was wounded in the shoulder, thank God. She had a fighting chance. Chevalier's words were stuttered and he frantically begged for forgiveness. "I'll tell you what. Let's just honor the original agreement, eh? You want Helena? She's all yours." He instructed his driver to let Helena go. She walked over to our side and embraced Napoleon. "Good. We're just going to go on our way then." What an awful, cowardly man. He doesn't deserve to raise that boy or produce any more. It needed to end. My heart was filled with so much rage I pulled out my pistol and shot him down below. Chevalier crumbled to the ground, crying in a higher pitch than Napoleon. I walked up to the other men who stood in fright. I didn't yell or scream at them, but I kept my tone reserved as I spoke how I felt.

"Ya better larn somethin', Monsieur Chevalier. You and the other men sit back and watch us break our bodies down to clean your house, fuel your war, birth your children, and expect us to cower before your presence when the only thing that separates us I just took away from you. You losing your pathetic excuse of manhood was your own fault, and there is nothing you can do about it." Chevalier continued to be defiant.

"Espèce de pute!" my blood boiled, and I stepped on the wound. His screams were loud enough to wake up the neighborhood.

"Vous reste deux options. donne-nous le garçon ou je tire sur toi et tes amis dans les rues comme des chiens!" Chevalier was horrified by my second language. He screamed at his men to give Felipe back then cursed my name.

"You will pay for this, you witch!"

BANG!

I fired one more bullet into Chevalier's leg and watched him scream in horror. I stepped off his wound and graciously took our crew and walked away, with Felipe embracing his mother.

* * *

We came to a mutual agreement that Montreal was no longer a safe city for me, so the girls got together and bought me a boarding pass for Halifax. It was a bittersweet goodbye to everyone, especially Napoleon. She thanked me for helping her with her son and wished me luck with Tommy. She said if she had time or the war ended she would bring her son down for a visit. Who knows. Tomorrow is the first day of December, if we wanted, we could find time to celebrate the holiday, and they can meet my oversized ball of fur Mindy. Heaven knows I can't wait to hold her again.

Halifax, Nova Scotia
12.06.1917

1918

XVIII
JANUARY

A lie can travel halfway aound the world while te truth is putting on its shoe.

MARK TWAIN

LONDON, ENGLAND
GEORGE

Arthur and I were on opposite sides of the wall waiting for King George to see us.

Today is Private Holmes' award ceremony and his royal majesty requested us the day before in his study. The only thing that was going through my mind was the secret I made Tommy keep. It wouldn't do anybody any good if the King discovered Tommy's real age. Arthur has been made aware, but he has his own troubles with Sam Hughes, the disgraced war minister who's going after anybody that had a hand removing him from office. Sam accused Arthur of embezzling thousands of dollars. Sam argues Arthur lived the life of a rich man and disregarded the well-being of our men on the front lines. His words spew nothing but venomous lies regarding neglecting the soldiers, but unfortunately before the war, Arthur had lost his fortune in the real estate market and against his better judgement he used war bonds to pay off his debt. To me it was nothing more than a farce as Mr. Hughes lined his pockets with any bribe he received. The coward was using taxpayers' money to launch a smear campaign against the man who had shown only fortitude and tactics as leader of the Canadian Corp.

The King was quiet when we walked into study. He was standing over his desk looking at something and had our backs against us. We stood at attention long enough for him to turn around and see us. "At ease," he said. Our shoulders relaxed and he went back to his original interest. "You can sit if you like." We sat in the chairs quietly while he revealed a stamp book. "I'm close to filling this book up. Colonel McFarland, do you collect stamps?"

"No, your Highness," I answered.

"One can learn a lot from collecting stamps. They are miniature gateways to the world." He sat in his office chair and waited for us to speak. Arthur was the first to break silence.

"Your Highness. May I ask why you requested us?"

"Colonel, I am under the belief that you know the Private personally?"

"Yes Sir."

"Tell me about him as if he was human."

"The boy is well-mannered. From the moments I've shared with him, his only flaw is his reclusiveness."

"How old is he?" I hesitated to answer, so Arthur obliged.

"His early twenties, your reverence."

"How old was he when he enlisted?"

"Eighteen, Sire." I prayed the King didn't see through my lie. He seemed unphased by my answer and continued.

"Tell me about the town he's from. Parry Sound, is it?"

"No, Sire. It's Owen Sound. It's a small shipping town off the tip of Georgian Bay."

"Ah, yes. Shipping. I heard he worked as a chicken picker." The King must've read Tommy's file.

"One of his jobs, yes. He also worked for the same man in the local butcher shop."

"Interesting. The boy has a good work ethic."

"He wouldn't have been able to take out two pills-boxes otherwise." The King smiled at my remark.

"I guess not, Colonel. I guess not." The smile was replaced with another question.

"Is there anything concerning the boy?"

"In what sense, Sire?" I answered.

"Does he have any unpleasant behaviours?"

"None that I am aware of, your highness. Unless you have heard of anything."

"Well, now that you mentioned it. Senator Talbot is demanding an audience. Would you know why that is?" I swallowed my fear and told the king the truth.

"Yes, my King. Senator Talbot had a son who was the commanding officer of Sergeant Holmes' company. It was discovered that the former Captain had committed espionage during his tenure at the front. I was investigating the matter myself and unfortunately Captain Talbot was declared diseased at Shorncliffe Hospital in May. We suspected Sergeant Holmes had witnessed one or two crimes committed but since the Senator's reputation was at stake we felt it was best to honour a legacy and bury the incident." The King sat silently in his chair with his hands pressed together.

"This is unfortunate news, Colonel. I, however, identify the predicament you were in and must admit if the shoe was on the other foot, I would do the same. Is the Senator aware of his son's wrongdoings?" Arthur jumped in to take the bullet.

"Not that we are aware of your Reverence." The King nodded his head and chose his words slowly.

"Let's keep it that way. We will adjourn for now then assemble before the ceremony. You can leave now." Arthur and I stood at attention, saluted our King, then left. From Kew Palace and Waterloo Station, Arthur and I maybe spoke ten words to each other.

* * *

Tommy's train docked at 17.00, the busiest time of the day. Arthur and I waited in the car while Private White went inside the station to get him. A few minutes went by, and Arthur felt it was the right time to talk about Tommy. "The King was right about being concerned about the boy."

"It isn't something I can't fix, Sir." Arthur looked at me like I was mad.

"There are things about this war that we still don't understand, George. One of them being the human condition. The boy may be an impeccable soldier, but he is still flesh and bone and should never be underestimated." I was getting tired of swallowing my pride, but our history made it too difficult to revolt.

"Yes Sir," I answered. He pointed out the window and saw the men approaching the vehicle. I got out to open the back door for the new Sergeant and the private.

"Welcome to London, Sergeant Holmes," I said with a smile.

"Thank you, Sir," is all Tommy said when he got in. He was shocked to see Arthur in the passenger seat.

"General Currie!" He gasped.

"At ease, Tommy. Good to see you." Tommy held his hands close together as if to stop them from shaking.

"You alright, son?" I asked.

"Yes Sir, it's just been very overwhelming the last couple days." Arthur gave me his classic judicious face. I fired back by instructing Sergeant Holmes to remember he is still on duty no matter the individual you will be standing with. The boy's response was my saving grace. He snapped out of his delusions and returned to his normal self.

"Understood, Sir!" He said with pride. I looked back at Arthur and nodded with pride. Once again, neither of us said a word the entire drive.

After we checked Tommy into his hotel room we drove to 10 Downing Street. The British Prime Minister was holding a gala in Tommy's honour. Arthur said The Prime Minister is much more flamboyant than our King so it should be a good warmup for tomorrow's ceremony. Tommy wore a fresh Sergeant Uniform with his two service medals he earned from Vimy Ridge and Passchendaele. His chevron was freshly sown and made him shine like a true patriot. As the night progressed Tommy became recluse. Attendants kept asking for the boy and he was nowhere to be found. Bless Private White as he was finding him in all sorts of areas. He would not disclose what Tommy was doing, he just assured me he was okay. Simultaneously Senator Talbot had his eye on the boy whenever he graced us with his presence. As far as I was aware, the two never shared a conversation, but I kept getting distracted by General Currie and the royals. After the gala was finished Sergeant Holmes told me they had a brief talk. What was said was something Tommy kept to himself. As much as I disagree with what Arthur has said, I was beginning to think he was right.

* * *

The next morning was quaint. Tommy struggled to wake up but was present in uniform at 9.00. King George wanted a rehearsal to ease the boy's nerves. It also gave him time to get to know Tommy on a personal level. Most of the discussion was about the town of Owen Sound and Tommy's newly found fame. Nothing of his age or his actions in battle. Tommy was dismissive of that talk when the King brought it up. "There have been many men before me who show the same level of courage," he said, then looked to someone else to change the conversation. As time passed and the pews began to fill with every sort of politician from the Triple Entente to witness this event unfold. Tommy secluded himself with Private White to calm himself and be clear-headed before everything began. When it came time for Tommy to fulfil his part, he was perfect. He walked down the aisle with dignity and respect. Showing pride in who he was as a soldier. I had my men stand and salute Tommy as his medal was draped around his neck. The King's speech that followed was mesmerising.

"Sergeant Thomas William Holmes showed the utmost courage and gallantry on the battlefield. At the young age of twenty, on his own initiative and single-handed, Tommy Holmes ran forward and threw two bombs, killing and wounding the crews of two machine guns. He then returned to his comrades, secured another bomb, and again rushed forward alone under heavy fire and threw the bomb into the entrance of the 'pillbox,' causing the nineteen occupants to surrender."

I looked out to the crowd to see if they invited Tommy's parents. To my amazement they were empty, but once I looked back in the King's direction. He looked at me with a sour expression. "He was nineteen?!" He asked.

MOMENTS LATER
TOMMY

I sat in a chair in an empty hallway, contemplating why the King was angry with me.

To my right was the office of the King who was screaming on the other side. I didn't understand what he was screaming about. I only snuck out with Private White to have a couple of swigs. I was still cordial by the end. I felt confused and annoyed by the situation. I was told by Otto I would be granted a leave but haven't heard a peep since. Silence was deadly at the front. It was how Holloway was killed. All this silence is making me see him as clear as day crawling across no man's land. Talbot ordered us to gather Intel because he was under the impression the Germans retreated. We couldn't even get past the ladder before he was shot in the head. The thought of him mangled made my shoulder twitch. The twitch sent Shockwave to my hands, and they wouldn't stop. I kept my hands tucked in my thighs but that failed as well. The shockwaves spread down to my leg, and it bounced like I was in the middle of an artillery strike. I spoke the Chronicles prayer and Roy's voice came to life. "I told you that doesn't work." I looked at the chair across from me and saw Roy having a cigarette while wearing the same outfit the day he died. The wound in his head looked infected, but Roy was unphased. "They're in there because you lied about your age." I did my best to ignore him. I knew he was a figment of my imagination. I just needed Abe to settle me down, or perhaps a good substitute. Roy wasn't having it. "What's the matter, little brother? Can't handle the truth?"

"Stop! get out of my head!" I looked around to see if anyone was close by.

"Ain't nobody here except for us, Tommy Boy."

"You're dead, Roy. There is a bullet wound in your head!" He felt his forehead and moved some of the loose skin around.

"Huh, odd," was all he said before the doors opened and the higher ups exited. The last two to leave were Colonel McFarland and General Currie. Both men had sour looks on their faces. The Colonel was the first to approach me.

"We still have one more event to attend." I nodded my head and stood at attention.

"Understood, Sir." The Colonel's breathing was deep. He felt compelled to be human.

"I want to be clear on something. I hold no resentment towards you. Every good soldier needs to remember who's in charge. Keep your chin up." The Colonel started walking down the hallway and I followed suit.

* * *

When we arrived at Blenheim Palace I was greeted with a standing ovation. The richest of people wearing outlandish attire. The kind of people that'll never step foot in a trench. The women I understand, but the men were all lean with perfect posture. None of them had any military honours, apart from Lord Churchill. When he shook my hand, it felt like it was going to be crushed. "Good on you, boy," he said before others took him away. Col. McFarland left me alone as well to talk with the guests. I was strolling around looking for the bar. I needed a drink to stop the shakes. The bar was within range, and I ordered myself a whiskey. Instead of a glass the bartender grabbed a bottle of Old Blue Ribbon and said;

"This is reserved for heroes, son," then placed it in front of me, followed by a glass with ice. I poured myself a glass and couldn't believe how smooth it was. It was like drinking bittersweet water. While I was enjoying my whiskey I was greeted by an Old British man in a fine-knitted suit. He was a bald man and had a moustache with wax at the tips.

"What's your poison?" He asked. I showed him the bottle and he seemed impressed. He waved the bartender over and had him pull out a bottle of American Whiskey. "Have this a go," he said. I finished my first drink and got him to pour me a glass. I got two sips down before my throat was on fire. The Old man laughed at my expense. "You're that brave Sergeant I keep hearing about," he said.

"Sergeant Thomas William Holmes, at your service," I needed to be careful. Whenever I drink, I let my intrusive thoughts win.

"Call me, Peter," he said. We shook hands and started a friendly conversation. He asked where I was from and what battles I was in. Giving me nods and showing signs of intrigue. He then asked for my Captain's name, and I gave him Otto's. The man looked perplexed and asked if he was my only commanding officer and I said no, but didn't reveal Talbot's name. I refuse to speak of him after what he had done. Peter refilled my glass and asked me why. I was about to tell the man how the bastard murdered my brother and comrades until Private White intervened.

"So sorry to interrupt, Senator. But, Sergeant Holmes, your presence is required."

"Not a problem," I uttered. I stood up from the chair slowly as the alcohol had taken effect. I didn't feel angry, I didn't feel any pain, I simply felt numb, and that's the way I liked it.

The private guided me to Col. McFarland where he was standing next to a Canadian Soldier maybe ten years older than me. His name was Private Duke, and he was my assistant. "What do I need an assistant for?" I asked. Col. McFarland gave a lengthy answer.

"Tommy, the war effort needs you back home. People need somebody to tell them they still need to fund the war. You're going to be travelling to every major city across Canada telling your story. Private Duke over here is to ensure you have everything you need to get the job done. You understand?" The whole idea sickened my stomach. I wanted to go home to rest, to get away from this insanity. Now I'm stuck on a train for God knows how long with a man I've never met. Private Duke shook my hand and offered a smoke. I grabbed my bottle of Blue Ribbon and joined him outside. There were a group of men outside smoking and drinking amongst each other, laughing up a storm. When I heard them laugh, I pictured Redfern crying in agony when he was wrapped up in barbed wire. My heart filled with rage, and I drank to suppress it. Private Duke looked at me oddly.

"You okay, Sir?" He asked.

"Yes, Private. Just tired is all."

"Have a couple more swigs, then. I'll see if I can talk to the Captain and get you to bed." I looked at him and shook my head.

"I'm tired of this charade, Private. I joined the war to be a hero, not a piece of jewellery the army can flaunt around." The private listened carefully, then offered his rebuttal.

"But that's what heroes do, Sir."

"No, they don't. Heroes don't wear a three-piece button-up suit made of wool. They die on the battlefield protecting their friend's. Have you ever been to the front, Private?" The numbness set in. I stopped caring.

"No, Sir."

"Do you want to go? Do you want to kill some Huns?" To the man's credit, he was honest.

"If I'm going to be honest, Sir. My skills are best suited behind a desk. As good as that medal looks on you, I would never pass for it." My drunken mind formed an idea. I took off my medal and held it in my hands. It was a cheap piece of metal with a burgundy ribbon.

"Try it on," I sneered. The private reluctantly took the medal from my hand and placed it over his heart. "It looks good on you," I said. He grew a faint smile but then took it off his uniform. He placed it back in my hand where I gave him an offer.

"Wear this when we get back home. It looks better on you anyways."

"I don't follow, Sir."

"When we hit port in Montreal, wear this and give them my name." The private thought for a moment and declined my offer.

"I'm sorry, Sir. I don't want to face a court martial." I can't say I blame him. I just offered him some of my whiskey and did my best to enjoy the evening. It wasn't enough as I spotted

Roy impersonating some of the guests. If I hadn't been drinking, I would've attacked him.

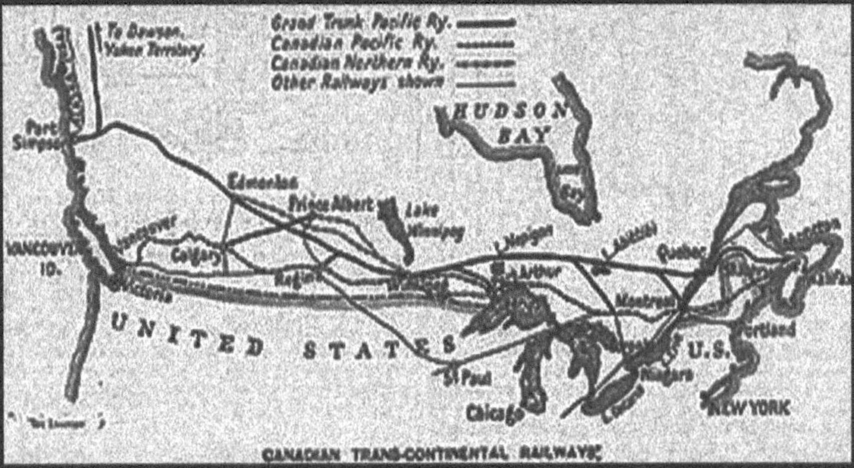

Canadian Pacific Highway
1906

XIX

TOMMY

The definition of insanity is doing the same thing over and over and expecting different results

ALBERT EINSTEIN

DAY 1
HALIFAX

The air was quiet. The sounds of the ocean tide hitting the shore echoed across the ship as we docked into port. It was a heart-breaking to see Halifax destroyed. Duke and I stood silently as we waited for our ride, observing the locals, feeling nothing but sorrow for the lost souls. Men were dragging and carrying dead bodies off carriages then tossing them into a mass grave. Women were tending to the casualties with dishevelled looks and bloody aprons. Children were moving around pieces of wood and stone like they were drunken sailors. I heard from Otto Annie survived the explosion, but heard nothing else. I kept looking for her as we drove out of the city. With no success I saw nothing and turned to Abe instead.

DAY 5
OTTAWA

Prime Minister George held a banquet for us and showed me off to other politicians. General Currie was there but Col McFarland was not as he was called back to the front. He said nothing else and continued to socialise with the other guests at the banquet. I should be grateful for the nice food, but I hated every minute of it. Every so often some rich man would approach me and ask what the war was like, how many men did I kill, if I've ever been wounded. I couldn't give any of them an honest answer, so I lied. "They said it was nineteen prisoners', but it was actually thirty." I didn't care what they knew. Each one of them wouldn't have the stones to step onto no man's and watch their friends and family get shot.

DAY 8
TORONTO

Peggy was right about Toronto. It's a imitator of London. Too many people roam about the streets and not pay attention to where they are going. On our way to the Mayor's office, we almost got run over by several horses and vehicles. In the elevator we were crammed full of men smoking cigarettes and chatting amongst themselves over frivolous subjects. The mayor wasn't a bad person. When he greeted us, he poured us drinks from his whiskey jar. It was the Old Blue Ribbon; I knew the scent and aroma instantly but preserved myself to not go overboard. One round of drinks turned into several and for once it was me carrying Duke back to the hotel. I can't say I blame him. The man had to endure two drunken men bickering over the French when he himself was from somewhere in Quebec. He kept saying the name and I remember it starts with a "C" but given he always tells me when I'm a few in, it's difficult for me to remember. He knows better than to expect me to remember that. I mean, if he just switched places with me to begin with, he wouldn't be having this issue.

DAY 15
SAULT STE MARIE

I befriended some men who were hiding in a cellar. I was out having a stroll outside of the hotel I was staying and came across a cellar filled with alcohol. I couldn't help but take another bottle of whiskey. I'm their hero, right? I don't foresee a reason why they would object to my liberties. What made matters more awkward was coming across four men wearing prison uniforms. We stared at each other well over a minute before I offered them a sip of the bottle. Each one took a gulp and gave a small smile. "Do you have any food?" One of them asked. I didn't have the heart to tell them no, so I just walked away. I don't wish to know of anyone's problems. I have my dead brother talking to me already.

DAY 27
REGINA

Duke picked me up from the town jail this morning. I had no recollection of what happened, but the perfect

Duke remembered everything. After I made my speech at the town square, I went drinking with some of the boys who returned from the front. We went to some tavern where the beer flowed like water. We didn't pay for the tab as the patrons got together and paid for everything. At least that's what I was told. I was lied to by one of the soldiers and was stuck paying the bill. Out of rage I broke the Manager's nose and flipped a couple of tables before the RCMP arrived. Duke said the man was lucky his eyeball didn't pop out with how close the cuts were. When the RCMP showed up I managed to fight them off for a while until reinforcements arrived. They took me to jail and tried to prosecute me until the Mayor stepped in and told them I was a war hero and that it was all just a big misunderstanding. As my punishment, we stayed in Regina for another night so the Mayor can make himself look good in front of Sam Hughes. The man's been exiled from the government and is still making moves. I should've told him how Major Corrie felt about his 'perfect' rifle. In fact, I was inches away from telling the man how I felt until Duke instructed me to go out for a stroll to clear my head.

Across from the city hall stood a church four-stories-high. The bell tower stood proud with a Union Jack waving across the night sky. It reminded me of what I said in the speech earlier that day. "The heroes that you should worship are not me. I am just a soldier, giving his life and blood to defend my King and my country." It sickened me; like I was about to vomit. Out of anger I broke the bottle and wounded my hand. I stared at the wound and laughed. I didn't think giving my blood would be so literal.

DAY 41
CALGARY

I woke up in a hotel room alone with nobody around and panicked. I didn't know where Duke was. My whiskey was gone, and the door was rigged to only open from the outside. When Duke comes back, he and I are going to have a talk, and he will be reminded of who his commanding officer is.

DAY 43
EDMONTON

I missed my speech at the city hall. Duke told everyone I was too ill to attend so he spoke on my behalf. Not a lot of people were happy about it. Various people from the crowd heckled Duke and criticized him immensely. The offer to switch is still on the table.

DAY 58
VANCOUVER

Duke and I fought outside a tavern early in the morning. The whining pig is upset because I broke his nose. Well, that's what he deserved for dumping all my whiskey into the streets. He can't blame me for having to relive the horrors of trench warfare when the yellow coward has "objected' to going there. The man kind of reminds me of Talbot. His posture, his clean-cut skin, that rich entitled attitude. He wasn't a monster like Talbot, but one could ponder if they were related.

I need to find a way to get more whiskey before we cross the border into America. I'm still insulted by that. The army said I would be back home on leave but now they're shipping me to a country that's three years behind everyone else. If they think they're going to expect an accurate portrayal of a hero. They are gravely mistaken.

DAY 80
BORDER CROSSING

We were stuck at the border for several hours due to a snowstorm. While everyone else was taking shovels and ice picks to get rid of the snow, I was searching each car for alcohol. Car by car, bag by bag, I went digging. I'll be honest there were a few moments where I was guessing my judgement. It felt more like I was in a trench raid gathering intel from my enemies. Instead of finding maps, I found men's undergarments. I doubted my sanity for a moment. Only for a moment, until I saw an American with a black bottle of alcohol. We went into his cabinet and had a few rounds until he gave me his spare bottle. "Take this. You look like you need it more than I do." The man sounded nothing like Grieve. I can't remember where Grieve said he was from, and it made me upset for the rest of the day; So upset I opened a fresh bottle and passed out before Duke got back on the train.

DAY 110
MILWAUKEE

The train ride from Minneapolis to Milwaukee was a violent one for us. Duke and I are no longer on speaking terms unless it is time for an appointment or gala to attend. The speech today was good in my opinion. I told my story AGAIN to all the people in power and they fell for every exaggeration I made. The

American General I met saw through my nonsense and asked the only smart question I heard. "How in god's name did you take out that pillbox by yourself?"

"It was two, sir. The second pillbox came close to tagging me, but my buddies drew their fire."

"How did they do that?"

"They did what we back home call 'chirping'. It's when you yell out insults to your enemy."

"Ahhhhhh. Psychological warfare. Astounding." Some rich man took over the conversation and I went back to my whiskey and hoped I wouldn't see Roy.

DAY 141
CHICAGO

Duke gave in and took my credentials and medal. Good riddance. I was finished with the army. If anything, I was the impersonator, and Duke was the 'hero' they're looking for. He's heard my speech enough to know it by memory and he's relatively my size. Maybe an inch taller. We shook hands and bided a bitter farewell. I kept my uniform for the sole purpose of showing my father I've become the man he expected me to be. I wrote to him during our layover, I hope he gets it by the time I get back to Owen Sound. My train to Toronto leaves in an hour. I had a moment where I hoped Annie would be there. But who was I kidding? Talking to my dead brother is more logical. I haven't heard from her in forever. She wouldn't even recognise me as I resemble a bloated whale in a soldier's uniform.

DAY 145
TORONTO

I snagged a couple bottles of whiskey with the last of my money along with a 1-way ticket to Owen Sound. I spent most of the time sitting on the bench trying my best to ignore Roy. He kept telling me nobody's going to remember me. Not even Mr. Boyd. In Roy's defense I have zero interest in working for that lazy oaf. I just want to relax on the deck, and enjoy my peace and quiet. The constant noise might be the reason why I feel so compelled to drink. When I get out to the countryside, I'll be able to relax and remember I'm no longer at the front.

DAY 146
OWEN SOUND

I expected Father to keep my homecoming quiet and not to tell anyone. I was expecting to be invisible and go about my travels in peace. I was expecting to be woken up by the beautiful sunrise over the small city. Instead, I was woken up by nonsense. When the train docked a crowd of people were singing a song.

For he's a jolly good fellow
For he's a jolly good fellow
For he's a jolly good fellow
That nobody can deny.

When I looked outside, I saw a large gathering of people with signs that said, "Welcome home, Tommy!" In big, black lettering. I loathed the idea of me going out there. I just wanted peace and quiet. I stayed in my seat as everyone left and continued to do so when the train was empty. The more I stayed inside, the louder people

sang. The conductor finally approached me and gave me an odd look.
"Is all that for you?" He asked. My breaths were deep as I nodded. "Well, soldier boy. I can't let you stay in here and hide from everyone. You're gonna have to face it." His words angered me, even though he was right. He gave me a couple of extra minutes to gather my things before he kicked me off. It gave me enough time to grab Abe out of my bag, have a little swig to numb the senses and embrace the crowd. When I walked outside there were roars of cheers and applause. The noise was loud enough to give me a headache. To my benefit, the headache made the sunlight more unbearable and made me keep my eyes closed until I was on the other side of the crowd. The people wouldn't stop grabbing me, trying to shake my hand while yelling in my face telling me what a fantastic job I did. It was revolting. I hated it. And when I saw Father standing next to a vehicle with Mother all I felt was resentment. It was a one-sided conversation on the way home. When Father asked why I wasn't talking I just said the train ride was long from Chicago.

DAY 150
OWEN SOUND

I drank the last of my alcohol last night and my body is paying for it. I woke up with the shakes along with my mouth feeling like there's chalk inside. I guess my face was pale and sweaty as Mother thinks I have the flu. She took care of me and made me drink lots of liquids. Everything tasted atrocious. I couldn't even digest water without having the urge to vomit. While Mother was tending her garden, I looked through Father's liquor cabinet in his study. All his liquor was gone. The whole house was dry, and it angered me. If I just had even a sip my shakes would stop instantly.

Later in the evening the family had dinner at the table. Essie, Margaret, and Annie all set the table and prepared a large feast. It was her famous roast with boiled potatoes and vegetables. For some reason Mother thought it was my favourite dish until I told her it was Roy's. Her eyes swelled up instantly and she had to leave the room. When I asked what was wrong Essie looked at me and shushed me. “Her heart is still broken over Roy,” Annie said to me. Of course, Roy had to add in his two cents.

“Why don't you ask the big man how he feels about me?” I passed along the message and Elizabeth merely said;

“Father doesn't talk.” It was an awkward dinner, along with an even more awkward evening. I didn't see Father with a glass at all. There's no possible way he stopped drinking.

DAY 156
OWEN SOUND

I was out wandering the streets in the morning to clear my head. The shakes have stopped but I'm constantly feeling cold. I'm constantly craving a drink, and the entire town is dry. It was heart-breaking. I fought for everyone's freedom, and I can't even have a drink in my hometown. My luck improved when I ran into Mr. Boyd. He’s into the bootlegging business and said he needed extra security on his runs. He was willing to pay me double what I was making at the butcher shop plus I had access to a percentage of liquor he moved. His whiskey wasn’t awful. It wasn’t as good as Old Blue Ribbon, but it did the trick.

DAY 167
BOGNOR

I'm currently sitting underneath a tree with a bottle of whiskey that was smeared with blood. I'm the only one here as Mr. Boyd and the others are dead. I should've seen something like this coming. I'm ashamed to admit it was my drinking that blinded my judgement. A true soldier can sense a battle approaching. After the hell I've been through I should've seen the betrayal long beforehand.

Mr. Boyd and I started the run in Craigleith to pick up a few cases of gin. I had a couple of swigs before and was feeling comfortable. Mr. Boyd sat in the back while he had someone deplorable driving the truck. I didn't bother to remember his name. Might have been Frank or something, I don't know. He was a large man who kept asking me questions and being overly hospitable. "Wow. I'm sitting next to a war hero." My response was bleak.

"Don't call me that," I said. The man went quiet, so Mr. Boyd broke the tension.

"Don't mind him. Our young friend has seen some depraved things. I do want to ask you, Tommy. Were your parents at the ceremony?"

"Nope." No one saida word after that.

When we arrived at Craigleith the man was bugging Mr. Boyd over an outstanding balance. Mr. Boyd said he'd give him the money on our way back from Kitchener. The job was supposed to make multiple stops along the way. One of those stops was in Bognor. There was a tavern out there run by two cousins whose names I chose to forget. They had issues with the owner of a secret pub in town. People kept flip-flopping between the two spots and I guess it caused friction. At least that's what Mr. Boyd told me. He obviously knew about the business and to his credit, when he isn't stressed, he knows how to do business. The man owned a butcher shop for ten years. It wasn't his fault the bank went broke and seized his shop. At least that's what he claimed. The longer we drove the more annoyed I was with Mr. Boyd. Well, truthfully it wasn't what Mr. Boyd said. It was what Roy was saying to him. "Don't believe a damn word this liar says. We kept that place running. Not him." My heart skipped a beat every time Roy spoke. His presence was so real I almost yelled at him from the passenger seat. What stopped me from doing it was Mr. Boyd handing me a six-shooter when we got to the tavern. When I surveyed the barn there wasn't a need for a gun. It was filled with people and live music. Why the need for violence? "What's this for?" I asked.

"These guys are trouble," Mr. Boyd answered. Roy chimed in with an indignant retort.

"They're only trouble because you're a waste of skin!" Much to my delight nothing happened then. It wasn't until later things went sour.

* * *

Before coming back into Bognor there was a car blocking our road. The same two cousins at the tavern were holding rifles and called out Mr Boyd.

"Aye, Boyd! Get yer yella arse out of that car and pay us the money you owe!" Mr. Boyd looked to me for protection.

"Tommy, go out there and flash the pistol!" I looked at the mad like he was stupid.

"You get out first," I answered. I had a couple drinks and was numb enough to put my life above his. It was the wrong move on my part because Boyd got only a few sentences in before the men opened fire. Mr. Boyd's blood splattered all over the windshield while the bullets broke the glass. The driver was killed as well while I slid out the side and emptied the six-shooter into the two men. When the dust settled, I checked the pulse of Mr. Boyd to see he was dead. I felt nothing. No grief whatsoever. All I did was take my bloody hands and grabbed the first bottle of whiskey from the back of the truck and sat by the trees. I had every intention of drinking from the bottle. But seeing my bloody handprints all over the bottle unsettled me. It made me feel Mr. Boyd's death would've been avoided if I didn't pick up the bottle. It was time to stop drinking or else it would get somebody else killed. I contemplated walking back but I wouldn't arrive at the house until sunrise. The Men aren't going to need a car where they're going.

DAY 172
OWEN SOUND

The town found out about the shooting, but nobody suspects I was there. Thank goodness I dumped the car downtown. Coincidentally Duke was arrested in Ottawa over impersonating an officer. My decision to quit drinking still stands. Even if I die without it.

DAY 175
OWEN SOUND

All I wish is to stay in bed and get over this wretched sickness, but Father keeps parading me around town like a puppet. It's like doing the horrendous war bonds again. Except for a whiny little rich boy named Duke I have Kaiser John Holmes giving me orders and telling me what to say and how to say it. Mother chose to stay silent about it. "Just listen to your father for now and hope the war ends next week." It pained me to see her in such a weakened state, but I couldn't help but feel anger for her cowering before him like a dog. When we were all children, we would hear Father come home late in the evening drunk and angry. He'd yell at Mother; call her every nasty name that you can think of, then have no memory of it the next day. Unfortunately, if the army were to find out I went AWOL they would give me a real court martial, and not just some petty disciplinary hearing coaxed by a monster. I had to stay under the roof and that meant living under the thumb of an even more selfish man that is my Father. Every gathering we go to he gets me to lie or say outlandish things to make my stories more interesting. While I'd be talking to someone, he would correct me by telling the person another version of what happened. Roy was never the type to question Father's judgement, and even he called malarky on a few of Father's remarks. "No, he did not kill the Colonel of that battalion you oaf!" I'm not sure how much more I can handle without rummaging through Father's stash and taking his gin. About that, the man got smart and moved his liquor into the cellar. The man is lucky I won a medal.

DAY 180
OWEN SOUND

The shakes are gone but my heart feels like it's being bonded by barbed wire. Each day I wake up, the more torn and shredded it feels. Getting dressed is difficult, bathing is demanded, a smile is non-existent no matter how hard Essie tries. The whole family can sense my disturbance. They know something is wrong with me. Elizabeth and I had a walk yesterday and no matter how hard she pried I gave her different excuses. Elizabeth didn't buy it for a second. It doesn't matter what she thinks of me anyways. Both her and I know she wouldn't dare stand up to him. She's even too scared to bring any boys around because If Father sees one, he'll chase them away. It was like each member of my family was wanting a way out.

Shortly after our walk we retreated to our separate rooms where we got dressed for dinner. Father insisted I wear my uniform every time we had company over. As each day progresses, I'm finding life's plan for me was to be a character in someone else's story. What is the point of living if I'm casted in a silhouette? This thought overwhelmed me at dinner time. So badly that I wanted to vomit. Father forced me to sit at the dinner table while Mr. and Mrs. Bumstead sat at the table and ate their food quietly. I doubt they will return for another visit. Mr. Bumstead grew tired of Father's charade within minutes of us sitting at the dinner table. Roy was laughing the entire time. "Hey Father. I didn't know you were at The Somme. Tell me, how many Huns did you kill?" "Hey Father. You were at Buckingham Palace with the king? We didn't see you." I wanted all the noise in my head to go away. Only liquor can cure that, but the cellar is always locked. You would need an axe or piece of iron to break it open. Maybe if I stole Father's keys, I could sneak in. What would Annie think, though? She would be embarrassed by my behaviour if she was here. Over and over my mind fluttered with these thoughts and my body grew tense and shook violently. I suppressed my emotions as best I could, but I had to be excused to the water closet where

I vomited repeatedly. After a few minutes my body stopped shivering and grew very tired. When I tried to stand on my feet I slipped and hit my hand off the back of the toilet, knocking loose a bunch of letters. Why were there letters on the back of the toilet? When I picked one of them up my jaw hit the floor. They were all letters from Roy when he was still alive.

DAY 181
OWEN SOUND

I was staring at my clothes beam with a necktie knotted like a noose. After reading the letters from Roy. I don't want to exist anymore. Roy tried desperately to get Father to stop me from joining. The last one Roy wrote to Father was the day before he died.

DEAR FATHER

You lied to me! You gave me your word Tommy would not enlist! You wrote in your last letter you threatened Tommy with disownment. Tommy may be rebellious, but he would not DARE join the army if it was at a price of his family! I hope you're proud knowing you had your sons killed to fill your ego.

This is goodbye.
Elmer Roy Holmes, Sgt

Once I was dressed, I put my head through the loop and took a second to process what I was about to do. I was fully committed to ending my life, ending the life of a war hero. There are some who would miss me, not enough to cure the illness that's inside my head. Without a second thought I leaped off the bed to finish the job. Like everything else I've done, it failed. The beam couldn't support my weight, and it broke. It enraged me. God wants me to stay alive and suffer for man's mistakes. Roy was cheering me on, coaxing me into succeeding. "I tell you what, chicken picker. You were always more defiant than me. Let's see you try that again!" His voice was silenced when Father knocked on the door.

"Tommy?! Are you okay?!" Father asked in a panic.

"I'm fine," I said, in a raspy voice.

"Well, quit stalling! We're expecting company any minute." I quickly collected myself and got dressed. Maybe after everyone leaves, I would try again.

Mrs. McClung along with other elitists came to hear me speak but was about to be entertained by Father instead. I couldn't bear to see myself in the army uniform, so I wore the suit Father and Stan made for me instead. It aggravated Father but he played along to the crowd and showed support. I'm certain when he showed off my newly recovered medal from Duke it was out of spite. Father was so petty and so childish that half-way through Mrs. McClung had enough and stormed out of the house and took all the guests with her. The man had the nerve to blame me for it too. If I had just worn the uniform like Father expected. He wouldn't have had to over explain himself and lose his temper. That irritated me and made me lose my calm. "FATHER YOU ARE NOTHING MORE THAN A LEECH!" Father slapped me violently in front of the family. The girls all went upstairs while Mother went outside. The slap wasn't painful at all. In fact, all it did was make me ask for more.

"Is that all you got, Father?!"

THWACK!

Father hit me again with his other hand. The one with the rings. The ring cut the inside of my nose and let blood seep into my mouth. The second I tasted my blood I grabbed Father by the scruff of his neck and threw him on to the table. The legs buckled under the weight and the table caved in. I had my hand wrapped around his throat with my hand gripping tighter and tighter. Father began to make gurgling sounds. Just like the sounds Talbot made before he asked me to take his life. Talbot wanted to die because he couldn't face his crimes. I wished I killed him, but instead I was too weak, and I just handed him the razor. All the man did was laugh then drag the steel from ear to ear. The memory of all the blood gushing out of his neck made me stop and think about what I was doing. Father doesn't deserve to take the easy way out. He doesn't deserve to be grieved. The man deserves the same level of pain and isolation I feel. I spared his life but not his liquor. I rolled him over to steal his keys and grabbed his precious bottle of Whiskey. I left the house with Mother sitting on the front porch in tears.

DAY 183
UNKNOWN ROAD

I wasn't going to go back to the house. Not after what happened. I didn't know where to go. I just kept walking down an old dirt road. I think it was the same road the slaves used to escape the south.

DAY 185
CHATSWORTH

I was woken up by farm animals licking my face. I wasn't sure where I was until I saw an old man on his porch ask me what I was doing sleeping by the barn. I couldn't say much without my stomach growling for food. “Let's fix yuh somethin’ to eat and we can talk at the dinner table.” His name was Wallace, and his wife was named Elise.

DAY 190
CHATSWORTH

It's been five days without alcohol, and it feels good. My hands may be shaky, and I might be flush for a bit, but I am going to be okay. Wallace and Elise are good people. In fact, we had crossed paths before. I was standing behind them when they found out their son died. It was the same day I felt proud to be a patriot. I can't say I share the same sentiments, but if they were able to smile after losing their son then I can at least put forth the effort. They are giving me food and a place to sleep in exchange for work on the farm. It felt good to be useful again. It felt even better to hear appraisal for my work.

1919

XX

JUNE

If everyone fought their own convictions, there would be no war

LEO TOLSTOY

WAR AND PEACE

OWEN SOUND, CANADA

ANNIE

The city isn't as beautiful as it used to be.

There used to be smiles and joyful townsfolk whenever I would walk downtown, even in winter. Today is a sunny day with clear skies yet there are few who roam and less who talk. I have been sitting outside the train station for an hour waiting for Aunt Nellie to pick me up, and it feels almost apocalyptic. Thank heavens Mindy is with me. It's a miracle she is still alive after the explosion. Every time I look at her cute button nose, I cry because it was the first thing I saw when I found her trapped under the rubble. I lost Angeni and all my stepsiblings. I couldn't bear to lose her. Captain Cockburn luckily was close by and helped me lift the debris and get her out. I'll always be grateful to him because of it. It was sweet, when we parted ways in Frederickton he thanked me for saving his life. Turns out when he had a bad heart and my outburst got him a medical discharge.

I didn't want to come out this way. I was considering rebuilding our home in Halifax but both Dad and Aunt Nellie insisted I go live in Owen Sound. They're trying to get Soldier boy and I to reconnect, I suppose. I'll be honest I feel that is a farce of a dream. Tommy is a war hero and with a new scar on my face I feel unrecognisable. I was struck in the head by something during the explosion and there's a line that runs down past my right eye to my cheek. It's not as disfiguring as I make it out to be. Even with the dirty looks I get from the housewives I can face my reflection and say I did my best and take the plunge.

After a while, Mindy was getting restless and kept meowing for food. The poor girl hasn't eaten since yesterday. I gave up thinking Nellie was going to pick me up, so I grabbed Mindy by the carrier and walked around town looking for canned meat. I had little money left and hadn't eaten myself, but Mindy was more important. I went to a food market I used to go to only to find it closed with a woman sitting on the front steps. "Sorry, miss, we're closed," she said.

"Do you know where the next food market is?" I asked.

"If you head east for eighteen miles, I think there's one there." All I could do was sigh. The woman looked at me with a saddened look. "What are you looking for?" She asked.

"I just need some canned food for my cat," I answered.

"Ah, well, I got plenty of that! Come on in!" The woman didn't even charge me for the food. She just asked for some company. We talked about many things and shared our stories of woe. The poor woman had to run the business after her husband lost his legs and did it single-handedly until the flu came. When I commended her for being so brave she said something that resonated with me. "There will come a time in everyone's life where you are going to encounter hardship. You can either cower from it or face it with a smile. I chose to smile."

"Does your husband feel the same way?" I asked.

"Oh, that bag of bones stays in the house all day and yells at the birds. The Germans should've finished the job if you ask me." I couldn't help but giggle at her response. I didn't feel the need to share Tommy. It was too difficult for me to share without getting emotional. In the end I gave the woman a hug goodbye and wished her all the best. Mindy rubbed up against her leg as the good girl that she is.

* * *

Aunt Nellie was waiting for us when we got back to the train station. She wasn't dressed as formally as normal. She wore a dress that flowed with a bonnet to match. It was bittersweet to see her as our last encounter was despicable. Part of me still holds resentment, but I have become too tired to be indignant. When I saw her, I gave a fake smile and a hug. She gave one back but had sadness in her eyes. "My poor baby. What happened to your face?" She asked. I gave her a short answer and she hurried me into the car. "Before we go to my house I have a surprise for you." I gave her an annoyed look.

"Aunt Nellie. I apologize but I am too weary for surprises," I uttered.

"Nonsense. You'll love it." She started the engine and off we went.

It was a one-way conversation as Aunt Nellie drove down the highway. She tried to ask miniscule questions and after a few attempts she gave in. "I guess there's still an elephant in the room?" I kept my attention on Mindy and chose not to answer. "Fair enough. I uh, I just want to say woman to woman; I'm sorry. I should have warned you Emily doesn't like Indians." I looked away from Nellie to hide my tears. Thoughts of holding Dakota in my arms had me shivering. I held my shawl tighter and composed myself.

"They're indigenous, not Indian. India's on the other side of the world." Nellie chose her words carefully.

"Can we agree to disagree? If you wish me to address them as indigenous, I will do so in your presence. I just ask for two things in return."

"What's that?"

"Remember the people who gave you the spirit to fight and remember who they stand with on the totem pole. A noble cause means nothing when petty differences divide a house." I was too tired and nauseous to argue. I was fed up with fighting after I shot Monsieur Chevalier. I know what I did was justified but reliving it in my nightmares is a burden I don't wish on anybody.

"Yes ma'am," I uttered. She smiled and patted my thigh.

"Think of it from this perspective. You have more time on earth than I do. After I'm too old to fight you'll be the one who takes my place. At that point you will have as much leverage as me and be able to implement the changes we need. You understand?"

"Yes ma'am," I said. The rest of the drive was quiet until she made a sharp turn onto a gravel road. That road took us through a valley filled with trees. We were concealed from the outside world as we approached a small farm in the distance. We drove past a lone man working in the fields. His face was hidden and Nellie kept driving. We stopped at a small house where an elderly couple sat on their front porch. The woman stood up in a panic and ran past us. Nellie pulled the car to a stop and gave me a look. "Just give me a second. They're a little funny," she said, then left me in the car. I followed the old woman grabbing the farm hand by the arm and walking him inside. The old woman covered his face and sent him inside while she had a few words with Nellie. I was confused by the whole ordeal and wanted answers. I honked the car horn to grab Nellie's attention, and she got back in the car frantically.

"What's wrong?!" She asked me.

"What's happening?" I asked her in return. Nellie gave me a cock-eyed grin.

"I found your soldier boy," she said. My eyes widened.

"WHAT?!" I gasped. I rushed out of the car and was ready to attack. I didn't understand why my feelings for Tommy were so strong, but they were and all I could do was wait patiently. Aunt Nellie said Tommy was as fragile as me and advised me to tread softly. It was a tall order to ask. All I have of him is three vague letters - nothing else. I want to say so much but words are finite by comparison. I could feel my heart gradually pumping faster as each second passed.

When he finally walked out, he was a different man. He looked more sophisticated and genuine. His hair was brushed and slicked back, with a small beard to compliment it. His clothes were more casual, yet tasteful. Above all else he retained that captivating smile I saw when I first met him. By the look of awe in his face I could tell he was just as surprised as me. We walked towards each other without saying a word, too scared to say the wrong words or wrong ideas. He was the one who broke the ice.

"Hi," he said to me.

"Hi," I said back.

"You look different." My eyes teared up and thought my scar made me ugly.

"It's a painful reminder."

"What is?"

"My scar." Tommy looks closely at my face.

"I'm sorry. I'm only seeing it now." He rubbed his thumb from the top of my scar to the bottom of my chin.

"I meant you look beautiful is all." my cheeks went rosy red.

"Is this where you live?" I asked, distracting my urges to kiss him.

"No. This is Wallace's house. I'm staying over in the barn." He walked me over to the barn out back and showed me his little hideaway. We spent a few minutes there talking softly, telling each other stories. After a few minutes he showed me around the farm and all he chores he does. The only things he said Wallace did on his behalf was to send out the livestock. Tommy said after what he saw in France he never wants to kill again. I understood and told him it didn't make him any less of a man and he graced me with another smile.

* * *

I spent the night alone with Tommy in the barn and woke up this morning feeling anxious. Yesterday felt like a dream, like it didn't happen. Yet sleeping peacefully next to me in Tommy. When I woke up the first thing, I saw was the scar on his back. It looked like it'd aged for a while. It's a line from his right shoulder blade to his lower left. I took my finger and followed the line down. It shocked Tommy and woke him out of a dead sleep. It took him a few seconds to wake up, but his eyes were focused on me.

"Good morning," he said.

"Good morning," I said back.

"How did you sleep?" He asked me. All I could do was smile.

"A bit rough, but, once I got there, I was a log."

"Good. Sorry if all I have is hay for a bed. I haven't gotten the courage to sleep in a bed." I looked at him oddly.

"What do you mean?" I asked him. He looked at me with pain in his eyes. His voice was cracking but he continued to speak.

"I uh, I hated everybody last year... more so myself. I was drinking a lot and while I was drunk, I tried to hang myself. I tied my tie around the beam where I dried my clothes, and the beam broke from my weight. Instead of breaking my neck I broke my bed instead." My heart sank. I felt so many emotions running through me. I was saddened yet angry, worried yet calm, grateful but aggravated. I needed to know more.

"Why were you drinking?" I asked. Tears dripped down his face as he continued to share.

"I always wanted to be like my father, except for the drinking part. When I was young, he used to get so inebriated he would be violent. The scar you felt on my back was from him. I broke one of my sister's dolls and he was too drunk to care how hard he was hitting me with the belt. The worst part was that the next day he didn't remember what happened and blamed it on me. He said I would be a man and suck it up. That made me hate drinking until I met a very cruel and evil captain named Talbot. I don't know if you remember the night I was with your dad but on the same night I threw up on Talbot." My mouth dropped in awe.

"You didn't?!"

"Mh-hmm. When he found out my name, he made it a mission to torture me. The first week we were at the front lines all my friends got killed because he sent us out on day raids. The day the Germans hit us with gas was the worst. My friend Charlie was trapped in the wire and couldn't get his mask on." He stopped to compose himself, then continued.

"Grieve and Holloway were next. We were given an order to attack, and they were killed trying to rescue me. I felt so angry at him I told Sergeant Broadhead but uhm..." Tommy's breathing intensified.

"We don't have to keep talking about it if you don't want to," I offered.

"I prefer to talk about it, actually," he said with a faint smile. "The Sergeant found out Talbot got paid by the Germans to give away our position and was a day away from telling Colonel McFarland until Talbot found out. Talbot tortured Broadhead for an hour looking for his paperwork until we were hit with artillery and the shrapnel pinned him to a barn door. As far as I know everyone still thinks Sergeant Broadhead was crucified."

"So, Talbot got away with it?"

"No. He was wounded at Vimy ridge then died in the hospital."

"Good." His smile grew into a frown.

"Yeah... when we took down the Sergeant and I found his canteen and it was filled with whiskey. It didn't take me long to finish because I loved the feeling of being numb. Most of the boys drank as well so finding some was just as easy. Not like here." His smile returned and his tears were gone. "I hope this doesn't make you think any less than me." All I did was hold his face and rubbed the scar on his cheek.

"If we're going to be candid, I must tell you I shot a man in Montreal. I'm not proud of it but, it was for a good cause. I hope you don't think any less of me for it." Tommy's smile never altered.

"I'm just grateful you're here," he said softly. We kissed then huddled into each other's arms. "Can I tell you something?" He asked.

"Sure," I whispered. He looked into my soul when he spoke.

"I love you." My heart skipped a beat and told me what to say back.

"I love you too." We kissed again and spent the rest of the day in the barn, then found a small place to live in a few months, then had a family of our own. Where we taught our children not to give into hate and to ensure love and peace triumphed. Even on the days we feel defeated, we just look into each other's eyes and remember the hardships we went through to earn our peace.

The end.

Tommy Holmes Married Annie Middaugh on January 28th, 1921. They remained together until Annie passed away in 1940.

Tommy passed away on January 4th, 1950

After the war ended Tommy became a pilot for the Toronto Harbour Commission for 15 years.

On Aprilt 18th, 1935, Tommy's war medals were stolen from his house and were not recovered until November 1st, 2022 where the Canadian War Museum acquired his Victoria Cross, preserving his legacy as one of the youngest VC winners in history.

In 1928, Nellie McClung and Emily Murphy helped influence the Alberta Government to pass the Sexual Sterilization Act.

In 1929, The Famous Five went to England to overturn the Supreme court in an appeal forever known as
''The Persons Case''.

In 1960, all women in Canada were granted the right to vote.

IN MEMORIAM

GEORGE FRANKLIN MCFARLAND - TORONTO, T. H. CORRIE - OWEN SOUND, DAVID RUSSELL DOBLE - OWEN SOUND, G. D. FLEMING - OWEN SOUND, W. D. MERCER - OWEN SOUND, ROBERT POLLOCK - OWEN SOUND, J. KYLE - LINDSAY, H. D. BURKE - TORONTO, JOHN DUNCAN CAMPBELL - OWEN SOUND, LINTON EWART DOUGLAS - OWEN SOUND, JAFFRAY EATON - OWEN SOUND, DAVID EDWIN HOWES - SHALLOW LAKE, WILDER REGINALD KERR - ST. CATHERINES, HENRY STRACHAN MULLOWNEY - OWEN SOUND, WILLIAM HARVEY SMITH - MEAFORD, ROBERT ALMON SPENCER - MEAFORD, COLEMAN BOYD ADAMS - HANOVER, GEORGE WEBSTER BUTCHART - OWEN SOUND, COLIN STANLEY CAMPBELL - OWEN SOUND, FREDERICK CLINCKETT - TORONTO, JOHN MILTON DOBIE - CHATSWORTH, JOHN A. D. ELDER - R. R. 2 - LONDON, GEORGE ARTUR EWENS - OWEN SOUND, CHARLES ARTHUR FINLEY - MEAFORD, NORMAN WILLIAM MUNRO - GUELPH, MITCHELL WHITE RICHARDSON - DURHAM, JOHN ERNEST RITCHIE - CLARKSBURG, JAMES THOMPSON ROBB - OWEN SOUND, THOMAS ALLEN - DURHAM, REG. C. FERGUSON - CLARKSBURG, PERCY EDGE - OWEN SOUND, THOMAS JOHN RUTHERFORD - OWEN SOUND, WILLIAM STEWART WILSON - HANOVER, JAMES E. G. ACTON - OWEN SOUND, ALEXANDER ADAIR - OWEN SOUND, CHAS, ROBIN ADAIR - R. R. 4 - MOUNT FOREST, WALTER IRWIN ADAIR - R. R. 4 - MOUNT FOREST, HAROLD ARTHUR ADAMS - MEAFORD, PHILIP HENRY ADAMS - BIG LAKE, WILLIAM CHARLES ADAMS - FLESHERTON, JAMES AGNEW - OWEN SOUND, HENRY FLOYD ALNSWORTH - MEAFORD, ROBERT OLIVER ALEXANDER - OWEN SOUND, ALFRED WATSON ALLEN - OWEN SOUND, WESLEY GORDON ALLEN - R. R. 2 - SHALLOW LAKE, HUGH ANDERSON - OWEN SOUND, ALFRED ANDREWS - SHALLOW LAKE, HENRY NORMAN APLIN - HOLLAND CENTRE, HILLIARD ARMSTRONG - MARKDALE, JOHN ARMSTRONG - EUGENIA, JOHN ARMSTON - EUGENIA, LESLIE ARMSTRONG - OWEN SOUND, WM. HERBERT ARMSTRONG - OWEN SOUND, HERBERT JOSEPH ATKINSON - TORONTO, MILES STANLEY ATKINSON - LIVERPOOL, ENGLAND, WILLIAM ATKINSON - OWEN SOUND, MIKE BAILEY - HANOVER, WESLEY GORDON BAILEY - CHESLEY, HAROLD EDGAR BAKER - MEAFORD, JOHN BAKER - HEATHCOTE, JOHN WESLEY BAKER - HANOVER, JOHN BAKER - WOODFORD, SAMUEL BAKER - OWEN SOUND, WESLEY GEORGE BAKER - OWEN SOUND, THOMAS WILLIAM BALLARD - MEAFORD, PERCY BARBER - OWEN SOUND, ALBERT HENRY BARRETT - LONDON, S. E. ENGLAND, WALTER GERALD BARRETT - OWEN SOUND, NORMAN RANSON BARTLEY - OWEN SOUND, WM. THOS BATCHELOW - OWEN SOUND, GEORGE CECIL BAXTER - LONDON, ENGLAND, THOMAS LEE BAYLEY - ASSINIBOIA, SASK., HARRY BEAMISH - DUNDALK, WALTER JAMES

BEARE - OWEN SOUND, ROY JOHN BEATON - R. R. 3 - OWEN SOUND, ADAM BEATTIE - OWEN SOUND, ALBERT CLARK BEATTIE - OWEN SOUND, PRESTON ANDREW BEATTIE - R. 5 - MARKDALE, JAMES HENRY BEATTY - OWEN SOUND, WILSON BEDELL - KEMBLE, AMOS WILLIAM BELL - ANNAN, FREDERICK RUSSELL BELL - R. R. 2 - ROCKLYN, GEORGE BELL - THORNBURY, GEO. ALEX. BELL - R. R. 3 - OWEN SOUND, JAMES BELL - OWEN SOUND, JOHN CLINTON BELL - OWEN SOUND, RICH. ELMER BELL - R. R. 3 - OWEN SOUND, FREDERICK HILTON BELLAMY - FLESHERTON, ROY CLIFFORD BENEDICT - R. R. 1 - SILCOTE, ALEXANDER BENNETT - OWEN SOUND, JAMES ARUTHUR BEST - OWEN SOUND, WALTER JAMES BEST - OWEN SOUND, LAIRD DOWLING BINNS - MARKDALE, ARUTHUR BISSON HULL - P. Q., THOMAS CLIFFORD BLAKELY - FLESHERTON, FRANK CECIL BLAKEMORE - LIANGENNECH, SARMARTHEN - WALES, CECIL JAMES BLYTH - VARNEY, ALBERT ROY BOGART - OWEN SOUND, JOHN BOLGER - EAST BARNET, HERTS - ENGLAND, ARUTHUR FRANCIS BOND - OWEN SOUND, JOSEPH LEO BOND - CHATSWORTH, JOHN HENRY BORDER - OWEN SOUND, STANLEY DAVID BORDER - OWEN SOUND, ERNEST HENRY BOSLEY - DUNDALK, WILLIAM BOSTOCK - MEAFORD, WM. ARUTHUR BOTT - R. R. 3 - OWEN SOUND, WILLIAM BOUGLAS - TODMORDEN, LORD GEORGE BOCINGDON - R. R. 1 - DURHAM, WILLIAM RALPH BOWEN - MARKDALE, WILLIAM FRANKLIN BOWES - CHATSWORTH, JAMES NOBLE BOWAN - EDINBURGH - SCOTLAND, HARRY WILLIAM BOYCE - OWEN SOUND, JAMES BOYD - FORT WILLIAM. , WIGTOWN - SCOTLAND, JAMES SAMUEL BOYD - MEAFORD, STANLEY ALLAN BOYD - ROCKLYN, PERCY HUBERT BOYLE - CLARKBURG, FREDERICK BRACKENBOROUGH - FEVERSHAM, THOMAS BRADLEY - ALLAN PARK, WILFRED PERCY BRAGGINS - ALDERLEY EDGE, CRESHITE - ENGLAND, ROBERT WILLIAM BRANSCOMBE - PECKHAM, LONDON - S.E . ENGLAND, GEORGE RICHARD BREEN - OWEN SOUND, NORMAN WICTOR BRIDGE - MARKDALE, GEORGE SYDNEY BRIGNELL - OWEN SOUND, GEORGE BRITTEN - MEAFORD, OSCAR BORADHEAD - OWEN SOUND, SIDNEY WILLIAM BROOK - MEAFORD, LEONARD NORVAL BROOKS - POINT AU BARIL, THOMAS BROOKS - OXFORD - ENGLAND, LEWIS BROTHWELL - FLESHERTON, ALFRED ELIAS BROWN - MARMION, ALVAH BROWN - OWEN SOUND, HECTOR CAMPBELL BROWN - OWEN SOUND, JOHN ARMSTONG BROWN - MEAFORD, JOHN MOFFAT BROWN - OWEN SOUND, WILLIS CLARKE BROWN - OWEN SOUND, WILLIAM STANLEY BROWN - OWEN SOUND, THOMAS BROWNLEE - HANOVER, ROBERT HENRY BRUCE - SHALLOW LAKE, JACOB BRUINSMA - HANOVER, STANLEY SHOWELL BRYANS - R. R. 3 - CHATSWORTH, JOHN CLARENCE BRYON - DURHAM, CHAS ISAAC BUCHANAN - R. R. 2 - FLESHERTON,

SAML. HANSON BUCHANAN - R. R. 4 - MARKDALE, WILLLIAM REID BUCHANAN - VANDELEUR, ELGIN LANCELOT BUCKLEY - KILSYTH, CLEMENT BURDIS - LETCHWORTH, HERTS - ENGLAND, REGINALD HERBERT BURGESS - GREAT TEW. OXON - ENGLAND, EDWARD BUTTERFIEL - OWEN SOUND, JOHN JOSPEH BYERS - R. R. 4 - OWEN SOUND, WILLIAM PERCY BYLES - OWEN SOUND, ROBERT ALLEN CAMERON - TORONTO, RODERICK GEO CAMERON - NORTH KEPPEL, ALEXANDER CAMERON - R. R. 1 - BOGNOR, GEORGE JAMES CAMPBELL - COLPOY'S BAY, GEORGE WILFRED CAMPBELL - PRICEVILLE, JOHN THOMAS CAMPBELL - R. R. 5 - TARA, ROY EMERSON CAMPBELL - OWEN SOUND, WM. FAWCETT CAMPBELL - OWEN SOUND, FREDERICK CALDER - NORTH KEPPEL, WALKERTON, EVERTON CARGOE - FLESHERTON, GEORGE CARR - OWEN SOUND, W. E. CARR - OWEN SOUND, IAN WALLACE L. CARRUTHERS - PORTREEVE - SASK, JOSEPH CHARLES CARSON - OWEN SOUND, THOMAS CARTER - MEAFORD, JOHN THOMAS CASCADEN - MACPHERSON, G. J. CATCHPOLE - OWEN SOUND, A. V. CATTON - DURHAM, C. A. CAVELLE - PRESQUE ISLE, THOMAS CHARD - FLESHERTON, W. G. H. CHARLTON - OWEN SOUND, S. W. CHEER - OWEN SOUND, LORNE CHERRY - CREEMORE, T. H. CHISHOLM - CHATSWORTH, C. H. CHISLITT - CEYLON, J. M. CHRISTIE - OWEN SOUND, CAMPBELL CLARK - ELMWOOD, CECIL CLARK - KILSYTH, E. H. CLARK - CLARKSBURG, FREDERICK CLARK - CLARKSBURG, H. S. CLARK - OWEN SOUND, A. B. CLARK - MEAFORD, K. E. CLOCK - MEAFORD, ALEXANDER COBEAN - OWEN SOUND, WILLIAM COFFIE - LONDON, ENGLAND, JAMES COLE - DOLLARD, SASKATCHEWAN, R. A. COLHOUN - TYRONNE, IRELAND, C. C. TILBRIGHT - SURREY, ENGLAND, SAMUEL COMFORT - MEAFORD, DENNIS CONFREY - STOCKTON, ENGLAND, ARTHUR CONNOLY - MARKDALE, J. M. CONNOLY - OWEN SOUND, F. J. CONNOLY - OWEN SOUND, A. C. COOK - HORNCHURCH, ENGLAND, V. S. CROFT - MEAFORD, W. H. CROFT - MEAFORD, R. A. CROSS - OWEN SOUND, D. B. CROUCH - KENT, ENGLAND, N. C. CROWE - OWEN SOUND, J. E. CROWTHER - HOLLAND CENTRE, CHARLES CUMBERLAND - OWEN SOUND, WILLIAM COPSKEY - DESBORO, EDWARD CURRIE - SHALLOW LAKE, G. R. CUTTING - SHALLOW LAKE, E. S. DANARD - OWEN SOUND, G. P. DANIEL - DURHAM, C. H. DARLING - SIMCOE, W. P. DAVEY - OWEN SOUND, G. H. DAVIDSON - WILLIAMSFORD B. P. DAVIS - LEITH, J. A. DAVIS - HOLSTEIN, THOMAS DAVIS - OWEN SOUND, WILLIAM DAVIS - OWEN SOUND, W. C. DAVIS - HOLSTEIN, W. M. DAVIS - FLESHERTON, JOHN DAVY - OWEN SOUND, ALEXANDER DAY - NORFOLK, ENGLAND, G. A. DAY - OWEN SOUND, G. W. DAY - OWEN SOUND, F. E. A. DEER - STAYNER, A. J. DEMMANS - BADJEROS, ALBERT DENNIS - OWEN SOUND, JOHN MCGILL DERBY - HANOVER, THOMAS ALBERT DEVINE - TORONTO,

WILLIAM GEORGE DEVLIN - HANOVER, NORMAN ROBERT DICKSON - AYTON, HERMAN DITTMER - DESBORO, THOMAS BERT DICKSON - ORCHARD, HARVEY ROBERT DISNEY - HANOVER, ROBERT DOBBINS - OWEN SOUND, HAROLD WILLOUGHBY DODSWORTH - ELMWOOD, JOHN BRITTON DOLPHIN - TARA, STANLEY DOLPHIN - TARA, ALEXANDER DONALDSON - SAND POINT, IDAHO U.S.A, FREDERICK COOK - MEAFORD, JOHN B. COOK - HANOVER, WILLIAM JAMES COONEY - HANOVER, WILLIAM LESTER COOPER - OWEN SOUND, FRANK COPE - DERBY, ENGLAND, ALFRED EDWARD CORBETTM R.R. 1 - HANOVER, FRANK THOMAS CORKRAN - OWEN SOUND, FRED REG CORKRAN JR - OWEN SOUND, FRED REG CORKRAN SR - OWEN SOUND, HENRY DELBERT CORNELL - IRELAND, WILLIAM CHARLES H. COURTS - ENGLAND, ALFRED BENJAMIN COVE - ENGLAND, FRANK COX - OWEN SOUND, WILLIAM THOMAS COXON - OWEN SOUND, ANDREW CRALK - SCOTLAND, EARL CRANNEY - OWEN SOUND, JOHN CONCIDINE CRAVEN - HOLLAND CENTRE, SAMUEL CRAWFORD - OWEN SOUND, RUSSEL ALEX CREIGHTON - OWEN SOUND, GEORGE PLATT CREIGHTON - OWEN SOUND, WALTER SAMUEL DORAN - WOODFORD, CARL FRANKLIN DOUGHERTY - TARA, GEORGE HENRY DOUGLASS - OWEN SOUND, WILLIAM DOUGLAS - OWEN SOUND, HOWARD GEORGE DRUMM - WATERLOO, CLARENCE ALEXANDER DUDGEON - FLESHERTON, JAMES BROWNE DUFFIELD - SCOTLAND, HORACE ALFRED DUKES - OWEN SOUND, LAUCHLAN JOHN DUNBAR - PARKINSON, THOMAS EDMUND DUNN - OWEN SOUND, WILLIAM BRUCE C. DUNN - OWEN SOUND, ALLEN DANIEL DUNOON - OWEN SOUND, HENRY ERNEST DURANT - MEAFORD, ALBERT DYER - DORNOCH, GEORGE CHARLES EAD - WOODFORD, ROY ECCLES - DROMORE, SAMUEL JOESPH EDGERTON - DUNDALK, THOMAS IVAN EDWARDS - MARKDALE, DOUGALD BAIRD C, ELDER - LONDON, ADAM SCOTT ELLIOTT - WILLIAMSFORD, VERNON ELVIDGE - DURHAM, JOHN ETHERTON - WALKERTON, JEFFREY WILLIAM D. EVANS - OWEN SOUND, WILLIAM BROCK EVANS - MEAFORD, THOMAS HAROLD FARRILL - CAMPBELLFORD, STANLEY GLADSTONE FARROW - OWEN SOUND, JAMES FAWCETT - DUNCAN, FREDERICK WILLIAM FEATHER - TORONTO, HARRY JOHN FEATHERSON - SHALLOW LAKE, ALEXANDER FERGUSON - OWEN SOUND, ALBERT FIELDS - OWEN SOUND, GEORGE HENRY FLEMING - OWEN SOUND, ROBERT FLEMING - SCOTLAND, FREDERICK BRADFORD FLINT - OWEN SOUND, DAVID ALEXANDER FLOOD - SHALLOW LAKE, RAYMOND ARTHUR FLUKER - DETROIT, WILLIAM LAYRENCE FLYNN - FLESHERTON, CHARLES RICH FOAMES - WOODFORD, JOHN FRANCIS FORBES - OWEN SOUND, VICTOR FORD - ENGLAND, WILLIAM FOSTER - HOLLAND CENTRE, ROBERT WILLING FOSTER - WALTER'S FALLS, WILLIAM FOSTER - HOLLAND

CENTRE, WILLIAM EARL FOSTER - DESBORO, WALTER GEORGE FRANCIS - OWEN SOUND, GEORGE FRANKLIN - OWEN SOUND, MARK LANE FRANKLIN - OWEN SOUND, WILFRED GEORGE FRANKLIN - CAPE RICH, ALBERT EARL FRENCH - OWEN SOUND, BURLEIGH FRENCH - OWEN SOUND, CHARLES WILMER GALBRAITH - TORONTO, JAMES RUSSEL GALBRAITH - ARNOTT, WILLIAM DUNCAN GALBRAITH - OWEN SOUND, FRANCIS LEO GALVIN - OWEN SOUND, GEORGE CECIL GARDHOUSE - OWEN SOUND, ROBERT NORMAN GARDHOUSE - OWEN SOUND, STANLEY GARDHOUSE - OWEN SOUND, JAMES CLYDE GEDDES - OWEN SOUND, PETER JAMES GARDNER - BOGNOR, ERROL FRANCIS GAUDIN - HEATHCOTE, JOSEPH ANDREW GAWLEY - BERKELEY, WILLIAM HENRY GIBBONS - MEAFORD, GEORGE ALDEN GILCHRIST - OWEN SOUND,, ALBERT EDWARD GILES - ENGLAND, JOHN GILLESBY - OWEN SOUND, REGINALD ERNEST HANSON - MEAFORD, SAMUEL ALBERT HANSON - MEAFORD, PERCY HARDING - DUNDALK, HUNTER HARROW, - CEYLON, RICHARDSON KENDALL HASKETT, BROCKVILLE, JOHN HATTON - MARKDALE, CHARLES WILBERT HAVENS - DURHAM, ALFRED CIKIN HAWKINS - MEAFORD, EDGAR HAYWARD - STOWMARKET, ENGLAND, JOSEPH WILLIAM, H HAMLET - ENGLAND, WELLINGTON STANLEY HAYWARD - OWEN SOUND, ROBERT HENRY HAZEN - DURHAM, JOHN ROBERT HEAPS - DODDINGTON, ENGLAND, JOHN HEINCKE - HANOVER, GORDON HENDRY EDINBURGH - SCOTLAND, GEORGE EVERETT HENRY - FLESHERTON, MELVILE GEDDES HENRY - OWEN SOUND, ROBERT ORMISTON HENRY - CHATSWORTH, WALTER HENRY - SHALLOW LAKE, JAMES HERON - RAVENNA, JAMES FENWICK HERON - MAXWELL, GEORGE ALEXANDER HETHERINGTON - OWEN SOUND, CLIFFORD WILLIAM HEWGILL - HEATHCOTE, ALFRED JAMES HILL - OWEN SOUN, HARRY ROY HILTS - OWEN SOUND, HAROLD HOLLEY - BERKELEY, WILLIAM DELBERT HOLLEY - HOLLAND CENTRE, FREDERICK CLARENCE HOLLOWAY - MEAFORD, OLIVER WILFRED HOLMES - OWEN SOUND, THOMAS WILLIAM HOLMES - OWEN SOUND, WILBERT ERNEST HOOEY - OWEN SOUND, WILLIAM VEITCH HOPE - OWEN SOUND, AUSTIN CLARENCE W. HOPKINS - CHATSWORTH, WILLIAM JOHN HOPKINS - HANOVER, ERNEST HOPPER - EUGENIA, CLARENCE AUSTIN HORLOCK - HANOVER, JOHNSTON HOWARD - FEVERSHAM, ALBERT OSCAR GILLESPIE - BERKELEY, SAMUEL ROBERT GILLMORE - MEAFORD, GILBERT REGINALD GILMORE - MEAFORD, ENNIS DANIEL GIRLING - SHALLOW LAKE, ALBERT ALEXANDER GIVENS - HOLLAND CENTRE, JAME EDWARD GIVENS - HOLLAND CENTRE, JAMES GODDEN - LONDON, ENGLAND, EBY GOHEEN - DUNDALK, WILLIAM GOLEBY - NORWICH, ARTHUR GOUGH - OWEN SOUND, J. ALEXANDER GOULD - MARKDALE, THOMAS GRAY - ROCANVILLE, SASKATCHEWAN,

ANNADALE GORDON GRIEVE - BUFFALO N.Y, JOHN EDWARD GRIMOLDBY - OWEN SOUND, WILLIAM GRUNDY - DUNDAS, BENJAMIN HILL HABERT - OWEN SOUND, JOHN SAMUEL HALL - SHALLOW LAKE, AUSTIN DAVIS HALL - OWEN SOUND, JAMES RARMON HALES - FLESHERTON, CHARLES HALLIDAY - AYTON, PETER HAMILTON - IRELAND, ROBERT FERRIS HAMILTON - OWEN SOUND, THOMAS JAMES HANBURY - CHATSWORTH, WINFIELD SCOTT HANCOCK - SEATTLE, WASHINGTON, EDWARD ALEXANDER HOWEY, - CHATSWORTH, BERNARD HOWSON - OWEN SOUND, ORSTIN CLARENCE HOY – HOLSTEIN, J. JESSE HUGHES - DURHAM, ERNEST GEORGE HUMPHRIES - ENGLAND, JOHN WILLIAM HUNEMORDER - HANOVER, JAMES SCOTT HUNTER - ORANGEVILLE, WILLIAM FRANKLIN HUNTER - OWEN SOUND, ERNEST HUNWICKS - MEAFORD, HAROLD BRYON HUTCHINSON - MARKDALE, ROBERT IRWIN - FLESHERTON, RICHARD SHAPE JACKSON - MEAFORD, DAVID BUCHANAN JAMIESOON - TORONTO, ELWIN NEWELL JAMIESON - FLESHERTON, JOHN RALSTON JAMIESON - SCOTLAND, ROBERT IRWIN - FLESHERTON, ALBERT WILSON JARRETT - OWEN SOUND, GEORGE ALBIN, JENKINSON - HANOVER, HERBERT HAINES JOHNSON - MEAFORD, NORMAN JOHNSON - OWEN SOUND, RICHARD GEORGE JOHNSTON - MEAFORD, STANLEY JOHNSTON - ELMWOOD, THOMAS JOHN JOHNSTON - HORNING'S MILLS, CLARENCE AUBREY JONES - OWEN SOUND, ELLIS KAUFMAN - MANCHESTER, ENGLAND, ROBERT KEITH - HOLSTEIN, PATRICK JAMES R. KELLY - MARKDALE, DAVID MESTON KENNEDY - OWEN SOUND, ARTHUR HENRY KENNETT - THORNBURY, JAMES HILL KENEDY - RIVERVIEW, ALFRED JAMES KENT - PROTON STATION, HAROLD WINSLOW KERNAHAM - FEVERSHAM, EDWARD JOHN KENT - PLUMSTEAD, ENGLAND, ROBERT CHARLES KERR - DRESDEN, AMBROSE ARCHIBALD KINAHAN - RYDAL BANK, VICTOR KINDREE - OWEN SOUND, WILLIAM HAROLD KINDREE - OWEN SOUND, CHARLES ALFRED KING - MEAFORD , JAMES HARVEY KING - WALTER'S FALLS, JOSEPH JOHN B. KING - MOUNT HOPE, WILLIAM HENRY KING - MEAFORD, RUSSELL KIRK - BERKELEY, MALCOM GREENLESS KIRKLAND - OWEN SOUND, LLOYD RUSSELL KIRKTON - HOLLAND CENTRE, BERT KIRTON - OWEN SOUND ROBERT KIRTON - OWEN SOUND, ROBERT THOMPSON KNOX - PROTON STATION, FREDERICK KREH, WINNIPEG - MANITOBA, JULIUS CHARLES KUPSKEY - UNKNOWN, DESBORO WILLIAM JAMES LAIRD - CHATSWORTH, ROGER THOMPSON LAMONT - WOODFORD, PERCY SAMUEL LARTER - EASTON LINTON, RUSSELL LATHAM - OWEN SOUND, WESLEY LATHAM - OWEN SOUND, ALLISTER LAUDER - DURHAM, THOMAS ARTHUR LAUDER - DURHAM, WILLIAM LEWIS LAW - OWEN SOUND, DAVID WILLIAM LAYCOCK - MEAFORD, WILLIAM LEATH LAWRENCE - KIMBERLEY, PATRICK ADAM

LAWRENCE - BERKELEY, GARNET RAY LLOYD - MEAFORD, WELLWOOD ROY LOCKSLEY - MEAFORD, BENJAMIN CLARKE LONG - WOODFORD, FRED SYLVESTER LONG - MAXWELL, SAMUEL LONG - WOODFORD, REGINALD LOUCKS - MEAFORD, WILSON LOUGHEED - OWEN SOUND, WILLIAM LOWE - MEAFORD, JOHN NOBLE LUCAS CAMBERWELL - ENGLAND, ALEXANDER LUMLEY - OWEN SOUND, GEORGE DEWAR LUNNEY - ELMWOOD, DAVID LUSL - OWEN SOUND, WILMER MITCHELL LYNN - OWEN SOUND, JOHN JOSEPH LYONS - OWEN SOUND, WILLIAM ARTHUR LYONS - OWEN SOUND, ARCHIBALD ELMORE MACINTYRE - OWEN SOUND, JOHN MACLEAN - ST. MARY'S, DONALD SMITH MACMILLAN - CAPE RICH, ANDREW IRVONE MACNIVEN - OWEN SOUND, CHARLES ALFRED MAGGS - THORNBURY, GEORGE WILLIAM MAHER - CHATSWORTH, ALLAN BEATTY MALCOM - OWEN SOUND, SIDNEY ALBERT MANTON - LONDON, ENGLAND, EDWARD MARKHAM GRAVELEY - HUNTINGTON, ENGLAND, JAMES WILLIE MARSDEN - OWEN SOUND, JOHN ALLAN MARSHALL - OWEN SOUND, WILLIAM SIMPSON MARSHALL - MEAFORD, WILLIAM ANTHONY MARSHALL - OWEN SOUND, DANIEL MARTELL - CORBETTON, THOMAS LAIDLAW MATHER - PRICEVILLE, LYALL GLADSTONE MATHEWSON - MARKDALE, WILLIAM J. W. MATHEWSON - MARKDALE, CHARLES HENRY MAY - ROCKLYN, WALTER WELLINGTON MCALLISTER - DURHAM, JOHN MCALLISTER - EAST LINTON, DONALD J. MCARTHUR - MARKDALE, JOHN MCARTHUR, PAISLEY - THOMAS G. MCARTHUR - CEYLON, WILLIAM ALEXANDER MCARTHUR - HOLSTEIN, FRANKLIN MICHAEL MCASEY – MARKDALE, ANGUS MCAULEY - DUNDALK, WILLIAM OSBORNE MCBAIN - DESBORO, GEORGE ERNEST MCBRIDE - MARKDALE, ARTHUR JOHN MCBURNEY - OWEN SOUND, HUGH JAMES MCCALLUM - SHALLOW LAKE, JOHN WESLEY MCCARTNEY - MEAFORD, WILBERT ANDREW MCCARTNEY - CAPE RICH, ANGUS MCCASKILL - OWEN SOUND, CHARLES SANDERSON MCCAULEY - WILLIAMSFORD, EARL THOMAS MCCAULEY - OWEN SOUND, HOWARD ALFRED MCCAULEY - FLESHERTON, CHARLES MURRAY MCCLURE - WILLIAMSFORD, HAROLD FALCONER MCCONNEL - HILLSBURGH, CHARLES ELMER MCDONALD - OWEN SOUND, JOHN MCDONALD - ALLENFORD, JOSEPH MCDONALD - BIRMINGHAM, ENGLAND, LESLIE MOORE MCDONALD - OWEN SOUND, LORNE MCDONALD - WOODFORD, NEIL EDWARD MCDONALD - OWEN SOUND, PHILLIP GEORGE MCDONALD - DURHAM, DONALD MCDONELL – DUNDALK, ROBERT ELMORE MCDOUGALL - OWEN SOUND, HENRY CARTER MCENTOSH - PRICEVILLE, LEONARD MCFADDEN - MARKDALE, DAVID BLAINE MCFARLANE - DURHAM, HECTOR STEWART MCGILLIVRAY - DORNOCH, JOHN REGINALD MCGILLIVRAY - CHATSWORTH, NEIL JOHN MCGILLIVRAY - OWEN SOUND, JOHN MCGILVERY -

LONDON, WILLIAM JAMES MCGIRR - DURHAM, FRANKLIN FOSTER MCILRAITH - DURHAM, THOMAS JAMES MCILFATERICK - ROCKLYN, JAMES MCINTERNEY - PARRY HARBOUR, JAMES AUSMAN BOYD MCINNIS - SHALLOW LAKE, JESSE ALEXANDER MCINNIS - OWEN SOUND, DONALD MCKAY - MEAFORD, FRANK MCKAY - DURHAM, KENNETH RUSSELL MCKAY - ANNAN, HAROLD CECIL MCKECHNIE - DURHAM, HENRY FREDERICK MCKECHNIE - MARKDALE, ROY BROWN MCKENZIE - OWEN SOUND, JOHN JOSEPH MCKEOWN - PRICEVILLE, WILLIAMS JOHN MCKESSOCK - CHATSWORTH, WILFRED GEORGE MCKIBBON - OWEN SOUND, MALCOLME EBERTS MCKINNON - OWEN SOUND, CLARENCE SYLVESTOR MCKNIGHT - OWEN SOUND, DONALD DRYDEN MCLAREN - MEAFORD., ALEXANDER MCLEAN - PRICEVILLE, ALEXANDER MCLEAN - OWEN SOUND, COLIN MCLEAN - OWEN SOUND, WILLIAM JOHN MCLEAN - KIPPEN, JOHN MCLEOD - CHATSWORTH, MARK SNOWDEN - CEYLON, WILLIAM JOHN MCLEOD - PROTON STATION, JAMES HENRY MCMAHAN - HANOVER, COLIN ANGUS MCMILLAN - CAPE RICH, DOUGAL JOHN MCMILLAN - OWEN SOUND, WILLIAM JAMES MCMILLAN - OWEN SOUND, JAMES MCMULLEN - CEYLON, ALEXANDER DUNCAN MCNAB - BOGNOR, WILLIAM JAMES MCNAB - OWEN SOUND, ALBERT MCNALLY – MARKDALE, OGLE ALEXANDER MCRAE - OWEN SOUND, WILLIAM MOORE – ENGLAND, WILLIAM ERNEST MORGAN - EUGENIA, GEORGE BERTRUM MORRISON - OWEN SOUND, WILLIAM MORROE - OWEN SOUND, WILLIAM ANDREW MORROR - OWEN SOUND, ALBERT ANDREW MORT - AYTON, WESLEY ERNEST MORTON – DURHAM, MELVILLE EARL MOULTON - OWEN SOUND, LORNE MOUNTAIN – DURHAM, BENJAMIN PERCIVAL MUNNS - MEAFORD, WILLIAM THOMAS MUNRO – DURHAM, GEORGE THOMAS MURRAY - DURHAM, THOMAS JOSEPH MYLOW - OWEN SOUND, JAMES EDWARD NEATH - OWEN SOUND, REUBEN NEATH - OWEN SOUND, CHRISTOPHER NEGUS - KEMBLE, KOHN NEILL - OWEN SOUND, ALFRED NELSON - OWEN SOUND, WILLIAM NESBIT - PROUDFOOT, MUSKOKA, LEWIS NEWELL - DURHAM, SAMUEL ROBERT NEWMAN - OWEN SOUND, ARTHUR ERNEST NICHOL - OWEN SOUND, JOHN CRENTON NICHOL - DURHAM, NOEL NICHOLSON – ENGLAND, CHARLES WILLIAM NICOL - ENGLAND, FREDERICK WILLIAM NOLAN - OWEN SOUND, WILLIAM NORTON - OWEN SOUND, FRANK OLIVER - OWEN SOUND, FREDERICK WILLIAM OLIVER - MEAFORD, JAMES OLIVER - PRICEVILLE, STEWART CLARENCE OLMSTEAD - MEAFORD, WILLIAM JOHN OLTHOFF - HANOVER, ALBERT ORFORD - OWEN SOUND, CHARLES EDGAR ORFORD - OWEN SOUND, CLAUDE HARTLEY ORFORD - OWEN SOUND, HENRY OSBORNE - EUGENIA, ALBERT OSBORNE – ENGLAND, CECIL HERBERT OYNS - ENGLAND, GEORGE ERNEST PALLISTER - DUNDALK, FREDERICK DAVIS

PALMER - ENGLAND, LOUIS GUY MCREYNOLDS – BALACLAVA, WILLIE CROSS MCREYNOLDS - BALACLAVA, JOHN JOSEPH MEADS – PRICEVILLE, ALEXANDER MCVICAR - PRICEVILLE, HOWARD STANLEY MERRIAM - TYVAN, SASKATCHEWAN, WILLIAM HAMILTON MERRITT - OWEN SOUND, ERROL CARSON MESTON - COLLINGWOOD, THOMAS HENRY MEYER - OWEN SOUND, HERBERT HANSON MIDDLETON - ENGLAND, JOHN MILLARD - ENGLAND, CECIL MILLER - LONDON, ENGLAND, CECIL MILLER - CHATSWORTH, GEORGE EDWIN MILLER - CLAVERING, CHARLES CHAW MILLER - MEAFORD, GEORGE RUSSELL MILLER - OWEN SOUND, JACK ACKARD MILLER - OWEN SOUND, JAMES VICTOR MILLER - OWEN SOUND, ROY FRANKLIN MILLER - COLLINGWOOD, JOSEPH THOMAS MILLS - TEIGNMOUTH, ENGLAND, NEIL DUNCAN MILNE - ELMWOOD, HERBERT MINEARD - OWEN SOUND, AUBREY BRYON MITCHELL - OWEN SOUND, JAMES MOBBS - NORTH KEPPEL, STANLEY MONCK - BRANTFORD, WILLIAM ESTWORTHY PALMER - DESBORO, RUSSELL PALMER - MEAFORD, RICHARD PARKS - DESBORO, GEORGE HENRY PARTRIDGE - OWEN SOUND, JAMES ARTHUR PATERSON - MEAFORD, WILFRED DAVID PATERSON - OWEN SOUND, ALEXANDER CHARLES PATTERSON - MEAFORD, DAVID BROWN PATTERSON - OWEN SOUND, JOSEPH JAMES PATTERSON - CEYLON, GEORGE BERTRAM PATTTON - FLESHERTON, JAMES FRANKLIN PATTON - FLESHERTON, HAROLD NEWTON PEACOCK - OWEN SOUND, PERCY WILLIAM J. PEARCE - CHATSWORTH, RUFUS CRITCHLEY PEARCE - CHATSWORTH, OSWALD LOY PENNER - OWEN SOUND, ELMER PENROSE - THORNBURY, HAROLD EDWARD PERKINS - MARKDALE, HAROLD MARTIN PHILLIPS - ROCK MILLS, FRANK WILLIAM PIERCE - MARMION, VICTOR EMERSON PIKE - ALLENFORD, FREDERICK JAMES PINKERTON - PRICEVILLE, ISAAC ANDREW PINKERTON - PRICEVILLE, WESLEY POLLOCK – HOLSTEIN, CAMERON PORTER - OWEN SOUND, ERNEST POUNTNEY - OWEN SOUND, JOHN PRIDMORE - PARK HEAD, FRANK PRIEST - DUNDALK, HARRY CLIFFORD PRINGLE - OWEN SOUND, HAROLD WILGRESS PROCTOR - KIMBERLEY, JAMES PROUDFOOT - LEITH, ANTHONY PUST - DURHAM, NORMAN HORACE QUINLAN - OWEN SOUND, ROBERT ALEXANDER QUINTON - MEAFORD, JAMES GORDON RABY - CHARLEVOIX, MICHIGAN, EARL VICTOR RADBOURNE - OWEN SOUND, WILLIAM JAMES RADLEY - CEYLON, COLLIN BUNYAN RAE - BALACLAVA, GEORGE MILLER RAE - BALACLAVA, JAMES LESLIE RAVEN - MEAFORD, SETH ENOS RAWN - HOATH HEAD, STEPHEN RAYNER - ENGLAND, FREDERICK WATKIN REDFERN - OWEN SOUND , DAVID LESLIE REEKIE - CAMPERDOWN, HENRY REID - MEAFORD, JOHN KENNETH REID - OWEN SOUND, JOHN ALEXANDER REILLY - ANNAN, JOHN WESLEY REINHART - OWEN SOUND, WILLIAM

HICKMAN RENNIE - CAPE RAY, NFLD, JAMES ANDERSON REOCH - PORT ELGIN, GEORGE WITTER REYNOLDS - BEETON, ALBERT CHARLES RIBBONS - MEAFORD, EDWARD RIBBONS - MEAFORD, GEORGE BENNET RICHARDSON - FREDERICKHOUSE, HENRY MADEWELL RICHARDSON - ENGLAND, ROBERT ROY RICHARDSON - CHATSWORTH, WILLIAM ELMER RICHARDSON - PROTON STATION, JAMES RIDGE - ENGLAND, JOHN WELSEY RITCHIE - BERKELEY, WILLIAM GEORGE ROBB - OWEN SOUND, EDWARD ROBBINS - OWEN SOUND, ERNEST ALEXANDER ROBINSON - OWEN SOUND, WILLIAM STANLEY ROBINSON - MEAFORD, JOHN ROBISON - OWEN SOUND, GEORGE ROBSON - OWEN SOUND, JOHN SILAS ROBSON - OWEN SOUND, STANLEY ROBSON - OWEN SOUND, JOHN ERNEST RODGERS - SAUBLE FALLS, ALBERT HENRY ROE - OWEN SOUND, CLARENCE RODD – HOLSTEIN, HERBERT GEORGE ROSS - WINNIPEG, JOHN MILFORD ROSS - HOLSTEIN, LORNE JOHN ROSS - OWEN SOUND, PERCY JOHN ROSS - HOLSTEIN, JOHN ROSSITER - SARAWAK, CHARLES WESLEY ROURKE - PARK HEAD, URISH MEADOWS ROZEL - OWEN SOUND, ALFRED ROZELL - TORONTO, HUGH RUMLEY - WIARTON, EDWARD MILES RUSH - OWEN SOUND, WILLIAM THOMAS RUSSELLL - ENGLAND, GEORGE FREDERICK SAINSBURY - OWEN SOUND, ALBERT BOLTON SAMUELLS - OWEN SOUND, ALLISTER SAUNDERS - DURHAM, DONALD MCPHAIL SAUNDERS - DURHAM, NORMAN RUSSELL SAUNDERS - OWEN SOUND, WILLIAM HENRY SAVAGE - OWEN SOUND, EARNEST CARMAN SCARROW - OWEN SOUND, VICTOR SCHUERMAN – DURHAM, ARTHUR HENRY SCHILLEMORE - ENGLAND, ROBERT CHARLES SCHILLEMORE - ENGLAND, JOHN MILTON SCHOFFIELD - OWEN SOUND, ARTHUR HAMES SEAWARD - OWEN SOUND, JOSEPH SEGUIN - THORNBURY, CHARLES OLIVER SENSABAUGH - LION'S HEAD, ROBERT WILLIAM SHANNON - MEAFORD, WILLIAM JOHN SHARP - FLESHERTON, CECIL MATHEW SHARPIN - OWEN SOUND, JAMES SHEFFIELD - OWEN SOUND, ALBERT HENRY SHIER - OWEN SOUND, WILLIAM GEORGE SHINE - MEAFORD, ALEXANDER MILTON SHUTE - HOLLAND CENTRE, OLIVER SIEGRIST - OXENDEN, AMBROSE DAVID SILVERTHORN - WOODFORD, THOMAS HECTOR SILVERTHORN - MEAFORD, CECIL FRANK SIMPSON - ENGLAND, WILLIAM JOHN H. SIMPSON - OWEN SOUND, J. ELMER SMART - OWEN SOUND, JOHN SMITH - APELDOORN, HOLLAND, ARCHIE SMITH - COOKSTOWN, CLIFFORD MEREDITH SMITH - CORBETT, EDWARD WILLIAM SMITH - HOUGH LAKE, EMERSON CLAUDE SMITH - EUGENIA, FRANCIS WALTER SMITH - OWEN SOUND, JAMES SMITH - HOATH HEAD, JAMES ALEXANDER SMITH - HANOVER, RICHARD JAMES SMITH - MEAFORD, WILLIAM ALEXANDER SMITH - HANOVER, WILLIAM ALEXANDER SNELL - OWEN SOUND, RICHARD JAMES SOBY - CORNWALL, ENGLAND, HERBERT DICKINSON

SPARLING - CLARKSBURG, C. AUGUSTUS SPEARMAN - OWEN SOUND, JAMES SPEARMAN - OWEN SOUND, GEORGE EDWIN SPENCER - ELMHEDGE, GERAL LOUE SPENCER - PARK HEAD, PERCY RALPH SPENCER - OXENDEN, WILLIAM THOMAS SPRINGHAM - OWEN SOUND, JOSEPH ERNEST STAFFORD - BERKELEY, THOMAS RICHARD STEAD - OWEN SOUND, ERNEST STANLEY - OWEN SOUND, THOMAS RICHARD STEAD - OWEN SOUND, JACK STEELE - HAMILTON, GEORGE STEPHEN FORRES - MORAY, SCOTLAND, ALEXANDER CONACHER STEWARD - HOLLAND, FREDERICK GEORGE STEWART - ECHO BAY, JOHN CECIL STEWART - DUNDALK, JOSEPH AMBROSE STEWART - OWEN SOUND, NORMAN LESLIE STEWART - OWEN SOUND, ROBERT STEWART - HOLLAND CENTRE, THOMAS ELLIS STEWART - DURHAMWILLIAM JOHN. W STODDART - MARKDALE, EARNEST STONE - TORONTO, WILLIAM ARTHUR STUCK - OWEN SOUND, ERIC FRANCIS STURGE - ENGLAND, STANLEY CLIFFORD SUDDEN - CHATSWORTH, FRANK SULLIVAN - TORONTO, GEORGE WILLIAM SUTHERBY - POINT ANNE, ALFRED RECORD SWITZER - HANOVER, SHERWOOD TACKABERRY - OWEN SOUND, WILLIAM HENRY TAITE - MEAFORD, CLAYTON JOSEPH TAYLOR - RUTLAND, VERMONT, FRANK TAYLOR - ENGLAND, JOHN SAMUEL TAYLOR - BIRMINGHAM, NORMAN JOSEPH TAYLOR - MEAFORD, WILLIAM GEORGE TAYLOR - KEMBLE, WILLIAM DAVID TEDFORD - MANCHESTER, CONNECTICUT, ALEXANDER MCCAULEY TEDFORD - HOLLAND CENTRE, CHARLES JOSEPH WILSON - OWEN SOUND, WILLIAM WILSON - OWEN SOUND, W. E. WILSON - THORNBURY, W. H. WILSON - SARAWAK, J. F. WILSON - MEAFORD, H. S. WITMER - PARKHEAD, EDWARD WOINOWSKI - WILLIAMSFORD, A. M. WOOD - MARMION, E. J. M. WOOD - CONSHOHOCKEN, USA, WALTER WOOD - CHESLEY, S. B. WOODBRIDGE - CHESLEY, SAMUEL WOODHOUSE - PROTON STATION, GEORGE WOODS - OWEN SOUND, CUTHBERT WOODWARD - HEREFORD, ENGLAND, J. A. WOOLGAR - HANOVER, H. J. WRIGHT - OWEN SOUND, HUGH WRIGHT - ELMWOOD, G. H. WYLLIE - KILSYTH, F. S. YANDT - NEUSTADT, JACOB YOUNG - TORONTO, ROBERT YOUNG - OWEN SOUND, S. M. YOUNG - HAWKHURST, SASKATCHEWAN, W. R. YOUNG - ST. CATHERINES, ARTHUR ZIMMERMAN - HANOVER

www.ingramcontent.com/pod-product-compliance
Lightning Source LLC
Chambersburg PA
CBHW021004260626
47169CB00006B/1932
* 9 7 8 1 7 7 8 2 8 9 9 2 7 *